NEVER SAY DIE

A JACK WHITFIELD THRILLER

Book 2

JOHN W. MEFFORD

NEVER SAY DIE
Copyright © 2022 by John W. Mefford
All rights reserved.

This is a work of fiction. The events and characters described herein are imaginary and are not intended to refer to specific places or living persons. The opinions expressed in this manuscript are solely the opinions of the author and do not represent the opinions or thoughts of the publisher. The author has represented and warranted full ownership and/or legal right to publish all the materials in this book.

This book may not be reproduced, transmitted, or stored in whole or in part by any means, including graphic, electronic, or mechanical without the express written consent of the publisher, except in the case of brief quotations embodied in critical articles and reviews.

Sugar Hill Publishing

ISBN: 979-8-354335-34-3

Interior book design by
Bob Houston eBook Formatting

To stay updated on John's latest releases, visit:
JohnWMefford.com

"He who has a why to live for, can bear almost any how."
~ **Friedrich Nietzsche, German philosopher**

"I don't care how big and fast computers are, they're not as big and fast as the world."
~ **Herbert Simon, American economist, and political scientist**

1

Lyon, France

A flash of glinting metal.

Then nothing in the thicket of darkness.

I froze, halting my descent on the stone staircase outside my apartment building.

My eyes narrowed on the corner of the brick wall leading to the alley. Heart thrumming like a drum roll. Breathing choppy. My brain in go mode, alert. Code Red. Always Code Red until I knew otherwise. My new life.

A slow exhale.

The neighborhood was working class. The research I'd been given from my handlers—hidden faces known only to me as Simon—stated this area had virtually no crime. One of the safest streets in all of Lyon. But I knew Utopia didn't exist.

A second flash.

Shiny.

A knife.

Had someone from my recent past caught up to me?

I pulled my phone from my pocket and pretended to surf as I descended the staircase. Calm, but highly aware.

"Monsieur, monsieur."

I spun toward the door as the property manager and resident mom, Miss Patty, started to walk outside.

"No, hold on. Go back inside, please," I said, knowing she spoke good English.

"I thought everyone was in for the night. Everything okay, Monsieur Ellington?"

"Just fine, thank you. It's about to rain. I can smell it in the air."

"Then why are you outside?"

"Too excited to sleep. I'd like to walk by the Saint-Jean Baptist Cathedral, get a first impression of the structure at night. Begin the scouting exercise for my photography book."

A slow nod. "I see. Well…"

"Miss Patty, please go inside." My tone was direct, bordering on rude. I just hoped she wouldn't think this American photographer had taken it too far. Question my purpose for being in Lyon.

She pulled back into the hallway, the door still open. "I have a question for you, but it can wait. Drop by my place when you get back?"

"Okay. Yes, I'll do that."

I waited for the door to shut, then tapped my phone a few times and brought it to my ear. "Hey, Daniel. How's it going?" I asked a dead line as I ambled down the sidewalk, seemingly distracted. "Yes, been here less than a day, but Lyon is beautiful. Lots of historic buildings and iconic architecture. How's the real estate business heading into the summer?"

One set of eyes. At least one set. I could feel them on me, but

I kept up with the ruse.

I nodded. "Oh yeah? How did you get the seller to agree to that deal?"

Tucking the phone under my chin, I paused to tie my sneaker. I searched the darkness in scattered glimpses. Scouring for another datapoint. How many, size, additional weapons. Any nugget to add to my calculations. To increase my odds.

Nothing.

Had the would-be assailant left?

I continued walking. Just past midnight, and the sidewalks were void of people in this section of the historic city. A distant grumble of what sounded like a truck without a muffler. The fog had lifted somewhat, but a light drizzle fell from the low sky.

I chuckled. "Dude, that's hilarious. What happened after that?"

Twenty feet from the alley.

I shifted my eyes to a sedan parked along the curb. A light from across the street illuminated drops of water on the car's side windows. It also created a distorted view into the alley.

Ten feet away.

The angle changed, allowing me to see some movement close to the ground.

One man. Hunkered down.

Part of me wanted to haul ass in the other direction. Avoid a confrontation that could put a spotlight on me—the last thing I wanted. This mission, which would lead me to some serious facetime with one particular leader at Interpol, required me to blend in with the citizens of the city.

But the other part of me—the survivor—knew I'd never sleep tonight or any night in the future wondering if a foreign intelligence service had sent an agent to assassinate me. If I played my cards right, I'd pin this person down, force them to communicate their objective and who had hired them.

One step away.

I dropped to my knees.

The man flew out of the darkness. Swung his knife wildly at what would have been my chest. He tripped over me and flipped onto his side. A split second later, he was back on his feet. The knife closing in on my throat.

I spun away on one knee, got my first good look at my adversary. Stout, built like a fireplug. Some type of tattoo on his neck. But it was his eyes that drew my attention—they were on fire.

"Donne-moi ton argent," he growled, his eyes bouncing wildly left and right.

I'd taken a sprint French class on the plane. He wanted my money. He was nothing more than a common thief. One who'd almost killed me. The only way to stop someone with a knife was to get inside their arm's length. A dangerous proposition. I had no weapon, only my phone. And this guy was either on something or far too eager.

Maintaining a five-foot separation, I circled left. He followed suit, nimbly twisting the knife in his hand like a seasoned hibachi chef. His breathing pattern was like that of a panting dog. I jabbed a step in his direction. As I'd hoped, he took a roundhouse swing with his knife arm. I jerked my torso to the left, then lunged, clocking his chin with the edge of my phone. The blow stunned him, caused him to drop his defenses. The knife, though, never left his hand.

I went for his arm—the one with the knife—but he slipped from my grasp. Started to drive the knife straight for my shoulder. His eyes lighting up in the process.

An opening.

I spun into the man, grabbed his arm with both hands this time. But instead of trying to block his stabbing movement, I pulled his arm down—hard and fast, going with the flow—plunging the knife into the meat of his thigh. He cried out.

"You shouldn't have attacked me," I said, wiping sweat from my forehead.

The man grabbed at his leg, shouting French expletives as he hobbled into the dark alley. The bold instigator with a deadly weapon was now nothing more than a meek, wounded animal. He'd probably live. His bruised ego would sideline him even if the physical injury did not.

I took a moment. Bent over, hands on knees, and breathed a few calming breaths.

Time to move on.

I turned to walk away, only to freeze yet again when I heard a clinking sound. I started to look behind me, but a chain came out of nowhere, looping around my neck. Before I could grab at the chain, the person on the other end had yanked me off my feet. The force more mechanical than human. Zero oxygen. Every sound cut off.

As I was dragged along the alley on my back, my fingers pawed at the metal links. The chain wouldn't budge. The man pulling me was gargantuan, easily half a foot taller than my height of six-one. Vertebrae popped along my spine. Like I'd been stabbed by a dozen ice picks. A single, morbid thought—which would happen first: my spinal cord snapping or my head exploding?

A muted thud.

The giant yelped and dropped to the ground. His open eyes stared straight at me, unblinking. A hole in his forehead. When I looked up, another man was standing there.

He offered me his hand.

2

I pulled the chain away from my neck and gasped out a breath. "Who... Who are you?" My voice sounded like I'd swallowed nails.

"Talk later. We need to get rid of the body."

The man's accent was American English. Midwest, if I had to guess. The alley was dark, but I could still see the outline of the pistol in the man's hand. It was pointed at the ground.

"Where did the guy with the knife go?" I asked, up on an elbow.

"Walking out the other end of the alley, cussing up a storm."

"Were they working together?" I asked.

"Probably. And there might be more. Those types are like roaches."

"Do you think—?"

He held up his free hand. "No time to talk now. Look, this dude is big," he said, his eyes glancing toward the street. "I can do it myself, but it'd take me a while. Police make the rounds."

"I can help." I pushed up to my feet but kept an eye on his gun.

He tucked the pistol in his pants and picked up one of the dead man's arms. "Let's drag him to the far end of the alley. I think I saw a random grocery cart about a street over. I'll grab that. Meanwhile, try to find something to cover him with."

"Then what?"

"Best bet is to wheel him down to the Rhone River and dump him. Unless you have a better idea."

I had to maintain a low profile while on this mission. Being associated with any type of murder would flush those chances down the proverbial toilet. And I couldn't let that happen. "Let's do it."

We dragged the body about fifty feet in quick order.

"Back in a flash." The man disappeared around the corner.

I started a slow spin in the alley. Two-thirds around, a dumpster near a metal staircase. I hustled over, slid open the side, and peered into the metal bin. Too dark. I turned on my phone's flashlight and pointed the beam inside. It was stacked with dark, plastic garbage bags. I pulled one closer, ripped open the top. The smell nearly knocked me over. I tried a second bag. Just more trash. I threw it to the side. Then something promising caught my eye.

Paint cans.

Which could mean…

I crawled into the dumpster and dug like a man possessed.

The tips of my fingers hit a mound of coarse fabric.

And there it was.

A canvas tarp.

I pulled it toward me and found two more tarps. A few holes, lots of splattered paint, but damn near perfect for our purpose.

Once I heard the wheels of a shopping cart rattling my way, I grabbed the tarps and a few cans of paint, and threw them over the side of the dumpster. Then I hefted my own body out, hopping deftly to the ground.

"Check it out," I said, pointing to my finds.

"Nice work," my rescuer said, nodding at our new tools. "Let's wrap this body up and get him in the cart."

When he turned, ambient light hit his face. Pale, smooth skin. Not a single crease. He couldn't be a day over twenty-five. He had short, cropped hair. Wiry physique. Beyond his appearance, something about his demeanor stood out: he'd just killed a man, yet he had not panicked. Stone-cold cool.

And now we were working to cover it up. Hell, I'd been forced to do worse in the last few weeks.

I wanted to tap the brakes, ask the young man a number of questions, but I knew time was of the essence. Without a lot of discussion, we wrapped one tarp around the massive body and folded it into the oversized cart. Then we stuffed the two additional tarps on top, along with the cans of paint.

"You didn't see any painter's clothes in there, did you?" he asked.

I shook my head. "Want me to go back and check again?"

"I was joking. No time anyway. Now comes the risky part. But something tells me you've waded in the risk pool before."

"I was thinking the same about you. I've got questions—like your name—but we'll talk after."

"Call me Casper."

I pointed at my chest. "Zane," I said, using the fake name I'd given Miss Patty and every other person in France.

We pushed the cart to the end of the alley and looked up and down Rue de Bugeaud—Bugeaud Street. Since I'd memorized the map of the area near my apartment building, I wasn't surprised to see four spotlights off to the east, illuminating the pillars of a church, Saint Pothin Immaculate Conception. One of many architectural wonders throughout this colorful city.

With only a handful of casual walkers around, and none in our immediate vicinity, we set out on the most direct route to the Rhone, moving west on Bugeaud. Many of the streets in Lyon were full of trees, either along sidewalks or in the medians. The street we were on had no trees, although six- to eight-story buildings hulked on either side of the narrow road. We walked about fifty yards and pulled into the first cross street—sans any trees—to hide briefly in the shadows.

"Safe so far," I said.

Casper's eyes never stopped moving. I figured his brain was doing the same. "Let's see if we can make it two in a row."

We pushed the cart back onto Bugeaud. Not five seconds later, two cyclists whirred by us.

"Shit," I said, holding my chest. "Scared the piss out of me."

"You and me both."

"Hey." I looked over my shoulder to watch a third cyclist zoom by without paying us any attention. "You concerned we might run into trouble at the river? It's coming up on one in the morning, but there's no tree coverage or anything by the river."

He worked his jaw as though he were chewing tobacco. I'd known a few folks on my home turf of Donelson, Tennessee, who chewed. My former life.

"We're about three blocks away from the crime scene," Casper said. "Even wrapped in this tarp, if we place him in another dumpster, he'll be found in less than twenty-four hours. The river current will take him downstream. Much more difficult to determine the original location of the crime."

The way Casper talked about crime scenes made me ponder his background and why he'd seemingly materialized out of obscurity to help me out. Hell, his nickname was Casper. A ghost. Could Simon have assigned me a covert guardian angel in case I got in trouble? Some might consider that an act of kindness and respect. But I couldn't go there, not for a group that had murdered my wife.

"High reward, but high risk," I said to Casper. "But I don't think we have an option at this point."

"Since it's my bullet in the guy, I was hoping you'd say that. Let's go."

We sauntered along Bugeaud, trying to act casual, even if my instincts told me to race to the river. We passed three sets of walkers, and another cyclist zipped by us. Everyone minding their own business. Perhaps I'd been too paranoid.

At the street just next to the river, two cars moved along at a leisurely pace. Off to our left was the Passerole de Collège, a footbridge that spilled onto the peninsula across the Rhone near the entrance to Collège-Lycée Ampère, a famous school founded over five hundred years earlier. If my wife, Anna, were here with me, she would soak up the city's rich history. She'd taught AP World History at the local high school back home. Before Simon had killed her and abducted my daughter.

"See the opening to the chute?" Casper pointed across the street, toward an enclosed slide under a canopy of trees.

"That drops to the path by the river," I surmised.

He nodded. "Tip the cart over and push the body down the chute. But let me go first."

"Got it. I'll follow behind the body. Then we'll carry him across that path and drop him into the river in the shadow of the bridge. Quickly."

With no more than a nod, Casper took a running start and dove into the metal chute as though it were a slide at a water park. I rolled the cart the final few feet to the opening, then hunkered down and tipped the cart upward.

The body missed the chute, instead crumbling to the ground.

"Crap." I walked around the cart and tried to move the body. It was like lifting jelly. Very heavy jelly.

"Hey, Zane, any problems?" Casper called up the chute.

"Give me a sec." With my back to the chute, I wrapped my

arms around the man's chest and used my legs to surge upward. A car screeched to a stop on the street just in front of the bridge. Peopled yelled in French through open windows.

I'd been noticed.

Were these people simply late-night party animals, inebriated, with nothing better to do than harass me? I hoped so.

My eyes landed on the man in the back seat—the one I'd knifed—and all hope splintered into a million pieces.

A different man got out of the car from the front passenger's side. A spear of light bounced off his bald head. But it was the gun that he pulled from his waistband that really caught my attention.

With the dead body still in my arms and the bald man closing in fast, I had only one choice. I launched myself backward through the chute. A sharp ping sounded against the metal; the bald man had fired a shot.

Seconds later, I crashed into Casper.

3

Silence all around, if only for a moment. Did the bald guy think he'd killed me?

Casper moaned, and loud voices spilled from the street above.

Casper pushed me off him and scrambled to his feet. "Who the hell is shooting at you?"

"No time for questions." I rolled away from the corpse and started to make a break for it, but Casper didn't follow me. Instead, he tugged at the arms of the dead guy. "What are you doing?" I hissed, exasperated. "A gunman is right above us. And I don't think he's very happy about his buddy being killed."

Casper anchored his feet and dragged the dead man no more than a yard. For the first time since Casper had saved my life, stress marks pulled at his eyes as sweat poured off his face.

"Can't afford to leave the vic here. Gotta get him in the water," he said behind a grunt.

Without further debate, I grabbed dead man's legs, Casper holding the top end. We shuffled across the wide path to the edge of the river. Swung the corpse once, and it dropped into the water ... four feet from shore. Maybe not as far as we'd like, but far enough for now.

"Damn, he was heavy," Casper said, working his shoulder.

A brief chirp, then a blue and red halo shining over the trees on the street above us. I nudged Casper. "We've got company."

He cursed under his breath at our conundrum. How to avoid being arrested or gunned down by people just waiting for us to make an appearance at street level?

Instead of making a run for it down the path that lined the river, we decided to walk right into the mouth of the danger.

We strode toward the steps at the bottom of the footbridge, arriving at the same time as a group of young people. They were chatting, laughing. Probably just wrapping up a night of bar hopping. Or whatever young people did today. Not a care in the world.

We followed the crowd up the staircase, and I took in the whole scene. Two police cars with lights flashing were wedged together in front of the bald guy's car, an older model Peugeot, white. He was handcuffed and being interrogated by two cops. Two other cops were speaking to the man I'd knifed. He had his hands on the side of the car. His injured leg was wrapped in a towel, streaks of crimson down the side.

"Follow me," Casper said.

We made a U-turn and started walking across the footbridge toward the peninsula. Unfortunately, the young partiers went in the opposite direction, heading east on Bugeaud in the direction of the cops.

"You see that tall cop talking to the bald guy, the one who shot me?" I said. "When we walked past, he shifted his eyes to us, then he started talking into his shoulder mic."

"Not a good sign."

"It would seem not. Let's just hope we seemed casual enough.

Keep going."

"Bald guy won't shut up, though," Casper said. "Perps love to shift the blame. I guarantee you he's yapping about us right this second."

"Will the cops believe him?"

"In my experience, it depends on a couple of factors. How convincing is the perp? And, more importantly, is the cop at the end of his shift? If he's tired, he could just want to end the night and take the perps in to get booked."

We could only hope. "No cops around when the bald guy shot me," I said.

"But the Peugeot was double-parked, right? Cops stopped to talk to them, then might have seen the gun. It's illegal to carry a gun in France."

"But you have one."

Casper glanced at me. A blank stare. There was a deeper story there. One I hoped to learn more about once we got out of this mess.

A man and a woman walked in our direction, holding hands, but their eyes were on the scene behind us. No surprise there. I was dying to take a look myself, but there was no way I could do that without being obvious. Casper and I were almost halfway across the bridge when a whistle blared from behind us. We glanced at each other, briefly, ever so slightly. Then, without saying a word, we both turned all the way around.

The tall cop was speed-walking toward us, blowing his whistle like a madman. He paused just long enough to yell some type of instructions. The couple who'd just walked past turned and stared at us.

"Now we should run," Casper said.

And we did. With a chorus of whistles and loud voices trailing us, we hustled across the footbridge. Casper took almost two steps to my longer stride. I was used to running long distances—I'd been a decathlete in college—but never with cops or thugs on my tail...

Well, until recently.

"Be on the lookout for cops up and down Moulin," Casper said as we approached the street on the far side of the footbridge.

Moulin—one of the French leaders of the resistance during World War II. Casper and I would have far too much time to read about French history in a cell if we didn't lose the cops. A few cars motored north and south on Moulin, but no police cars. "Do they have unmarked police cars in France?"

"Only the DGSE, that I know of."

The French intelligence agency. Casper had known that answer off the top of his head.

We hit concrete, and a new decision had to be made. The Collège-Lycée Ampère—a prestigious private school—stood directly in front of us, on the far side of Moulin.

"Do you know your way around this city?" I asked, doing a quick check over my shoulder. Before Casper could reply, I pointed behind us. "I think the tall cop ran the four hundred meters in college."

Casper looked for himself. "The last thing we need. Follow me."

We went left at the school, ran about a hundred feet, then hooked a right on Gentil. No doubt the cop had seen which direction we were taking. "He'll call in backups and give them our direction," I yelled.

"That's why we went left."

When we reached the end of the short block, Casper unexpectedly skidded to a stop. I tried to avoid him but slipped on the concrete, falling onto my hands and knees.

"Sorry I didn't warn you."

"I'll live." I got to my feet, and blood oozed from my palms.

He stuck his neck around an extension of the school and looked up and down Bourse. I did the same. A few walkers near the corner to the north, a cyclist and two cars headed in the opposite direction.

"No cops." We sprinted up the sidewalk toward the walkers. They were standing in line at a McDonald's, which was built into the façade of the large white building. Most buildings in the heart of Lyon were shades of white with red terracotta-tiled roofs. Continuing to push farther north, I ran across Mulet.

"Yo, Zane."

I whipped my head around. Casper had turned right on Mulet. I caught up to him in about twenty yards. "We're headed back toward the river, you know."

"Right. And the walkers will tell the cops that. We want to leave markers that we're moving in a different direction than we actually are."

I liked the way his mind worked. As long he was on my team. And for now, that was my assumption. Given my experiences—specifically in the betrayal department—no one received blanket trust, even if that person had a Midwest accent. The next block down, Casper turned left. We were moving north again on Bourse. "Do you have a destination in mind, or just scramble until we lose them?"

"We already lost them. Not wise to stop until we reach a safe place to hunker down."

"Which is?"

"A bookstore, almost due west of here. But we'll take the long route there. Ever been to the opera?"

"Once. Back home."

"Lyon's opera house is at twelve o'clock."

At the large dome we went left, then cut directly in front of the darkened building, crossed another street, and took another left onto Desiree, a tiny road enveloped by buildings on both sides. Casper slowed to a jog and used his T-shirt to wipe sweat off his face.

"You're in pretty good shape," Casper said. His eyes briefly landed on me before scanning our surroundings.

"Comes in handy in my profession."

"And what is that?"

"Photography."

He clapped out a laugh. "No, really, what's your gig?"

I gave him a flat look. "What about you?"

He paused for a second.

"Just tell me when we're safe," I said.

"I like that answer."

We picked up our tempo and continued our fast-paced tour of the peninsula, generally moving west and north, before turning sharply south

We were on a street named Lantern. Wider, more cars, people, and shops. Plenty of shops. Clothes, pastries, cafés, cheese, coffee. The works.

A siren blared, but I couldn't pinpoint its location.

"Quick, in here." Next to a bookstore, Casper opened a scarred wooden door and marched up a single flight of stairs. He unlocked a door and walked inside a small apartment. He went to the window, pulled down one slat of the metal blind, and peered down at the street.

"See anything?"

He shook his head. "With the maze of buildings, it's hard to figure out where the sirens are coming from."

I meandered into the tiny kitchen and turned on the water to wash the dried blood from my wounded hands. "How long have you been in Lyon?" I asked as I looked around the place.

"Not long. Hey, I'm going to stay on watch here at the window, make sure we don't have any unwanted visitors storming the building. Why don't you grab a couple of beers?"

He'd dodged my inquiry. I'd get to the bottom of it eventually. After drying my hands on a towel, I opened the small fridge and pulled out two bottled beers, Heineken. As I closed the fridge door, I noticed a white substance on the linoleum floor next to a closet. I lowered to a crouch and tasted the granules to confirm they were sugar. The size of the sugar pile only grew larger as it disappeared under the crack of the door. Casper must have accidently spilled a package of sugar.

"Hey, Casper…" I opened the pantry door, and my breath hitched.

A man with duct tape over his mouth grunted at me, his eyes pleading for freedom.

A second later, a metal object poked the back of my head. "You're too nosy," Casper said. "And now it's going to cost you."

4

I cursed myself for letting my guard down, for not maintaining constant eye contact with everyone around me. Especially the person with a gun. My relative newness to the shadowy world of espionage was no excuse.

Casper was a man with a past, not unlike myself. But his motivations were unknown. Sure, he'd killed a man to save me. But I knew that event didn't have to align with his true objective. He was an American in Lyon, France. Beyond a few hints of some type of knowledge of how police operated—which could have come from a criminal perspective just as easily as a law-enforcement one—he was an enigma.

I cursed myself a second time. This whole damn episode had diverted me from the mission assigned by Simon: kidnap the head of Interpol's Cybercrime Intelligence Unit and take him to a small house outside Grenoble. All to ensure that three of the unit's most high-profile investigations were shut down. It was a mission I could not fail. And that had nothing to do with my natural-born competitiveness. Simon had implanted an electro-vile in my arm. If I did not succeed, or if I bailed on the mission altogether in order to be with my daughter, Simon would release a deadly concoction of drugs into my system, killing me within minutes. Alternatively, if I dared to have the device surgically removed, Simon would be notified, and I'd be dealt the same fate. My daughter had already lost her mother. She couldn't lose her father.

"Why don't we just kick back and drink our beers?" I suggested. The man in the closet was looking downward, as if he'd lost all hope.

Casper chuckled. "Nice try. I'll direct this conversation, Zane. If that's your real name. So, what are you really doing in Lyon? And don't bullshit me."

I had no idea what he was getting at, why he didn't trust me. Whatever crime he'd committed here, he wasn't vested in my world, this twisted international spy game created by Simon.

"Casper, dude, you can look up my credentials." I'd stated that confidently, knowing how adept Simon was at manipulating information in various systems across the globe. "I'm a photographer. And a damn good one. I'm in Lyon to scout locations to include in my upcoming European photography book. Miss Patty can vouch for me. She's seen my work."

"Who?"

"Miss Patty, the resident mom at the small apartment building I'm staying in. You know, near the..." I left the last part unsaid, even though the man in the pantry was hardly in a position to do anything with the knowledge.

"You were sent here to find me, weren't you?" Casper said.

"Say what?"

"You heard me."

"What are you talking about? You're the one who found me."

No response, although I could hear his rapid breaths. I didn't understand what had provoked this line of questioning. But he was clearly spooked by something—or someone—from his past.

The guy in the closet had tats up and down his arm. I had a few of my own, although many were now fading. Simon had sent me a homemade formula to begin naturally erasing the tattoos I'd been given prior to my first assignment in Macau.

My eyes zoomed in on one tattoo in particular, and my train of thought stopped. The man had a Nazi swastika inked on his neck.

"Look, maybe I've been a bit hasty." Casper lowered the gun, and I turned to face him.

"You think?"

"I just panicked when you opened that door. Jumped to conclusions that you might have been... I don't know."

I blew out a slow breath, realizing I had a hundred questions for the young guy. I started with the most important one. "You mind putting the gun away?"

He looked beyond me at the man in the closet. "Duct tape is still unbroken at his ankles and wrists, so I'm good with that."

I picked up the two bottles of beer and offered him one. "I think we need to chat."

"Let me check one more thing." He walked past me and looked inside the man's ears. "Still intact."

"What is?"

"Earplugs. He can hear basic noises, but not individual words." Casper shut the door with his foot, then took the bottle from me. "Thanks." He used the edge of the counter to pop the top of his beer, took a generous swig, and walked into the sparse living room. Plopping down on a gray couch, he set the gun on a side table. I knocked back a big gulp of my beer while moving to the window. With one eye still on Casper, I glanced outside. A typical late night. No sign of the police, or even a black-clad SWAT team about to raid the building.

"Does Lyon have a SWAT team?" I sat on the back of a leather chair that had more scars than my knees and hands.

"No clue." He bolted upright and grabbed his gun. "Why? Did you see someone outside?"

I held up a hand. "Chill. Nothing out there. Just curious what you know about the police in general."

"You want to know my story. And I want to know yours."

"I already told you mine. You haven't given me the same courtesy."

He blew out a breath, wiped a hand across his face. "I'm an MP."

"Military police?"

He nodded. "On leave."

I waited for more. It never came, so I realized he was only going to reply to questions. I had many.

"You said you were on leave."

"Yep."

"From?"

"Stuttgart, Germany."

"Baumholder is the largest Army base outside of the US."

He squinted an eye at me. "You've done your homework."

"It's just a random fact. And I told you, I was not sent to hunt you down. That's not my line of work."

"Says the man who has a stride like he could win the Boston Marathon. People your age aren't in that kind of shape for no reason."

I chuckled. "My age? Okay, I'm thirty-six, which probably feels like about seventy to you. And you're…"

"Twenty-three."

"A kid."

"I've seen more than any kid should have."

He tugged at a loose thread on the couch and then picked at a fingernail. I'd just had a gun to my head, yet it was Casper who seemed worked up. Was he suffering from some type of PTSD? He was an MP, so I was unsure how much battlefield experience he had. I shifted my eyes toward the kitchen pantry.

"He's a lowlife. No need to worry about his rights. He should be rotting in jail." Casper chugged his beer.

"So why isn't he?"

"In jail?"

I nodded.

"Who knows? Maybe law enforcement doesn't think he's important enough to pick up."

"Why did you pick him up?"

He shrugged and went back to pulling at loose threads, not uttering a word.

"Look, I respect your desire to do your own thing and all, but you put a gun to the back of my head."

"I wasn't going to shoot."

"Tell that to my machine-gun pulse."

"I know how to use my weapon safely."

"People can get itchy trigger fingers."

"I just…"

He didn't speak for a few seconds, so I walked back over to the window to see if any unexpected visitors were in the vicinity. All clear. And then Casper finally spoke again.

"The guy in the pantry is a low-level grunt for the Corsican Mafia."

I just stared through the slats of the blinds to the outside.

"They're some bad dudes, Zane. Money laundering, racketeering, extortion, even drug trafficking. Makes the old French Connection look like a weekly poker club. But that's not my fight."

I turned, my eyes stopping on the blank white wall, which served as the backdrop for my mind to surf through the events of the night. A gear clicked, and I looked at Casper. "The two guys who tried to rob me, kill me… Are they part of this Corsican Mafia?"

A single nod.

"You were following them. That's why you were there to save me."

Another nod. "I think they're just foot soldiers, though."

"Damn." More than cops might be looking for Casper.

"Again. I'm not trying to break up the mafia."

"Okay, so tell me...what *is* your fight?" I asked. "Why did you kidnap that guy?"

"He knows stuff."

"Stuff." I shrugged, growing frustrated with his dodge game. "Look, Casper, or whatever your real name is, I appreciate you saving my ass back in the alley, but I need to know what I've stepped into here."

He scratched his scalp through his cropped hair, took another swig of his beer, and set the bottle next to his gun. He finally looked me in the eye. "There are disturbing rumors on the base. An officer has ties to a Neo-Nazi group."

"If you were trying to shock me, you accomplished your goal."

"I'm no shock-jock, man. I'm not lying about the rumors, though."

I nodded. "But what does a low-level grunt in the Corsican Mafia have to do with this officer or the Neo-Nazi group?"

"We need evidence confirming that the officer is tied to the Neo-Nazi group, or some way of showing the rumors are unfounded. The Corsican Mafia has loose ties to this same Neo-Nazi group, and—"

"And you think this low-level guy has information about your Army officer dancing with the Nazis?" I pointed at the pantry with my beer.

He shook his head, stood up, and began to pace. At the kitchen, he turned and faced me. I could see green arteries snaking down the side of his head. "There are reports that one of the Neo-Nazis wants to defect, and the Corsican Mafia is holding the guy as a favor for their demented Nazi friends."

My head was almost spinning with that story. If it were true. But why would he make it up? "And you want the man in the pantry to tell you where they're holding the Neo-Nazi defector so you can get to him and find out if he knows about any ties the Neo-Nazi group has to your officer."

"Bingo. By the way, my real name is Cletus. Cletus Jacobsen."

"I'll call you Casper."

5

The Q&A session with Casper lasted a couple of hours. I asked some probing questions, which prompted him to inquire more about my background. On and on it went. I held steadfast to my fake persona, restating that I was a photographer, and my interview chops came from a stint at a newspaper. That appeased the MP. For now.

Casper asked me not to turn him in for kidnapping the mafia grunt. I wouldn't have done it anyway, even if I did question his methods of operating in a foreign country as a representative of the US Army. When our taxi pulled up to my apartment building, he said he appreciated having a non-military person to talk to about his operation. We exchanged cell phone numbers and decided to touch base at least once a day. A minimal time investment. I owed him that much; the man had saved my life. Plus, he seemed to know who was important and how things worked in this city. I couldn't pay for that kind of insider knowledge.

One concern: Casper hadn't mentioned sharing the progress of his Neo-Nazi investigation with his commanding officer. Maybe it had been a verbal oversight.

I slept in restless sprints, then finally gave up. So many concerns, questions, thoughts—none of them conducive to rest and relaxation.

I also worried about my own mission. I couldn't sleepwalk through kidnapping one of the top officials at Interpol. The odds were stacked against me succeeding. Familiar territory. But just like with my first mission—where the ultimate goal had been to locate a world-renowned hacker and force him to steal the secret algorithm code from the Asian online giant Alibaba—I questioned Simon's true intention for the bold abduction.

On the surface, the purpose seemed rather straightforward: Simon wanted three key cyber investigations to be shut down. The question was *why*. The only answer I could ascertain was the simplest one: Simon would be implicated somehow if those investigations proceeded. If that was the case, then my mind had already jumped to the next step: could this mission be an opportunity for me to finally uncover who ran Simon? And if I found out the details of Simon's criminal involvement in the cyberattacks, could I somehow use that as leverage to secure my freedom? Of course, they had the ultimate power, holding the virtual syringe that could kill me at a moment's notice.

I'd successfully completed my first mission, allowing me to get my daughter Maddie back, just long enough to get her settled in with her aunt. Simon had demanded I complete three more missions before I'd be released from my "contract." Three more times putting my life on the line. Three more times my daughter could lose her remaining parent.

There was a knock on my apartment door.

"Hi, Miss Patty."

The slender woman, who had gray hair pulled into a ponytail and soft features, placed her hand over her heart. "You had me worried, monsieur. When I awoke, I realized you had not stopped by my place. I feared the worst."

"Sorry I didn't drop by. It was so late. I didn't want to disturb you."

"I guess you don't know me. I'm a bit of what you Americans call a worry worm."

I smiled at her motherly qualities, with no intention of correcting her comment. "Well, I'm all in one piece."

Her eyes stared at my hands. "You fell."

"Tripped on the road while I was looking at the stunning architecture. It's not the first time I've made such a klutzy move. Probably not my last either."

"Would you like any hydrogen peroxide?"

"It's nothing."

"Very well." She started to walk away, but then stopped and turned toward me. "Lyon is a beautiful city with a rich history, Monsieur Ellington. But beneath the surface, there is an element of unsavory behavior that most Lyonnais find abhorrent. These criminals have no scruples. Please watch yourself. They prey on foreigners who do not know the ways of this land."

I took that warning with me to lunch. I ate pizza and drank wine, my thoughts churning on Miss Patty's words. Her warning had been direct. Was it born from a personal experience?

6

My target destination this afternoon was in the 9th arrondissement. The route I would take to reach the destination was not intended to be direct. In fact, it would be the opposite.

I grabbed a cab and, using very rough French, asked the driver to take me to the La Basilique of Notre-Dame de Fourvière, which sat in the 5th arrondissement. I was dropped off at the bottom of the steep incline on Saint-Barthélemy, near the entrance to the Parc des Hauteurs—the hillside park on the east side of the massive church.

With my camera strapped around my neck, I began the upward trek along the winding path lined with lush greenery, trellis after trellis adorned with colorful flowers and vines. I brought the Nikon D850 to my eye and took several shots of the pink flowers. As much as it was an automatic action—Anna's favorite color was pink—I'd done it with intent. If I were to be questioned by law enforcement, I would need my camera to be filled with many pictures of Lyon.

I came into contact with several tourists along the path. The United Nations was well represented. I heard at least six different languages spoken, including a couple of families speaking Mandarin. That reminded me of my recent foray in Hong Kong, one I was lucky to have survived.

At the top of the park, I paused on the suspension bridge, dubbed "The Four Winds." The views from this position were spectacular. Vieux Lyon—Old Town—sat on the east banks of the Saone River. It was surrounded by mansions with hidden courtyards from the Renaissance era. I took a slew of photos to show off my interest in all types of architecture and lighting and angles.

As I fell in line with other groups walking toward the Basilica, I was filled with a sense of awe at its greatness. The structure had been built following the Franco-Prussian War in 1894, relatively new by European standards.

The moment I stepped into the main sanctuary, there were muted gasps all around, even from me. My eyes were struck by the light caught in the elaborate gold mosaics, which told the story of the Virgin Mary in the history of France and the Church. One mosaic that stood out featured the arrival of Saint Pothin in Lyon. I bypassed the more detailed tour of the church and headed outside again, to the Esplanade de Fourvière.

I had a hefty walk ahead of me—the next phase of my expedition—and I was grateful when the steamy sun slid behind a cotton-ball cloud.

"Hey, will you take our picture?" A young woman with bright red hair and a brighter smile was nestled against a young man, possibly a boyfriend. Given her accent and the Alabama Crimson Tide logo on her T-shirt, I guessed she was from the American southeast.

I hesitated, just wanting to move on with my plans.

"It's okay. You don't have to," the young man said while subtly shaking his head.

They looked to be college-aged and in love. I really wanted to keep walking, but I didn't want to be a jerk.

The young woman held up her phone. "Here you go."

I smiled—on the outside—and took the phone, snapped off a few shots as they posed this way and that way. The young lady eagerly took back her phone, and the couple surfed through the pictures, giggling every few seconds.

A hint of melancholy came over me. While I missed my little girl, I knew she was safe with her Aunt Zeta in Dallas. I'd see her again, hopefully soon. But my wife? I'd yet to allow myself to fully deal with the grief from her horrific murder. I'd been so spun around with these missions that I'd buried my emotions. The anguish. I had to finish this work and get back to my Maddie. No other way for me to handle things than to laser focus on the endgame. If I opened the painful floodgates to my grief, I'd be down for the count, unable to fulfill my forced obligation to Simon. I'd be lucky to do anything more than breathe.

"Merci beaucoup," the young woman said with a soft giggle, and then she kissed her boyfriend. His eyes glazed over—the same response I used to have when Anna kissed me.

Not now, Jack. Not now. I shoved those thoughts into a distant compartment in my mind and walked toward the expansive grounds on the north side of the church.

Smaller buildings ran endlessly along the walkway until it crossed in front of the metallic tower of Fourvière, a miniature version of the Eifel Tower and one of Lyon's most iconic symbols.

I descended the steep hill along a flight of steps until I was under a dense canopy of trees, the sun barely poking through. There were tourists along the route, but only a handful. I'd taken this direction as a test, one that I'd assess when I reached my next destination. The trail reached a Y, and I veered right.

At the bottom of the hill, I turned left on Montauban and

walked alongside the road. The directions I'd mapped out in the apartment had matched reality. After a quarter mile, I cut across the road, walked down a small hill, then made my way into Bar Le 42. The swanky bar—all dark wood and muted lighting—was half empty this midafternoon. Wanting to enjoy the sights, I found a table near the back windows overlooking the Saone River.

I ordered a beer and pretzels. Surfed my phone. And waited ... for the refreshments, yes. But mostly for anyone I recognized, someone who might have followed me during my tour of the Basilica.

I thanked the waitress when she dropped off the order, then took a long pull on my Heineken, ending with an "ahhh." Glanced around for the umpteenth time. Saw no suspicious characters, which I knew meant nothing really, but still... It was something to be grateful for in that moment. I checked scores of the NBA playoffs back home, specifically the Memphis Grizzlies. I'd attended a few Grizzlies games with my buddy Daniel, the only person from my previous life with whom I'd connected since the start of this nightmare. And that was only to help me get Maddie settled with her Aunt Zeta. Simon had given us all of twenty-four hours to complete Maddie's transition from captivity to freedom under the watchful eye of a caretaker of my choosing. Just another in a long list of reasons to loathe every person associated with that group.

The Griz were up 2-0 in their first-round series against the Jazz. There was a highlight of Ja Morant seemingly float through the air before dunking over the Jazz center. While I craved returning to my old life, I recognized that was likely never to happen. Outside of being with my daughter, it was difficult to picture a new life in Donelson without Anna at my side.

Not now, Jack. Not now.

More snacking, more surfing, and I became more comfortable that I hadn't been followed. My mind drifted back to the events of the previous night. It had taken quite a bit of coaxing to get Casper to share the details of why there was a man tied up in his pantry. But when he did, I was amazed. I'd never associated Lyon, France, with the mob. But where there was money and commerce, crime wasn't far behind.

Before I was almost killed three times in an hour, I would have thought Lyon too picturesque a city for such violent behavior. My research had essentially stated as much.

Casper had said he didn't intend to harm the foot soldier in the pantry. I'd almost questioned his sincerity, but I held back. He seemed to have a lot invested in the search for answers, for the defector from the Neo-Nazi group. He was dedicated to his job, to the orders he was given. However, it made little sense to me why his superiors had sent him on a solo mission to prove or disprove evidence that a US military officer had ties to a Neo-Nazi group. In my old life as a "simple man" and owner of a small accounting firm, I had consumed a decent amount of news to stay up on the latest. I'd read stories about the military trying to uproot small pockets of hate groups within the ranks, but never heard of the military indicting an officer for those crimes.

I owed Casper a great debt for saving my life. How I might repay that debt, I couldn't predict. But I wouldn't allow it to put my Simon mission at risk.

There was a squeal of laughter behind me, and my eyes darted from my phone to the window, where I saw a troubling reflection. And this time, it wasn't my mug.

The Crimson Tide couple had just walked into the bar. They'd followed me from the Basilica.

My trust radar fired off a strong warning signal.

7

I'd yet to take any substantive steps toward the kidnapping of the Interpol official. Still much to be done in terms of surveillance, planning, and execution.

And watching my back.

Who could this young Bama couple be working for?

I recalled the early stages when my life had flipped on a dime. I'd discovered my wife murdered and my daughter kidnapped. Was then thrust into a position that required I use skills I didn't know I possessed.

Truth be told, I winged it most of the time in a world to which I was not accustomed. I did have a mentor of sorts during that first mission, even if she didn't realize it. An agent working for China's version of the CIA: the MSS. Su Lien was savvy, athletic, and determined like few others I'd met before or since. Because we had a shared common goal—to shut down a trafficking ring—we'd essentially worked as partners.

But it was the young woman we'd rescued, twenty-year-old

Cai Chen, who'd publicly embarrassed the Chinese Communist Party. She was the leader of the new protest movement. And some would say I'd aided her in the effort. The MSS had good reason to want to eliminate me.

Could the MSS have convinced these two young Americans—from the southeast region of the US, my stomping grounds—to show up in France and keep a bead on me?

I imagined Su would say, *"Absolutely. Yes."*

Which is why my internal alarm was going off.

A tap on my shoulder.

"Hi there." The young lady gave me a round wave, her face split with an effervescent smile.

"Hi."

"You must think we're stalking you or something." She giggled, looked over at her boyfriend, who was sitting at a table nearby, then turned back to me.

"You're reading my mind perfectly," I said flatly.

Her jaw dropped.

"Just kidding, of course." Which I wasn't, but no sense in starting something that may be nothing. Hopefully.

She giggle-snorted this time, which then led to a louder howl. A few of the patrons gave us the eye. "On our way to the bar, I was telling Evan how I felt like maybe I'd been a bit rude to you back at the Basilica. Just lost in my own weird world."

I nodded and attempted to smile. I must have pulled it off, since she kept talking. "Anyway, I guess it's fate that we ran into you here. Now I get to apologize. So ... I'm *so* sorry. Forgive me?"

One of my eyebrows inched higher. "Sure. But for what exactly?"

"Not introducing myself." She stuck out a hand, and I shook it. "I'm Karma. And that big lug is my boyfriend, Evan."

"Karma and Evan. Nice to meet you. I'm Zane."

"I like that name. Where did you come up with that?"

That eyebrow moved higher on my forehead. "I'm sorry?"

Another giggle-snort. "I thought you could read my mind." She waved at Evan to join us and continued. "Evan and I are already thinking about future baby names."

"Oh? You're expecting?"

"Hell no," Evan said.

Karma crossed her arms and tapped her foot.

Bad Karma?

Evan adjusted. "I mean, we want to have kids eventually. Down the line. After we're married, get two dogs, and grow tired of each other."

"What are you talking about?" she said, her face all scrunched up.

"That's what my parents told me how it works." He shrugged. "Just ignore me."

She rolled her eyes and put her arm around him. "He's a little clueless, but I still love him."

"Well, it's nice to meet two folks from the States. Native to Alabama?" I was eager to hear their answers.

"He's from Auburn, our hated rival. But at least he ended up at the best school on the planet. I was born and raised in Tuscaloosa."

"Nice."

"You from the Southeast?"

"Actually, I was raised in Pennsylvania, went to school in New York."

"Where?"

"NYU. One of the best photography schools in the country."

She touched my shoulder, then quickly pulled her finger off while releasing a hissing sound. "Ooh, aren't you too hot to trot. That's a fancy, schmancy school. We're just a couple of hicks."

If she only knew the same label could be applied to me, having attended the University of Tennessee.

Or maybe she did.

"Well, we're sorry to have bothered you. Again," Evan said with a side-glance to his other half.

"You want to join us for a drink? We'll even pay," Karma said.

"I need to get going, but thanks anyway."

I breathed a sigh of relief when they walked away. I got my stuff together, paid my bill, and headed for the exit. Right past their table.

"Hey, Zane." Karma tugged on my shirtsleeve. "Let's trade numbers. We might be interested in paying you to do a professional photoshoot of us in Lyon."

"Well, I…"

The phone number transaction was completed before I knew what had hit me. I said they could give me a call. Of course, I didn't say I'd answer it. "It was nice meeting you, Evan and Karma."

"You never made a snide comment about my name," Karma said. "Almost everybody does."

I shrugged. "To each his own. Or her own."

"What can I say? My mom was a bit of a hippie. But at least you didn't say 'Karma's a bitch.'"

I laughed all the way to the door, wondering how I could have missed *that* one.

8

The city bus dropped me off in the heart of the 9th arrondissement. I walked the neighborhood, stopping to take pictures of homes, boutique hotels, and various angles of the Saone River. Having a master zoning plan wasn't a viable option for old cities like Lyon. Therefore, the photos would serve not only as my cover, but also as a guide for this mission. What was where, and how would it all connect to my target. I only hoped my visit here would be reasonably short and successful.

Failure was not an option.

I turned onto the street that housed the head of Interpol's Cybercrime Intelligence Unit, Pierre Amadou. The ex-pat, born and raised in Cameroon, had been in the position for six years, one of the longest tenures for any given role at the agency. Before that, he'd served in associate positions in the same unit, was schooled in the UK, and had even served an internship for the FBI in the States. His resume was long and impressive. And from what I'd read about him in the dossier supplied by Simon, his scruples were impeccable. I could only guess how they knew that: Simon had considered bribing Amadou but realized it would lead nowhere? Or perhaps they had actually attempted to bribe the man and failed. And now, desperate, they'd ordered me to kidnap the official.

Not at easy feat, especially without a support team.

I stopped across the street from Amadou's house to take a snapshot of a small pond, complete with lily pads and frogs. A small oasis surrounded by older buildings and even pockets of trees. I swung around and snapped a few shots of the front of Amadou's home, which was more of a complex, most of it fenced in, with a healthy array of shrubs and trees adding to the coverage. There was a small driveway in the front that fed into a one-car garage. Based on property specs and a high-level design of the home, I knew there was a larger parking area in the back, adjacent to a smaller bunkhouse. Unlike most homes in Lyon, the two-story main house was designed using contemporary architecture with its minimalist lines that merged with the natural landscape.

I walked to the end of the street, turned right, and made my way up an incline until I reached a small cluster of trees on the side of a hill. This position offered me a cleaner view of the entire complex. Even with trees blocking parts of the back and side yards, I could see the bunkhouse. It was detached, and from what I'd learned, no one currently lived there. Amadou's mother-in-law had stayed with his family up until a month ago but had since returned to the UK. Amadou would occasionally leave his family in the larger house to take agency calls from the bunkhouse. According to the dossier, though, the most pressing concern were the security guards who accompanied Amadou to and from work, or to any other meetings throughout the city. Strangely, the security detail would escort Amadou on some trips and not on others. I surmised that they based it on potential threats the agency had picked up through internet chatter, or even directly through one of its investigations. If it was below a certain risk threshold, Amadou could travel without the security detail.

My decision on when and how to pull off this unlikely abduction centered first and foremost on the presence of the security guards. Additionally, I would ascertain any patterns on the routes to and from the Interpol headquarters, as well as any other habits. The data-gathering would start this evening. Hopefully. As I'd learned from my MSS counterpart, people change their rituals without notice and for no easily identifiable explanation. And it was up to those in our profession to be fluid and think on the fly.

Knowing I couldn't afford to have any residents view me as a suspicious person and call the police, I took another two dozen shots and started to walk toward the bus stop. With my luck, or lack thereof, the tall officer with the loping stride at the footbridge would show up.

Halfway to the Leclair bus stop, my phone buzzed with a text. Simon often wanted status updates on a moment's notice. I was relieved it wasn't them. "Casper the friendly ghost," I muttered after seeing the contact ID.

His message read: *Can you meet me at Bar Le 42 tonight at 8? Want to bounce a couple ideas off you.*

I stopped walking. The hair on the back of my neck stood up. Did Casper know I'd recently visited that very same bar? I wasn't carrying a tracking device. Maybe he knew someone at the bar who'd then relayed the info to him.

Chill, Jack. It's probably just a coincidence.

But I didn't believe in coincidences. Not in this new life, where trust and transparency were nothing more than fleeting concepts. If I automatically trusted everyone I met, it wouldn't be long before one of those folks put a bullet in the back of my head.

Would Casper be the one to pull the trigger?

9

Casper had already pulled a gun on me once. We'd patched up our differences but feeling the metal barrel pressed against the back of my head was not something I'd soon forget.

While I still thought Casper had more to his backstory than he was letting on, he seemed to have a decent moral compass. Sure, he'd murdered another human being, but it wasn't out of malice. He'd saved my life. Was he just supposed to stand there and watch the guy with the chain detach my head from the rest of my body?

Regardless, I wouldn't let my guard down again. I couldn't take the risk, not even with a fellow American who'd saved my life.

I typed in a quick reply to Casper—*See you at 8*—and jumped on the bus, taking a window seat on a row with no other people. The planned route of the bus would take about twenty to thirty minutes. I was eager to see Interpol up close for the first time. As my eyes scanned the landscape, my brain was cataloging every data point.

Flow of traffic at 5:15 p.m. local time (most of it moving out of the city).

Number of vehicles on the roads (rather dense).

Number of pedestrians (most of them getting on and off buses).

All of it. Anything that was important or even *seemed* important for me to successfully complete my mission.

The bus screeched to halt, and I arched my neck and peered through the front window. Road construction. Just like the States.

A moment later, the bus door opened, and a woman boarded. She engaged the driver for a moment, then sat right next to me. Using a small handkerchief, she dabbed her cheeks, nose, and the forehead, at least the small amount not covered by her veil. Based on the habit she wore… had to be a nun. She turned and smiled at me, and I reciprocated with a cordial smile then looked out the window. I watched men dig a hole for a few seconds, and my mind veered to the three main investigations that Simon wanted shut down. But not for long.

"I hope I didn't take the seat of your companion," the nun said in a thick but understandable French accent.

What was she talking about…? I glanced over my shoulder. There was a woman standing in the aisle, swaying to music coming faintly through her earbuds. "Nope, I'm all alone."

"I see. American?"

"Did my accent give me away?"

"I knew it before you spoke."

I gave a long nod.

"Americans just have this…" She tilted her head left and right as if debating which negative term to use. I'd heard stories about how the French felt about Americans.

"Cockiness?"

She smiled. "Confidence. You carry this confidence like others I've met from your country."

All that in about five seconds. "I'll take that as a compliment." "Please do." And then she crossed herself.

She opened her Bible and began to read. The construction workers were still blocking the bus's path, so I immersed myself once again in the tangled channels of my mind, this operation.

Simon had a consistent record of supplying a plethora of intel remotely important to my mission, but when it came to the actual cyber investigations, the information was notably thin. The mission dossier provided the high-level basics: the investigations involved ransomware attacks on three separate companies, in three different countries, impacting three different industries:

One, Green River, the top solar panel company in the United States.

Two, the Shanghai Stock Exchange in China.

Three, Kozlov Crude, the third largest oil and gas company in Russia.

Everything else I'd learned came from my own personal research. Green River, while relatively small compared to the other two companies, with revenues just under one billion, was a Wall Street darling. Its stock had tripled since the initial offering and was considered the new standard barrier in the field of green energy. Highly protective of its pristine image, the company paid the hackers their asking price of $50 million in less than twenty-four hours.

The Shanghai Stock Exchange, a.k.a. the SSE, was a unique configuration, considered "not profit-oriented." In the US, one might assume it was a non-profit, which would allow it generous tax breaks. But China operated on a different plane. The SSE was part of a state-owned enterprise with direct links to the Communist Party, and its chairman was appointed by the Central Committee. The value of companies listed on the SSE was $6.24 trillion. With over $100 billion in trades every day, I was not surprised to see the SSE as a target of a ransomware attack but was surprised they didn't have the most advanced security in the world to thwart it. The SSE reportedly paid the ransom—$500 million—after only six hours.

Moscow's Kozlov Crude appeared to be a run-of-the-mill, old-fashioned energy company. It made no real headlines, yielded a decent profit, and had just been chugging along for the thirty years of its existence. But the devil was in the details, specifically in its ownership structure. A majority interest was owned by a wealthy oligarch, Dmitri Popov. One of the minority partners, however, was the eye-catcher: Nicholai Putin. Yes, *that* Putin.

Kozlov's operations were completely shut down for seven days as the company worked feverishly to recover their systems without paying the ransom. Message boards indicated owners feared the bad PR for its business and for the leader of the Russian government. But no one was able to out-hacker the hackers, and Kozlov ended up paying a ransom of $100 million.

The bus finally inched around the construction.

"Dier merci."

I glanced at the nun. "Thank you…something?"

"Thank God." She couldn't hide her wry grin. "Nuns are people too."

"That's nice to hear." I lifted my sights to focus again on our journey to the Interpol headquarters. But in the background, my mind was still chewing on the three ransomware attacks. They'd hit three of the biggest countries in the world. Two were superpowers, while one (Russia) was constantly trying to bully its way onto the main stage. If Simon or someone related to the group was indeed behind all three of these attacks, this told me they had no allegiances to those three countries. Or, better stated, their allegiances were to money over country.

In my first mission, Simon had at one point demonstrated the characteristics of a benevolent organization—blowing up a trafficking ring and saving a girl. It was only after I'd rescued Cai

Chen that Simon revealed the true purpose of the first mission. It became crystal clear that Simon followed just one central edict: greed above all else.

We finally reached the roundabout and turned east on Marietton. After two blocks, we crossed over the Saone. I snapped a few photos looking north and south on the river, ensuring I picked up the view of the walking areas next to the bridge's railing, which appeared to be about three feet high.

"May I ask if you are a professional photographer?"

"Yes." I pulled my eyes off the road. "And yes, I'm a photographer."

"You look like you really enjoy your work. Or do you even call it work?"

"Sometimes I've used other four-letter words. No offense, Sister."

"Sister Jeanne." She extended her hand, and I shook it briefly before offering my fake name.

When we entered the Tunnel de la Croix-Rousse, the tires hummed in the tube, but traffic was light, moving at a steady speed. About a quarter of the way in, I noticed a door on the far wall. There was also a sign with a phone symbol. The architects had planned for emergencies. There were three additional exits at various intervals. I took more pictures all the way through the one-mile tunnel.

We emerged to a blinding sun. I glanced around, and everyone, including Sister Jeanne, had donned sunglasses.

"I can see you're new to the city." She touched the black rim of her sunglasses. "On assignment?"

"Working on my own photography book."

"Interesting. We have such wonderful historic sites in Lyon. Yet you took pictures of the inside of a tunnel." She giggled.

I shrugged, hoping to avoid further explanation.

The bus traveled another block and crossed the Rhone. Lush

trees lined both banks, with mostly white, six-story buildings serving as the backdrop. I snapped a few more shots of our surroundings, although I could still not yet see the Interpol building off to the northeast.

After two more turns, we finally hit Charles de Gaulle Way. The largest park in Lyon proper sat to our right, a pond in the middle of it. That park acted as a buffer between the back of the Interpol headquarters up on our right and Stalingrad Boulevard about a mile to our east. The location of the HQ building was not by accident.

As the road and river bent to the right, the bus slowed to a crawl just before we reached the massive headquarters. I focused on the entrance into the site, with multiple levels of security. An eight-foot metal gate was the most formidable structure. Ten feet in front of that, a wooden arm blocked the narrow entryway. A camera sat on a stone wall high above the action. From what I'd read in the dossier, people would have to show their ID to the camera, the arm would lift, and the metal gate would open. Once a person adequately passed that level of security, there was a second wooden arm and a strip of metal spikes on the road that could be raised or lowered as needed. Two security guards sat in a small building behind bulletproof glass for entry control. Once a security guard provided approval, only then could someone get access to the parking area.

The exit to the facility was right next to the entrance. As we motored past the main building—another modern architecture marvel—I took note of the lush vegetation that sat between the narrow sidewalk and the metal fence that rimmed the grounds.

"You know, I've always wondered what they actually do in that building." Sister Jeanne tapped a finger to her chin. "So secretive."

I mumbled an acknowledgement and snapped photos like a maniac.

I got back to my apartment and spent three hours poring through every picture. One thing was glaringly obvious: there was no way I'd be able to breach Interpol's security to sneak into Amadou's car and wait for him to leave work. I'd have to be much more inventive to pull off the abduction of the head of the Cybercrime Intelligence Unit.

I'd begin trailing Amadou in the morning. For now, I would go to Bar Le 42 to meet up with Casper.

10

I took a circuitous route to the bar, just to be on the safe side. Two buses, the second stopping four blocks north of my destination. As I walked along the west side of the Saone, I looked over my shoulder, taking a mental snapshot of every person to determine if they had been on the buses. So far, I was in the clear.

Half a block before I reached the front door, I heard my fake name being called.

I stopped and turned. At the precipice of an alley off to the right, the amber glow of a cigarette lit up Casper's face.

I approached. "Is there a reason you're hiding in the alley?"

He dropped his cigarette and snuffed it out with his shoe. "Not going to the bar. Change of plans."

"Why?"

"Got new information."

"About?"

A group of men strolled by, and Casper's eyes tracked them the whole way. Once they were a good twenty feet past us, he took two steps in my direction and spoke under his breath. "We don't need to be sharing this with the world. Follow me, and I'll tell you on the way to my car."

He walked deeper into the alley. I didn't budge. After a few steps, he realized I hadn't followed him, and he reversed course until he stood next to me. "You don't trust me."

"Is that a question?"

He chuckled. "Sorry I'm being so…"

He waited for me to fill in the blank. I didn't.

"Okay, fine. You're pissed," he said. "Makes sense, especially after I overreacted last night."

"I'll agree with you on that point."

People shouted from behind me—more like a gleeful cheer—and Casper glanced over my shoulder. "Look, Zane, I just need to show you something that's about twelve kilometers outside the city."

"You've dug a hole in the ground for me?"

He narrowed his eyes. "I'm not the bad guy here."

"This something that is twelve kilometers outside the city… Who gave you the information?"

He smiled, but it was uneven. "The man in the pantry."

"Is he still alive?" I asked, thinking about Casper wielding the gun like a madman.

"You think I'd…? Hell yeah, he's still alive. I don't kill prisoners. Some countries do, but not us."

He'd suddenly wrapped himself in the American flag. "What exactly did he share with you?"

"He confirmed the family running the crime organization. The Campanellas."

"Confirmed. So that's something you already suspected?"

He nodded. "Dominic is the godfather. He just got into town and set up shop at this villa that's—"

"Twelve kilometers outside the city. What's the objective of this, uh...?"

"Just surveillance."

"You think there's a possibility they could be holding that Neo-Nazi defector at this villa? Did the guy in the pantry tell you that?"

"He claims he doesn't know."

"And you didn't beat it out of him?"

"Hey, I told you—"

I held up my hand. "I know, I know." I scanned the area around us one more time, looking for anyone suspicious, but also using the time to gauge the risk factor: whether I could believe that Casper was not just telling me the truth, but the whole story.

"You've got to trust me," he said.

"Did you read my mind?"

"Maybe."

"I'll follow you to your car, but when we're in the dark in the alley, I want you to give me your gun."

"How do you know I'm packing?"

"I can read your mind just as easily."

11

Irigny, France

Casper exited the A7 motorway, and the loud engine in the old-model BMW quieted to a level where I could finally think. But just barely.

"Where did you find this piece?" I asked.

"The pistol?" He nudged his head at the gun, which was on the floorboard next to my feet.

"I was talking about the car. I'm assuming the pistol is straight from the US Army."

He nodded. "The Beretta M9. Standard sidearm of the Navy, Army, and Air Force since 1985. I would ask if you've shot one before, but I'm assuming you've never served in the Armed Forces."

I shook my head and peered out the window. We were heading east toward a countryside villa, and dusk had begun to give way to darkness, especially in the dense forests on the side of the road.

Even with the car moving at a slower pace, the engine was still deafening. It was also emitting a foul smell, something akin to rotten eggs.

"You feel comfortable this old BMW won't kick the bucket right when we need it the most?" I asked.

"No guarantees."

Wonderful.

We took a right down a narrow two-lane road, then another sharp right. "You know your way around here pretty well," I said.

"I know how to read maps. Comes with the job. Speaking of jobs, where's your camera?"

"Back at my apartment."

He glanced at me. "They say photographers never leave home without their cameras."

I pulled out my phone and held it at eye level. "I thought we were getting a couple of beers, not taking a tour."

Brakes squealed as Casper pulled off to the side of the road, parking the car about twenty feet in the woods. "We're on foot the rest of the way," he said while exiting the car. "Don't forget to grab the pistol."

"I thought this was only a surveillance."

"Can't be too careful. I figured you'd be thinking the same thing since the guy who you stabbed in the leg is the youngest son of Dominic Campanella."

Halfway out the door, I stopped moving. "You never told me that."

"I didn't?" He grinned, his pale features practically glowing in the darkness. "Okay, okay," he said. "Don't want you to think you're losing your mind. I'd been doing some research."

I tapped the top of the BMW. "So you knew all along. Wow."

"I knew the names of his sons. It was only after that escapade in the alley that I was able to match the names to faces."

"Dominic has more than one son?"

"You betcha. Salvadore is the dude you stabbed in the leg. Biaggio is the one who shot at you."

"The bald guy."

He nodded.

"What about the Neanderthal, the one who almost broke my neck?"

"Just a goon for hire. You all good now?" He circled the car and trekked deeper into the woods.

"Have you told me everything?"

"Just grab the gun."

I picked up the pistol, shut the door, and caught up with Casper just before a gravel road intersected the woods. I handed him the gun. "You know how to use this better than I do."

"You're trusting me now. A good sign, since we're teaming up on this."

I wanted to dispute his wording about "teaming up," but we'd deal with how to label our roles later. "Does this road lead to the main house?"

"Yep. A private drive. We'll need to approach from the back. This way." He cut across the driveway and then marched into the woods on the far side. I was right behind him.

We hiked about a hundred yards through dense brush and trees, pausing at the edge of the forest. The area opened up to a grassy field with just a few trees sprinkled here and there. Off in the distance, the two-story mansion was illuminated by spotlights.

"Should we be worrying about guards or cameras?" I asked.

"Probably not cameras. Dominic rented the place. Best I can tell, he's been here before. They might have guards, but the property is so huge, it would take a battalion to cover every square inch. My guess is we'll see some security presence near the home. But that's why we brought The Widowmaker."

I looked around before realizing what he was referencing. "You've nicknamed your pistol?"

"Of course," he snickered.

While keeping a constant eye on the main house, we rimmed the edge of the woods to reach the east side of the property. I heard the rush of water before I actually saw the slate-black creek.

"We'll need to cross this to reach the back of the house," Casper said.

I dipped a hand in the water to test the depth. No more than a couple of feet. "Okay."

"You afraid you'll drown in two feet of water?"

Taking that as my cue to proceed, I stepped on four embedded rocks and nimbly hopped to the other side.

"Quick feet. You must be a dancer or something. My ex loved to dance. She told me I have two left feet." Casper tried to follow my path, but he slipped on the first rock, fell backward into the water. Flailing his arms, he gained purchase and plowed his way to the other side.

"Guess I know why you two broke up."

He rolled his eyes. "Just a little farther to the back. From there, I'm hoping we can see inside—"

I'd just tapped his shoulder and put a finger to my mouth. I pointed over his shoulder, where a man circled the house with a semi-automatic rifle in his hands. Casper and I eased our way behind a tree trunk. The guard paused at a stone water fountain and scanned the area.

"You think he saw us?" Casper whispered.

"Better chance he heard you storming through the creek. Be prepared to draw The Widowmaker."

"I'm always ready."

Didn't I know it.

Casper smacked my arm and chin-nodded toward the guard, who'd just brought a phone to his ear.

"He might be calling for more men," I said. "Maybe we should live to fight another day." I tugged at his shirt, but Casper stayed put behind the tree.

"If more men rush out of the building, then we take off," he said.

"You do realize bullets are faster than people, right?"

I weighed the idea of getting caught or, worse yet, injured in an operation that had nothing to do with Simon's directive. I flipped my head around and eyed the path we'd used to reach this point.

"He's walking away. Let's go." Casper had walked ten feet by the time I turned around to protest. I hustled up behind him.

"You think this is wise?"

"It's necessary."

It had been hours since I'd eaten, but I still felt food moving up my chest. Fortunately, we avoided any other run-ins with guards and positioned ourselves behind one of the large trees on the back side of the house. Beyond a trampoline in the yard area, there was general movement through floor-to-ceiling windows on the first floor.

"The trampoline. Just a little closer." Without warning, Casper stepped out from behind the tree.

"Do you have a fucking death wish?" I hissed.

He just kept moving. I stayed put for about two seconds, then dropped to the ground and bear-crawled to the back of the trampoline. At about thirty paces from the home, we were still cast in darkness. Well, not completely.

"You might need to cover your face," I said.

"Now you know how I got my nickname," he said, but he didn't bother covering up.

We scanned the windows for any sign of people. I hit pay dirt thirty seconds later. "Bald guy holding a glass in second window from right."

"I see him. Biaggio."

"Police didn't hold him very long," I said.

"Once they got him back to the station, word probably got around on who his father was."

"Dirty cops?"

"Bribery will always be one of the best tools in a criminal's arsenal. If that doesn't work, they turn to extortion or blackmail."

Casper was young, but it sounded like he had some experience in this field. I was rather naïve about the role of the military police. I'd always thought their focus was on drunk or unruly soldiers, that kind of thing.

"Zane, I'm gonna run up to the house and take a quick peak in those windows that are partially covered by blinds."

I couldn't believe what I was hearing. "Do you want to get caught, or even shot? I don't."

"We can't waste this opportunity. I'll be quick." He rushed off without saying another word, scurrying toward the giant home. All I could do was tug at blades of grass, hoping one of the crime family's guards wouldn't walk outside. But hope itself was not a great strategy. Even if Casper could somehow defend himself, more guards would likely appear in quick order.

While Casper surveyed the first-floor windows, I kept an eye on the second level, looking for any sign of a man under duress. While doing so, I started to think about what would happen if Casper actually found this Neo-Nazi defector. Would he come back later to get him? Surely he wouldn't try to extricate him on the spot. The risk would be off the charts.

"Goonies never say die." My daughter often recited that phrase, and right now, it was just what I needed to hear. Anna and I had allowed our only child to watch *The Goonies* movie. Halfway through, we started to regret that decision. Maddie began to hide behind the couch, only occasionally peeking above it to catch parts of a scene. But when the movie ended, she claimed she loved it and wouldn't have nightmares.

"Goonies never say die," she'd said, flicking her eyebrows,

repeating the memorable line from the movie. Anna and I laughed hysterically at our sweet girl, who continued to play it up and repeat the phrase—even though she really didn't know what it meant.

But I did. Death wasn't an option. Never say die.

A flicker of movement at the third window snagged my attention. I focused and waited for the man to reappear, hoping it wouldn't be one of the Campanella boys.

The person walked by the window again.

Not a man.

A woman with black hair draped just below her shoulders. I waited to see if she'd return. A few seconds passed. From my vantage point, I couldn't see very far into the room. I glanced up at the nearby tree—the first branch was a good fifteen feet off the ground. I pulled myself onto the edge of the trampoline, crawled to the far edge and stood, achieving a better view of the second floor. A moment later, the woman reappeared at the window and looked out.

At me?

Sure felt like it.

For some reason, I didn't hide. Her dark eyes seemed to be calling out for help. She was distressed. And so beautiful. Even though my heart would always be with my precious Anna, I couldn't deny this mystery woman was stunning. I became curious as to why she was there at the window, seemingly despondent and anxious, at a compound run by a crime family.

I gasped.

Was she the defector from the Neo-Nazi group?

Out of nowhere, an arm wrapped around the woman's neck. She whirled, her hand drawn back, to take a whack at an older man with graying temples. He blocked her slap, and then the two appeared to wrestle and left my line of sight.

A little boy appeared at the window. He was crying, his hands pressed against the side of his face.

Casper and I just had to save this mom, her little boy. Simple as that. No way I could leave without helping them, removing them out of danger.

Voices shouted, and a dog barked. I scrambled backward, dropping to my knees on the trampoline. A dog was running in the back yard. More yelling and then a shriek.

Casper? Holy... "Hold on, man!" I started to crawl to the other side of the trampoline, but halfway across, it ripped. I fell to the ground.

A menacing dog growled at me, mere inches from my face.

12

People yelled in languages I didn't understand, and lights splashed throughout the back yard. I didn't move. And neither did the Doberman.

"You a good puppy?" I spoke as though I were addressing a toddler.

He stopped growling. A small victory.

Another dog barked off in the distance. How many were there?

Someone whistled, and the Doberman bolted away from me. I wiped the sweat from my face and took some deep breaths.

Footfalls coming toward me. More than one person.

"Stop or I'll shoot!" someone yelled in accented English.

They had to be chasing Casper.

Two dark figures ran right past me. I assumed Casper was the one in front.

"Stop!" the man from behind yelled.

As I crawled on the grass to the edge of the trampoline, Casper whizzed by. The man chasing Casper raised a gun and took aim. I lunged for the man's legs, causing his knee to bend awkwardly. He flipped through the air with a yelp.

When he hit the ground, the gun went off.

"What the hell?" Casper ran over to the man, who was groaning. "He shot himself."

Back on my feet, I grabbed Casper's arm. "Let's get the hell out of here before they unleash the entire Doberman army."

As we raced away from the house, I glanced back at the second floor of the house. The mystery woman was standing at the window, looking right at me.

And I knew I would see her again.

13

On the drive back into Lyon, I was ready to rip into Casper, but he beat me to it. He apologized for being sloppy, for allowing his emotions to take the lead. I asked him why he was so emotionally invested in this operation.

"This is damn important, Zane." He glanced in the rearview mirror before continuing. "We've heard rumblings over the last couple of years that the Neo-Nazis might try to pull off a terrorist attack."

That caught me off guard. "Against who?"

His head and shoulders shifted in all directions. "The intel is spotty. It would be horrible if they actually targeted our base or our soldiers. But think about how that would look if one of our soldiers or officers was involved in the terror plot. It would be catastrophic."

And yet, according to Casper, he was the sole operator for this mission. Just didn't add up.

"And you're the only one assigned to this operation?" I

pressed.

A brief nod, but he didn't elaborate further.

I was dumbfounded by the approach taken by his superiors. I knew soldiers weren't supposed to question their orders, but this seemed crazy. Without support resources, his leaders were risking his life, and potentially others' too—like mine. There had to be more details, and Casper was following instructions to keep them under wraps. Not much I could do about it now. I switched gears.

"On our way to the car, when I told you about the mystery woman, you agreed that she could be the defector," I said.

"The way you described the confrontation, it makes sense."

"But you'd thought the defector was a guy."

"My prisoner threw out a name," he said. "I thought he was screwing with me. I just assumed it was a guy. My bad."

"The name was...?"

"Bailey."

The BMW hummed along on the barren country road, and I waited to see if Casper would suggest the logical next step. For me, that would be rescuing Bailey and the little boy, who I guessed was her son. This mysterious woman had somehow found one of the few remaining soft spots in my heart, which had nearly been blackened by grief. And even after this surveillance debacle, I still was drawn to help her. After five minutes of silence, I voiced my concerns.

"You know we can't sit on the sidelines, right?"

He looked at me. "Correct. We need to rescue the woman."

"The boy too. Can't leave him behind."

"Right. Then the woman can hopefully give us all the intel on the Neo-Nazi group, and we can nail the bastards involved at the base."

I wanted to help, but I wasn't suicidal. "What kind of support can you call in?"

"I saw four more guards inside the house. The guy who shot

himself in the shoulder will probably live, but he won't be as effective with his arm in a sling."

He'd completely dodged my question. I thrummed my fingers on the door panel, expecting him to address the support question. He didn't. "We'll need help. Technically, you shouldn't even need me. The Army has people who specialize in this type of extrication."

"Army Rangers. No way I could get authorization to use them."

"Okay, so how about fellow MPs? Or just a few foot soldiers?"

His forehead slowly folded. "If you want to bail, I get it. You're just a photographer, albeit one with some pretty slick skills. I'll figure something out."

I chuckled. "Slick skills?"

"The way you took that guy down."

"I ran track."

"Not football?"

I shook my head.

"All kidding aside, sports are one thing, Zane. No offense, but you're not made for this kind of thing, fighting for your life."

If he only knew. "No way you can pull off an operation like that alone. So, if you can't get any other support…"

I waited for a signal that he could drum up assistance from somewhere, but his face didn't move.

I blew out a long sigh. "Just count me in."

He eyed me for second, as though questioning my judgment, and then he simply faced forward and kept driving.

We agreed to brainstorm later in the day.

After a few hours of sleep, I arose barely refreshed, but it was better than nothing. I rented a scooter and zipped my way up the A6 until I reached the 9th arrondissement, then headed east toward Amadou's place. The brisk wind hitting my face sharpened my mind. Got my blood pumping.

I reached Amadou's neighborhood, stopping at the same hillside perch I'd used the previous day. Looking through the long lens of my Nikon, I spotted two men standing next to a white SUV in the paved parking area behind the main house. I snapped a few shots and pulled up the pictures, zoomed in and studied the content. Both men wore black sport coats and sneakers. More importantly, they were the size of middle linebackers, with prominent jaws and scowls to match. Amadou's security team. They appeared ready for any adversary. Not a fight I could win.

Amadou exited from the back door of the house. With a phone to his ear, he walked like a man with great confidence. He wore a sport coat, the fit impeccable, his leather shoes high end. He reached the SUV but didn't get in as he continued his call. The taller security guard walked over and tossed a set of keys from hand to hand, as if trying to get Amadou's attention. Amadou finally ended the call, pocketing his phone. The three men began to converse. Amadou's jaw was moving at a high velocity, his hands turned to the sky. Agitated. Because of the phone call or the security guards?

I'd thought about setting up a listening device. But it was possible, if not likely, that Amadou had security cameras everywhere. Too risky for me to get in and out undetected, so I opted out.

Amadou walked over to another car, a blue Audi sedan—an S8. He touched the hood and pointed at the SUV. Again, agitated. I couldn't even form a guess as to what had him all riled up.

A woman walked out of the house, and I recognized her as his wife. She was tall, and most of that was legs—striking. She smiled as she approached her husband. She did all the talking, with Amadou nodding a few times when she pointed at the SUV. Then she leaned in close to his ear, obviously conveying a private message. He nodded again, and she went back inside the house. He shrugged and belted out a chuckle I could hear from my position. He slipped into the back seat of the SUV, while the two guards sat in the front, and they pulled out of the driveway.

Showtime.

14

I knew something was off the moment Amadou's driver turned south on Berthet. The previous day on the bus, I'd gone north on Berthet to get to Interpol headquarters. The most direct route.

A precautionary switch-up or were they headed to another destination?

The white SUV, a Renault Captur, went southbound on the A6, and I continued my pursuit. With no shortage of scooters in Lyon, it was fairly easy for me to blend in with other scooter riders, although the smaller engines made it difficult to keep up with the faster cars. Afraid I'd lost them at one point, I pulled away from the cover of the scooter pack to open my field of vision. Saw a Captur quite a ways up ahead in the far lane. I kicked it in as much as the scooter would allow and made it within three car lengths—Amadou was in the back seat, so I eased back on the throttle.

I still had no idea where they were headed.

We crossed into the 6th arrondissement but remained on the east side of the Rhone. This elongated journey could be nothing more than an intended misdirection play. I'd surmised that security guards were only used when there was sufficient risk to Amadou's life to warrant increased protection. If this was one of those times, maybe they needed to employ extra precautions, like taking a circuitous route.

Off to the east, a large park with the serene pond in the middle.

Red lights brought me back to the road—I was almost on top of the SUV. I pressed the handle brake. Turned the scooter hard right. Its back end bump-skidded across the road. I dropped my foot to the ground and rocked to a stop. My back wheel was just under the SUV's bumper—but I didn't make contact.

Amadou started to turn to look out the back window. I promptly dropped my head, as though I were inspecting the scooter for damage.

The SUV motored away and turned right onto Churchill Bridge. I pulled my heart out of my throat and allowed cars and scooters to fill in behind the Captur while I hung back. Two minutes later, the SUV turned into the Interpol entry area. I slowed my pace to see the metal gate slowly swing open.

Now the waiting game begins. I still had much to learn about his Amadou's habits—work or otherwise. I grabbed a Diet Coke at a nearby corner convenience store and found a shady spot under a scraggly tree across from the Interpol headquarters.

It only took a few minutes before my mind started wandering, drifting down memory lane. Quick snapshots of events, randomly taking center stage then fading to the next one. Maddie's fourth birthday, when she buried her face in her cake. My wedding day with Anna, when it felt like we were both floating above ground. Our last family meal together, spaghetti and meatballs. I had nothing else to pull me away, to occupy my mind. No dossier to read or risk-mitigation plan to develop. No injury to rehab. It was just me and my mind with more time than I could stand.

I needed a diversion.

Just then—as if someone upstairs had seen my inner demons approaching—a text popped up on my phone. It was from Aunt Zeta.

Thought you'd like to see your daughter in action.

I tapped the attached video and watched a twenty-second clip of Maddie running alongside Aunt Zeta's dog, Spots, through an obstacle course. Maddie giggled the entire time as the handsome Australian shepherd playfully barked and wagged his tail all the way to the end. Pure joy.

Ever since I'd settled Maddie in with Aunt Z, I'd spoken to my girl about every other day.

But sometimes words weren't enough. Sometimes she needed to *see* that I was okay. I queued up my phone, raked my fingers through my hair, and hit play. I spent about thirty seconds sharing general information about riding a scooter, the river behind me, and then I showed her my Diet Coke. "Please tell Aunt Z that you're allowed to have one soda, just because Dad is having one now too. Love you, Maddie. Talk soon, sweetie."

I tapped the send button. Before I could get emotional, another text came in. This one from Casper.

U on a foto shoot?

As I thumbed my response, the phone rang.

I answered with, "You didn't give me time to reply."

"So, are you?"

"Essentially, yes."

"You qualified your answer."

An eighteen-wheeler roared by, and the manufactured wind nearly blew me off the scooter.

"Damn, Zane, are you at the airport?"

"Not exactly. Just lots of cars and trucks driving by. But I am working. I'm on a scooter, moving around to different locations, depending on a few factors."

"Like what?"

I'd opened that door. "Weather. What's up?"

"Can't stop thinking about the fact that you saw the Neo-Nazi woman."

The image of Bailey's face flashed before my eyes so quickly it must have been lingering just under the surface. "And her son," I said. "What makes you think she's a believer of the same hate-filled Neo-Nazi crap?"

"Seems she's not a believer anymore. She's a *defector*, Zane. Maybe she woke up and saw the light. I don't know."

"What intel do you have on her?"

He chuckled. "I didn't even know the defector was a chick. I guess we still don't know for certain. That's one of the risks going forward. Probably not at the top of the list, though."

I replayed my run-in with the dog from the previous night. While I was able to charm the pooch, I knew we'd poked the proverbial bear—a crime family, no less. "I'm wondering what the Campanellas are thinking right now. Do they know who we are? Do they know why we were there?"

"Damn good questions. Wish we had the place wired for sound, but we don't."

"As much as I want to rescue Bailey and her son, a full threat assessment is needed first."

He snickered. "Threat assessment? You sure your name isn't Bourne?"

"Funny. I did see the most recent movie. What number are they on? It's all fiction, right?" I was attempting to divert the conversation away from me stupidly talking about threat assessments and similar terms.

"Look, Zane, I called because I don't think we have much time."

The exit gate opened, and a car left the Interpol facility. It wasn't Amadou's SUV.

"You're hesitant, aren't you?" Casper said. "I'll say it again, man. If you want to steer clear of this op—which I acknowledge could be dangerous—just say the word. I won't hold it against you."

"It's not that. I'm just wondering if Bailey and her son are still alive."

"That thought crossed my mind too. Dominic is a crazy sonofabitch. Who knows what kind of retribution he has in mind?"

I didn't want to remind Casper that his zest to push the envelope had most likely been the catalyst for pandemonium breaking out at the villa. "We can't do much about it other than get them the hell out of there. You must be calling because you've come up with a plan. Am I right?"

"Dude, I've been pacing in my apartment for the last two hours, tossing around a thousand ideas. I need someone to rein me in, tell me what's viable."

"I'm just a photographer."

"Yeah, but you're also motivated to get her out of there."

"Her and her son."

"Right. The son. That only complicates things more. When can we meet up?"

My days were going to be unpredictable from now until the moment I abducted Amadou. "After dinner."

"I'll take it," he said on a sigh. "I can't complain. I know you're doing important work."

I wasn't sure if he was mocking me on that last comment, but I held my ground nonetheless. He said he'd text me a meeting place later, and between now and then, he'd take the time to jot down a few ideas.

As I pocketed my phone, I felt it buzz. My spirits lifted, thinking it would be a reply from Aunt Z or Maddie about my video. I peered at the screen and my spirits took a nosedive.

A text from Simon.

Picked up new intel. As a result, you've got 3 days to kidnap

Amadou.

Heat climbed up my neck. "Are they fucking kidding me?" I said over the buzz of traffic. I quickly typed in reply.

Not possible. Need more time to observe patterns in movement.

I sent off the text and studied the traffic while I waited for a reply. It only took thirty seconds before the phone buzzed again. Simon had a two-word response.

3 days.

I wanted to chuck the phone into the river and just walk away from this whole damn thing. They were blackmailing me into kidnapping a high-ranking official of Interpol, a nearly century-old international police organization with almost two hundred member countries. If I successfully pulled off this abduction—and that was no foregone conclusion—I'd have countless governments and their police and spy agencies gunning for me. There would be virtually no place on the planet I could go without the risk of being arrested on the spot.

But as much as I hated all of the unknown people who comprised Simon—whether that be five, fifty, or five hundred—I couldn't say no.

The electro-vial made sure of that.

I gently scratched the area of my arm where the device had been implanted. A reminder that Simon held all the power, made all the decisions for me, and as a result, for my daughter.

I might be able to walk somewhat freely through society, but I was just as much a hostage as Bailey.

15

Thankfully, Amadou worked a normal workday and headed directly home at just after five in the white Captur with his security guards. Would that be his MO for the next three days? I had no way of knowing, which only added to my anxiety.

Just then, Casper sent a text directing me to Wallace Pub on Claire Street in the northern section of the 9th arrondissement. Three miles north of Bar Le 42. Two miles north of Amadou's home.

The bar, half full with patrons, had a red ceiling with lots of signage and country flags. The UEFA European Football Championship was underway, although the two flatscreens were playing rugby matches. A small stage held a drum set and other audio equipment. Between sports and live music, I imagined this would be a happening place on weekends.

Casper was sitting at a table in the corner, his beady eyes gazing at two dart boards on the far wall.

"Do you play?" I sat and picked up a menu.

He shook his head. "Sorry, I was just thinking."

"Your mind hasn't stopped trying to figure out how to pull off this rescue, huh?"

"Same for you?" he asked.

On two fronts, although Casper would hopefully never learn about my most important mission. "Pretty much," I said, then nodded to an empty shot glass on the table. "What are you drinking?"

"Russian Standard. I needed something to calm my nerves."

Vodka. The hard stuff. A waiter wearing a green Guinness hat walked up and took our orders. I went with his recommendation, a bottled beer called Duvel. Casper decided to go with a canned beer, Fortnight Pendragon.

The beers arrived, and I took my first sip. "So, any ideas float to the top yet?"

He picked up a napkin that had words written on it and flapped it a few times.

"Your ideas?"

He nodded. "That, plus the threat assessment. I know I said this before, but after logically reviewing how things went down last night, I don't think we have the luxury of time. A couple of days or so."

My stomach formed a knot. Basically the same time pressures coming from Simon. "Do you think Campanella could have moved Bailey and her son to another location?"

He tilted his head left and then right. "It's possible. Which is why we need to confirm they're still there."

"You want to make another surveillance run?"

He nodded.

"Let's say we're able to confirm Bailey and her son are in the house. Would we execute the plan—whatever it is—at that time, or wait?"

"And to answer your question, unless we see Bailey and her

son under extreme duress, I think we'll need to take some time to set up our plan. Twenty-four hours."

I nodded, sipping more of my beer. Thoughts bouncing between the two operations. One, a rescue of a little boy and a woman who had captured my attention. The other, a kidnapping of a high-profile law enforcement official. A rescue and a kidnapping. On the surface, they were opposing actions. But they were both inspired by one central theme: freedom. Freedom for Bailey and her son. Freedom for me and Maddie.

I refocused on Casper. He was smiling while jingling a set of keys. "Ready to take a trip?" he asked.

"Do the surveillance right now?"

He nodded. "I'd go by myself, but I'm a little tipsy. Can you drive?"

I snatched the keys from his hands, and we headed for the old BMW.

16

Irigny, France

One thing I could say about Casper—the kid learned from his mistakes. Instead of crawling right up to the windowsills of Campanella's countryside villa, we stayed in the woods and slowly circled the mansion. He'd also brought along a surprise tool.

"You going to let me use that cool gadget?"

He pulled the device away from his eye and smiled—yes, his face glowed in the darkness. "It's a monocular, as in one eye. PVS-14 night vision monocular. Forty-degree field of view, one-power magnification, automatic high-light cutoff, and submersible up to sixty-six feet."

"Impressive." As he brought the monocular up to his eye, I added, "What about two feet of creek water… How does it operate in those conditions?" I quietly laughed as he gave me the middle finger.

He studied the area for a couple of minutes, then handed the monocular to me. "Maybe the goddess of love will intercede, and you'll get a chance to gaze into Bailey's eyes again," he teased.

"Love?"

"Okay, lust."

I didn't like the sound of either one. I brought the monocular to my eye, adjusted the diopter to focus on the east side of the home. "She was a woman in distress. That's all that got my attention."

"Don't have to convince me," he said.

The chatter ended as we moved to the north side of the home. I kept the monocular on high, watching out for problems, like men with guns or angry dogs. Spotted Biaggio, the older brother, rummaging for food in the kitchen, alongside a couple of guards. No sign of Bailey or her son.

After checking the west side of the home—where we saw Salvadore with his leg propped up watching a soccer match—we moved to the south side, the back of the house. Within seconds, I saw a blur of movement on the second floor. Two windows down from where I'd previously seen Bailey and her son.

"See anything?" Casper asked.

"Maybe."

"In the house?"

"Fourth window from right. But right now, it's clear."

"Maybe you'll get another bite. Let's be patient."

And patient I was. I panned across the second floor a few times. Ten minutes passed, and I saw no one. In fact, I'd begun to question that I even saw a blur at all.

"Surveillance can be pretty mundane work." Casper sighed. "Want me to take over?"

I was about to pull the monocular from my eye when another blur snagged my attention.

"Whatcha got?" Casper sidled up next to me.

Bailey was at the window, fourth from the right. The magnification allowed me to see her dark eyes, captivating and intense, drawing me in. There was a story behind those eyes—a story I sensed was filled with tragedy.

"That's Bailey, isn't it?"

"Yep." She was wearing a gold, off-the-shoulder dress. Shiny sequins. Quite formal.

"They must have her hostage in that room on the second floor. For our purposes, that might be a good thing."

"Different room than last time," I said.

"Maybe she's sequestered to the second floor."

"Maybe."

A second later, an arm draped around her neck.

"Shit!"

"What? What's going on, Zane? Do we need to raid the place? I brought my pistol."

Holding my breath to keep the monocular steady, I waited to see how the struggle would play out. The same man as last time, presumably Dominic, spun her around so that her back was to me. She didn't take a swing at him. In fact, he was smiling at her, his hands now gently touching her bare shoulders. An embrace. Then a kiss.

"What are they doing now?" Casper asked.

I couldn't believe my eyes. I gave Casper a quick rundown of the scene.

"What the hell?" he said.

Bailey slowly turned to face the window, and Dominic pulled up behind her and kissed her bare shoulder and neck. I was able to get one long look into her eyes.

Tears were pooling.

17

Three days out

When I woke the next morning, Bailey's eyes were still haunting me.

"Big plans today, Monsieur Ellington?" Miss Patty asked from in her office

I'd just taken a sip of my orange juice. Every morning, she laid out a generous breakfast in the office near the front door to the building.

"Just more of the same, which means finding more awe-inspiring photo ops in this great city."

She smiled, although there was a strain at the edges of her eyes. "I'd love to see your work some time. Unless you want me to wait until you've published your photo book."

"Before I'm done, I'll give you a sneak peek," I lied.

For all I knew, she could be well-versed in the ways of professional photography. Hopefully, I would complete my mission—well, now two missions—and be long gone before she would ask to see them again.

Having learned a few traffic-pattern lessons, I scootered across town to the hill above the Amadou property in relatively quick fashion. Security guards loitered next to the white SUV. No change there. I pulled out the monocular from the cubby on my scooter—Casper hadn't asked for them back—and zoomed in on the home. The least-obstructed view was through the kitchen window. Amadou's two school-aged boys were eating cereal while looking at their phones. Mom was sipping coffee, and her husband paced nearby while speaking into his cell phone.

Through openings in the trees, I surveyed as much of the house as possible, paying particular attention to the access points. Once Amadou made his way outside and into the SUV, I flipped the visor down on my helmet—one wasn't required in France, but I wanted to give a different look in case I had another close-call with the target—and followed the SUV out of the neighborhood.

The Captur turned north on Berthet—the beginning of the most direct route to Interpol when traffic wasn't an issue. When they took the roundabout and headed east across the Saone, I had a good feeling about this trip. I followed at a safe distance through the tunnel before we turned north on the east side of the Rhone. Five more minutes of commute, and the white SUV pulled into the Interpol front gate.

Nine hours later, right after five p.m., Amadou and his security detail left the facility and traveled back home using the same route but in reverse. Amadou kissed his wife and kids, who were wearing soccer gear, in the parking area. Wife and kids then drove away in a red SUV—probably the family vehicle. Amadou headed for the kitchen, where he poured himself a drink and got back on his phone.

The next two days would need to follow the same routine if I were to have any chance at kidnapping Amadou. Just repeating

Simon's order in my mind nearly made my head explode.

I headed back to my apartment, slipped inside without running into Miss Patty, and promptly popped the top on a beer. Then another. During the second drink, I called Casper to see where he was at in terms of his operation, rescuing Bailey and her son.

It turned out to be a long call. Approaching the two-hour mark. We were getting nowhere. Then Casper released a string of curse words that would have made my old track coach blush.

"Did your hostage try to escape?" I asked.

"Not a chance. He'll be asleep for a while."

I was concerned Casper had killed the man. "Don't tell me you..."

He chuckled. "The guy was hungry, so I gave him a bunch of spam."

"Spam?"

"Yeah, mixed with some crushed-up Ambien. Dude's been out for about four hours."

I had to get him back on track. "Then why the expletives?"

"Spilled my beer. Back to the plan to extricate Bailey and her son. Okay, our best bet in keeping us out of the grave is to separate as many of the guards from Bailey and son as possible. Outside of setting the whole villa on fire, which might harm or kill our assets, our most viable option is to create a diversion."

"I'm listening."

The idea was simple but smart. There were only two of us, but the Campanellas wouldn't know that. Casper would pick up the supplies, and we would plan for a raid just before dawn.

Casper wrapped up the call, saying, "Thirty-six hours until go time for the rescue of Bailey and her son. You still in, Zane?"

"Absolutely."

"You didn't hesitate, not one bit. Not many photographers willing to put their lives on the line for this kind of cause."

"Not many MPs willing to partner with a photographer. You

saved my ass from these goons. I owe you."

"Plus, that woman, Bailey…she's really on your mind, huh?"

"Let's just get this done."

Given the new deadline from Simon, I had forty-eight hours remaining to kidnap Amadou, which meant I'd be executing my plan twelve hours or so after rescuing Bailey and son. But the call with Casper had sparked an idea on how to pull off my one-person operation with limited risk in the shortest amount of time possible.

But it would only work if Amadou's routine stayed constant over the next two days.

18

Two days out

After a night of decent sleep and another fortifying breakfast courtesy of Miss Patty, I followed Amadou on his morning routine. Thankfully, it played out just like the previous morning. Same security detail. Same white SUV. Same route to the Interpol building with no stops. The day started at just before eight—just like the day before. Would the evening routine follow its similar pattern, especially the part where the wife and kids leave for soccer practice after Amadou arrived home?

I breathed a sigh of relief as I motored past Interpol en route to a grocery in northeast Lyon. I'd exchanged late-night messages with Simon—all encrypted, as standard procedure. I needed supplies for the operation, and Simon had confirmed those supplies would be ready for me to pick up.

When this nightmare odyssey began, I'd thought Simon was an organization of at least a thousand people, if not more. I'd believed their ranks included subject-matter experts covering all aspects of information technology, biotechnology, medicine, languages, and of course, assassination and kidnapping. But over time, those thoughts had changed. I now believed the organization was most likely lean. A core set of people making the big decisions with minions executing various tasks. And those minions would have no clue they were part of a larger plan.

Like when they gathered supplies for my fieldwork.

I arrived at the grocery, found the mail kiosk, and asked for the package for Zane Ellington. The clerk handed it over without even asking for my ID. I tied the package to my scooter and proceeded to stop number two. I found the low-end, used-car lot on the eastern outskirts of the city. A bearded man chewing on a cigar helped set me up. Actually, the specific phrase he said over and over again was, "Let me set you up," as if I needed convincing.

After giving him two thousand euros, I drove off the lot in a black, dusty, nine-year-old Peugeot 407 SW. Every time I pressed the gas, the engine kicked and sputtered before accelerating. His final selling pitch was that the car had belonged to the estate of a wealthy landowner. An ox that had been used to plow the fields would have been more reliable.

I picked up some lunch at Subway and parked the Peugeot near the Interpol exit so I could review the contents of the package and start to visualize the execution of my plan. It certainly wasn't foolproof. In fact, it was riddled with a dozen holes, if every risk came to fruition. I'd come to realize that the term "risk-free" did not exist in the world of espionage.

Executing Amadou's kidnapping while he was en route with two security guards would require one of two things: a team of at least six people, or timing an explosive somewhere along the path of the white SUV to stun if not injure the guards so I could pull Amadou out and escape. But the collateral damage would be impossible to control. I couldn't risk killing dozens of innocent civilians.

I opened the package and reviewed the contents. At the top was a Sig Saur P226—the only gun I'd ever comfortably shot and that was at a gun range back home in Donelson. Also in the box was a taser, a syringe with the proper dose of propofol, and a flash-bang stun grenade. Everything I'd asked for. *Good job, minions.* Then I sifted through the countless photos on my camera and examined my makeshift map of Amadou's property. Collecting the data, moving the pieces, seeing how they best fit so that I could successfully accomplish my assignment.

I leaned back against the headrest and let it all run through my mind. Then I drove back to Interpol headquarters.

Casper had sent me a text saying he was going to get to sleep earlier than normal tonight, since he wanted to rendezvous with me at "O three hundred." I'd do the same ... after confirming Amadou's evening routine.

Like clockwork, the white Captur rolled out of Interpol at a quarter after five, moving south on Charles de Gaulle Way. The SUV turned right at the bridge and crossed the Rhone. I heard my phone ding as we entered Red Cross Tunnel. Probably Casper confirming our 3:00 a.m. meetup. I passed a slower truck, but quickly hit a sea of brake lights, and the procession halted.

"Wonderful." I sighed, slid the car into park, and craned my neck, looking ahead to determine the cause of the backup. Nothing was visible from my position. Probably a traffic accident, just like you see in every American city.

I grabbed my phone from the passenger seat to check the text. It was Simon. My gut immediately tensed into a knot.

URGENT UPDATE: CAN'T WAIT ANOTHER DAY. MUST EXECUTE PLAN TO ABDUCT AMADOU TONIGHT. PLEASE CONFIRM.

A fire ignited behind my eyes. Slamming my fist into the dashboard, I screamed an expletive until it felt like I'd popped a blood vessel in my neck. But I wasn't done. I chucked my phone into the back and smacked my hand off the passenger seat two, three, four times, and then I lost count. Anything to release the unbridled exasperation and fury that burned so deeply inside me. Dealing with Simon—being on the end of that leash—to carry out these vile acts not only sickened me, but also made me constantly second-guess my purpose in this world. They had turned me into a killer, and now they wanted me to kidnap a man responsible for doing good work. A man with two little kids and a wife.

I wiped both hands down my face and took in a deep, long breath. If I wanted to live and see my daughter grow up, I had no other option but to carry out the ever-shifting directive.

I fished my phone out from the back seat and thumbed a quick reply to Simon's text.

GO TO HELL!!!!!!!

But I didn't hit send. I glared at the words, knowing they represented just an inkling of what I wanted to convey to those fuckers.

Traffic had begun to move, and I shifted the gear into drive. The Peugeot poked ahead at an agonizingly slow pace. Fifteen minutes later, while stuck at a light and my pulse finally out of the red zone, I erased the previous words in the text and typed one new one.

CONFIRMED.

I hit send.

19

The last leg of the trip to Amadou's home proceeded without further delays. And that disappointed me greatly.

"I need more time, dammit!" I pressed the gas pedal to the floor and sped down the street parallel to Amadou's home, reaching the perch just as his white SUV turned into the large parking area behind the house. I pulled out my monocular and rolled down the window.

Amadou exited the car and waved goodbye to the guards, who promptly left. He walked toward the back door, where he was met by his wife. They kissed and talked, and his two kids ran past them kicking a soccer ball. His wife gave Amadou a pat on the backside—reminding me for a brief second of something my Anna used to do to me—and then the wife and kids piled into the family SUV and rolled out of the parking area.

"Good." I pushed out a calming breath. I had approximately two hours to execute my plan before the family returned. While it wouldn't be completely dark at the end of that interval, the sun would have set, giving me some modest cover. Any clouds that might roll in would be a bonus.

I leaned over and pulled back the lid of the package to scan my goodies. Given the tight window of time, I couldn't afford to take a passive approach. If there ever was a time for "shock and awe," this was it.

With my desired entry point in mind—the kitchen—I raised the monocular to have one more look before I went in.

Amadou was walking out of the house.

I silently begged him to turn around, go back inside. But he didn't. He marched straight to his car with a drink in his hand, slipped into the front seat, and started to back out of the parking area.

"What the hell are you doing?"

The blue Audi S8 headed north out of the neighborhood. I tossed the monocular into the passenger's seat, fired up the Peugeot, and tore a modest amount of rubber to get into position to follow Amadou.

"Where are you going, Pierre?"

I was halfway down Amadou's street when he took a right on Cottin. That was east, toward the river, where there was no direct route across the Saone. When I executed the turn onto Cottin, he had hit the T at the end of the road. If he went left, he could make his way back to the office. He went right instead. I reached the intersection and attempted to spit out the name of the road: "Boulevard Antoine de Saint-Exupéry." My French left much to be desired.

Before I caught up to the Audi, the southerly road took a sharp turn back to the north. Another quarter of a mile, and it cut back to the south. We'd just completed one of the most abrupt figure 8s I'd ever driven. With the sun-glazed Saone sparkling off to my left, and the Audi moving at a comfortable if not slow speed, I loosened my death grip on the steering wheel and pondered where he could be going.

I came up with zero answers. I didn't have enough data. No time to ascertain real patterns or habits. Something Simon apparently didn't care much about—my problem, not theirs. *Just get the job done, Jack. Or die.*

After another ten minutes, we were leisurely winding around the hill upon which La Basilique of Notre-Dame de Fourvière sat. It was even more breathtaking from this view, although I only took quick side-glances.

As time ticked by, I began to consider the idea that Amadou might simply be out for a casual drive. He had one hand on the wheel and his drink in the other, sipping leisurely, I found that interesting. He didn't seem concerned about being pulled over for drinking and driving. In the States, that would be taking a big risk. Maybe not as much in France, where wine was imbibed as much as water. Or maybe it was because of who he was, the big shot at Interpol.

Before we reached the A6, Amadou took the Alphonse Juin bridge across the Saone. But instead of continuing the easterly path across the Rhone, he stayed on the peninsula and turned south. We wound through several side streets, still at a casual pace, but I now got the sense that he was traveling to a specific destination. There were a number of bars in the southern half of the peninsula. Maybe he simply wanted to break free from the security detail to hang out with his buddies, drink a beer or two, and watch one of the Euro soccer games. I'd done the same plenty of times back home. My good friend Daniel and I would end up putting a wager on some portion of the game and then mercilessly razz the one who lost.

A heavy sigh escaped me. I'd never be able to go back to those days.

Up ahead, a sign for the Charlemagne Hotel, and then another for the Axotel Lyon Perrache. I finally understood. Amadou was having an affair. With his wife and kids occupied, he was meeting up with his mistress for a quickie at a hotel.

I strummed my fingers on the steering wheel, thinking through how I could still accomplish my end goal. Two options came to mind: abduct Amadou on the way in to the hotel, or on the way out. Easier to accomplish at night, but I wasn't in a position to choose. Another twist: we were in a public place with people everywhere. No patterns... I had no control over the situation.

Perhaps shock-and-awe wouldn't be the best tactic. I would need to entice Amadou to comply. And I now had an edge. I would threaten to expose him to his wife unless he walked quietly with me to my car.

After two lights, Amadou's Audi drove right past the Charlemagne Hotel. Half a block later, when he should have turned left to reach the Axotel Lyon Perrache Hotel, he didn't even brake. I shook my head, completely perplexed as to his destination.

One minute later, I had my answer. Amadou turned into a parking garage at Bayard and Charlemagne. I slipped in behind him. The garage was about three-quarters full, and he drove up to the third floor and parked. I turned into a spot on level two where I could see his car just above me. He got out of the car, still with drink in hand, and walked down the ramp.

He was headed right for me.

20

Instead of dropping lower in my seat, I froze. If Amadou didn't know I'd been tailing him, I didn't want any sudden movement in his periphery to attract his attention. Of course, if he'd seen my Peugeot following him, and he was hell-bent on confronting me, it wouldn't matter either way.

His footfalls echoed throughout the concrete structure. I shifted my eyes to my new box of tools. If he confronted me, I would grab the Taser and jab him with it, incapacitate him long enough to drag him into the back seat. Of course, there were countless ways this could go, so I mentally prepared myself to act on the fly.

I heard laughter. More than one person somewhere in the large echo chamber, all cheerful, both male and female. Were they up on level three or below us on two? Impossible to decipher.

With a brief pause in the ruckus, Amadou's shoe-clopping was nearly on top of me. I shifted my eyes to the side mirror.

Wearing a tan blazer—probably cashmere—he walked past

the back of my car. Paced another ten steps. Turned left into a parking space two down from me.

He unlocked a silver car of some kind—there was another car blocking my view—and pulled out of the space. I gave him a short head start, swiftly backed out, and raced to the garage exit.

His "new" car was a Renault sedan, the paint mottled in varying shades of silver and gray. The car was missing hubcaps on the two wheels I could see, and the back passenger window was covered in duct tape.

"Why are you driving that piece of shit with your kind of money?"

More importantly, why had he changed cars, and where the hell was he going?

I tailed Amadou to the southern tip of the Peninsula, across the Rhone, and through the 7th arrondissement. He stayed off the major highways, which made me believe his destination was somewhere close.

My supposition was incorrect.

Other than stoplights, the silver Renault never stopped moving south. Even as the city faded behind us and buildings became sparse, Amadou avoided the major highways. Approximately five kilometers south of Lyon, he turned right onto a small two-lane road. With the sun dipping below the horizon, we traveled west, crossing the A7 and two forks of the Rhone, before driving into the shadows of the tall trees lining the country road.

And that's when my stomach clenched into the mother of all knots. We'd just entered Irigny, the temporary home of Dominic Campanella and his thug sons, along with his hostages, Bailey and her son.

Allowing some more distance between our cars, I practically held my breath on every blind curve, hoping I'd see Amadou change course, away from the Campanella compound. But each time I came out of a curve, the silver Renault was still moving in that direction.

It was hard to tamp down the burgeoning hypotheses simmering in my mind as we motored through the countryside. The moment of truth was less than a kilometer away—the private drive entrance to the villa.

Amadou connected to the Campanella crime family? It was an incomprehensible notion, but one that I couldn't purge from my mind. Where this journey would end, I had no idea, but it had to end with me abducting Amadou. All previous ideas on how I might accomplish that had been discarded. From here on out, I was winging it.

In my old life as a small business owner of a four-person CPA firm, structure and predictability had been two of our most important pillars. But my childhood was anything but predictable. My mother died when I was young, and my absent father passed me on to his mother to raise me. It was the most uncomfortable relationship one could imagine, especially for a boy trying to navigate so many aspects of life, from sports to school, girls, work, what I wanted to be when I grew up, you name it. It was all uncomfortable. And Mama—what I called my grandmother—ruled my world like a tyrant, one who wasn't bashful to use a switch when I broke one of her rules.

Outside of Anna, I'd never been able to rely on anyone to help me traverse life's hurdles. And that included one time when I was held at gunpoint by an armed bank robber. Maybe that was why, thus far in this warped dance with Simon, I hadn't shriveled into a ball and just given up. I had survived every wild fast ball thrown straight at my head. And if I could ever figure out the people hiding behind the Simon façade, I would take one of those balls and ram it down their throats.

When I rounded the next bend, Amadou had just turned into the Campanella compound.

My mind began to spin, but I kept my cool. Drove down the

road, found the same general area where Casper and I had parked his old BMW.

Into the woods I went, Peugeot and all.

I grabbed my pistol and monocular, and set out on foot. Unlike the last time, I knew the lay of the land. A tremendous benefit. With my eyes and every other sense on high alert, I trekked through the woods and reached the private drive. No sign of Amadou's Renault. It had likely continued on to the villa, which wasn't visible from this vantage point. Crossing the gravel road, I made my way through the next set of woods. Eyes open for guards, human and canine.

Twenty feet from the edge of the woods and with the villa now in view, I stopped in my tracks. Lights were splashing wildly behind the home. Rotating spotlights, as if highlighting some star-studded Hollywood premiere.

Strange.

But further investigation into the light display would have to wait for now. I had to locate Amadou.

Locate. Extricate. Don't get shot.

Sheer madness.

I moved behind the last tree before the field opened up. Two men stood near the four cars in the driveway, their heads on a swivel. Both carried semi-automatic rifles. Movement from the left side of the house—two more men walking toward the front, guns at the ready.

Whether it was for Amadou's benefit or someone else's, the security presence had increased significantly since my last visit. I brought the monocular to my eye. The silver Renault was one of the four vehicles... and parked near the back. Apparently the latest arrival to this party. And an oddity at that, a far cry from the shine of the three other cars, which were newer Mercedes and BMW sedans.

Since the woods were thinner on the east side of the home—

therefore easier for someone holding a rifle to notice me—the smart path would be to approach the back area from the west side. That meant crossing the creek in the open field.

I kept an eye on the guards through my monocular. When they turned away from me, I bolted to the next tree about forty feet away. I made it safely, stopping to take a breath. I repeated the exercise three more times before reaching the tree near the bank of the creek bed. I peeked around the trunk. One of the guards was walking down the private drive in my general direction. Had he seen me?

His gait was mostly casual, his eyes panning the area. Maybe he'd seen a flash of movement and decided to investigate. Whatever his reason for drawing closer, it was bad news. Even if I could somehow take out this one guard, he had plenty of armed buddies.

And I still hadn't seen Amadou.

Still had no real plan.

I cautiously peered around the trunk. The man, wearing all black, had closed to within fifty feet of my position, so close I could hear his boots crunching against the gravel above the gentle rush of creek water. But his body language made me think he wasn't aware of me specifically.

How to play this? I could make a break for the tree behind me, but I was certain he'd spot me. On the other hand, if I held my position, there would be a confrontation. Unavoidable.

Me, the sitting duck.

Would I be killed? Brought in for questioning by the mob?

Would I be forced to kill again? Or could I simply incapacitate the guy, then go about my merry way?

Which way would the chips fall?

My thoughts were reaching a vortex, and I had a hard time reining them in. I didn't want to use my gun, only because I had no silencer. But if it came down to him or me, I knew what that answer would be.

Goonies never say die. I would have no choice but to choose my life over his.

If I survived this upcoming confrontation, where the hell would that leave me? I'd surely go from hunter to hunted. And with that, any prospect of extricating Amadou would roll right down the shitter.

Steps coming closer. I pulled my pistol from my waistband. Adrenaline spigot wide open.

I waited like some seasoned assassin.

Waited for the right moment to shock and awe.

21

Someone in the distance belted out a whistle. Not a casual whistle, but a trying-to-catch-your-attention whistle. The guard near me shouted something in response, maybe in Italian.

Receding footsteps. I dared to peek. He was walking back to the house.

Gun back into waistband. Monocular back up to my eye. No one seemed to be gesturing toward my area. I was safe for now.

I turned toward the creek. Three boulders protruded above the waterline. I bolted that way and, like a stone skimming the water, lightly tapped the tops of each rock to cross the creek. On the last one, my foot slipped just enough to send my other foot skyward. I thought of Casper, who'd done something similar, and how I'd razzed him. Oh, how fast the tables did turn.

My arms flailed as I tried to regain my balance. One foot dropped into the water, got wedged behind some other stone. While my upper body toppled like a chopped tree and slammed into the bank, my ankle came free, but awkwardly so. The pain shot up my leg, hitting every available nerve ending along the way.

I muted my groan as I dug my fingers into the turf. Having sprained each ankle numerous times, I recognized the condition immediately. I turned onto my back and stared up at the sky, now a deep purple. I could make out a couple of stars, seemingly attached to the ends of branches.

Grabbed a tree root. Pulled myself up. Put some weight on my bum ankle. Not bad.

With my eyes locked on the guards by the house, I hunched over and hobble-jogged from tree to tree toward the west side of the mansion. Pulled farther back into the woods and arced around to the rear of the home, lowering myself behind a large dead tree trunk.

And there he was. Amadou standing in the middle of three men and three cars, all of which had their headlights on. I took a quick glance up to the second floor—no sign of Bailey. I was supposed to be at this same location in about nine hours, but with Casper. Unfortunately, I couldn't see how I'd be able to pull that off. Casper, like me right now, would have to go at it alone.

And I still had no idea how I was going to grab Amadou and make it out with my life and limbs intact.

I heard the rumble of a diesel engine. Then a beeping sound, as though...

A large truck backed around the far side of the house, driving into the edge of the yard near the men, close to the intersecting beams of the cars' headlights.

More men materialized. Likely part of the security detail since they held semi-automatic rifles. A few of them shook hands, but not Amadou. His face was all business. One man emerged from the crowd. Shorter, thicker than Amadou. Touches of silver at his hairline. It was Dominic Campanella. He clapped his hands and motioned for someone to pull open the back of the truck. The din of chatter picked up as people jockeyed left and right to try to get a better view of what was about to be unveiled.

The metal door rolled open. Two men jumped inside and used electric screwdrivers to unscrew bolts from two wooden crates. On the side of each crate, one word was written: *Danger.*

The men opened one crate. A metal container was housed inside. They pulled back the top of that container, rummaged around. I focused my sights on Amadou, who was standing near Dominic and some other man I couldn't quite see beyond the cluster of men. Amadou's hands were at his hips like an anxious coach waiting for the officials to make the final call. He had skin in this game, although I doubted the cargo had anything to do with a sporting event.

There were a few *ooh*s and *ahh*s, and I swung my monocular back to focus on the men in the truck. One of them held up a metal object, like a doctor holding up a newborn.

I gulped when I realized what it was. Pulse flying, heart whirring, the whole nine yards.

A rocket launcher.

What the hell was Amadou mixed up in?

One of the minions broke from the pack, grabbed another rocket launcher from the open crate and started dancing around, tossing it in the air. A couple of guys urged him to stop, then others joined in. Dominic even yelled at the man, but he only laughed and danced more. If that weapon accidently fired, it could take out every person standing there. He had to be shit-faced or plain stupid. Maybe both.

A gunshot pierced the air—everyone, including me, jolted. Everyone except the rabble-rouser, who dropped to the ground. As he fell, another man pulled the rocket launcher from his hands.

I panned my monocular to the left. Amadou was still holding the pistol outward. All eyes were on him.

But my eyes quickly trained on something even more shocking. I knew the man standing to Amadou's left.

I had no idea what my old college buddy was doing at a gathering that involved the sale of illegal weapons.

22

Arms trafficking. That was my quick, uninformed guess as to the nature of this late-night meeting. But who, exactly, was the customer?

As Dominic's guards pulled the dead body from the pack, my sights stayed on Charlie Atwater, my track teammate at the University of Tennessee. That was him, wasn't it? My mind argued with itself. *It couldn't be! But it is!* I pulled out my phone and snapped off ten quick pictures of the whole scene, then brought the monocular back to my eye.

Charlie was pacing, smoking a cigarette. That didn't surprise me. Everyone in college had thought he had ice in his veins. One of Tennessee's better triple jumpers, Charlie was known for playing to the crowd, pumping up the fans before he'd begin his run down the ramp. And then he'd hop, skip, and finally take one giant leap into the pit. If it was a successful jump—and many were—he'd reach his hands toward the sky, then jump and twirl around, the movement followed closely by his trademark ponytail.

Charlie Atwater was one of the most adored athletes in all of college sports.

But Charlie had another side, and few knew about it. I was one of those few.

One night at a party, I found Charlie smoking weed. He admitted to having severe anxiety issues, which could only be mollified with heavy prescription medication. But because of the brain-fog side effects, he couldn't take the medication any time near a meet, which happened more weeks than not. I once asked why he didn't just quit the sport so he could find some peace in his life. His response? "I can't let go of the high I get from the fans. It's addictive, Jack."

When I didn't qualify for the Olympics as a decathlete, I'd married Anna, and for the most part, lost touch with the people from my track world. I'd occasionally wondered what had become of Charlie Atwater, fan favorite.

And there he was.

Had his life trajectory veered so far off course that he was now an illegal arms dealer? Or at least associated with one?

Charlie's attire was casual but high end, similar to how Amadou dressed. His ponytail was history, his dark hair now parted to the side, almost like a model. He still looked fit, other than the smoking part. What the hell was he doing hanging out with a dirty Interpol official, a crime family boss, and a cache of weapons usually found on military bases?

Loud voices carried above the din of the motors, and Amadou and Dominic seemed to ignore them. With Charlie standing somewhat off to the side by himself, Amadou approached the back of the truck and scanned the contents. I counted at least a dozen crates.

Fucking Amadou. He worked for an international policing agency, had a nice house, fancy clothes and vehicles… In reality, he was nothing but a murdering thug.

Was Simon aware of Amadou's character flaw, starting with a proclivity for murder? Was that why they wanted him out of commission? I doubted Simon would even care, if they knew at all. They wanted those cyber investigations stopped—and fast, probably because someone important in the Simon orbit could be implicated.

Dominic waddled up next to Amadou and started speaking. After a few seconds, he clapped Amadou on the back. Amadou scanned the truck's contents one last time and gave a pronounced nod.

I'd just witnessed the consummation of an illegal weapons deal.

The knot in my stomach was forcing its way up my chest. As champagne corks flew and everyone shared a toast in the yard, I picked at a piece of bark on the tree trunk and tried to make sense of things. Even just one thing would be good.

I came to this conclusion: despite the murder I'd just observed, or the arms deal, or even the presence of my old college teammate, I couldn't be so distracted that I allowed the night to pass without completing my mission. I had to figure out a way to abduct Amadou and take him to the location Simon had provided, a small house outside of Grenoble.

I couldn't do it with the guards hanging around. No way I would make it out alive.

An idea shot to the front of my mind. I turned on a stealthy dime and retraced my steps through the woods. Once I circled the property and made it to the front of the house, I turned back toward the villa. Movement near the vehicles. Brake lights on the silver Renault, Amadou's car. I high-stepped through the weeds and brush of the woods until I hit the private drive that split the two sections of woods at the front of the property.

Headlights cut between the tall trees. Amadou was about to round a curve in the driveway to reach my position. When he did so, I'd step into the Renault's path with my gun raised and demand that he stop. If he didn't, I'd fire one shot into the windshield on the passenger's side. Once he stopped, I'd get into the vehicle and, after disarming him, make him drive us to our destination.

Emboldened by both the audacity and simplicity of the plan, I stepped into the middle of the path. Raised my pistol. The Renault pulled around the bend and…

I dove back into the woods and hid within the brush. Just in time.

Another car motored just behind the Renault. Actually, two more cars. The vehicles rushed past. I had not been seen.

Change of plans.

I bolted across the drive into the last section of woods. Scurrying through the dark forest as my shoulders clipped trees, I made quick progress until I almost rammed my knees off the front fender of my Peugeot. I slipped into the front seat, revved the engine, backed out, and headed east on the country road.

It took a good kilometer, but I finally caught up. The two cars, both new-model BMWs, were still riding behind Amadou's Renault. I scratched my face, wondering who was in those cars and where they were going.

It wasn't long before a glimmer of understanding dawned. *Don't tell me…*

The trio motored up the first ramp of the parking garage. I stayed back in the uncovered lot this time. Hardly any time passed before Amadou drove out of the garage, right past me. The two BMWs were behind him.

I returned to my position at the back of the pack.

The trek north moved at an elevated pace. Perhaps the BMW folks planned to stay at Amadou's villas. Fellow thug houseguests.

Two minutes later, we were at Amadou's house, and the three vehicles pulled onto the property. Once Amadou had walked inside, the two BMWs headed out. Had to be security detail. The family SUV was back in its spot. The wife and kids had returned home.

Now I had a decision to make. Use the flash-bang and every tool at my disposal to pull Amadou from his house, which might injure his kids or wife, or...

"Bailey!" Ten ideas converged at the exact same moment. But it could work. Maybe. Hopefully.

At the heart of this idea was my newfound knowledge of several disturbing facts. The truck full of weapons at the Campanella property. Amadou murdering someone in cold blood. The number of people who had witnessed both, including my teammate from college.

My updated plan started with a risky premise: *not* kidnapping Amadou tonight. I could probably hold Simon at bay until mid-morning tomorrow, saying I was busy subduing the target and then driving to Grenoble. Once Casper and I rescued Bailey and her son, I could quiz her about Amadou and those weapons.

There was no guarantee Bailey would know a damn thing about the weapons deal or Amadou's involvement, but I couldn't rewind the clock and unsee what had gone down in the haze of headlights. And I couldn't magically remove Amadou's wife and kids from his house. My revised plan was the best chance—maybe my only chance—at gaining the information I needed to complete my mission

There was a consequence to this new plan. At some point, I'd have to share the information with Casper. The floodgates would open:

"Why were you at the Campanella property?"

"Who are you really?"

"Why are you here?"

I would tell him only what was absolutely critical for him to know—nothing about Simon. I hoped I could trust him.

I checked the time on my phone. I had just over four hours to figure out my story and try to get some rest.

23

I dozed fitfully, worried about oversleeping and missing the planned rendezvous with Casper. My anxiety level made sure that didn't happen.

I escaped my apartment building in the thick of the night without waking Miss Patty. A small miracle. Walked four blocks amidst a heavy fog hovering over red-tiled rooftops of the downtown area. A slight chill in the air, but not uncomfortable. I spotted Casper's ancient BMW, but he wasn't inside.

Someone whistled, and I whipped around to follow the sound.

"You like your coffee black?" Casper was standing at an outdoor counter of a restaurant with signage in red and blue lights.

"Messob?" I said, pointing to the sign.

Casper walked up, holding two large cups of coffee. "Best Ethiopian food around. Anyway, the coffee's black. Hope you like it the way."

"As long as it's caffeinated." I took the cup and blew at the steam pouring out of the crack in the lid.

He nudged his head back toward the restaurant. "They also happen to make the best coffee of all the places open this late, or early."

"How many places are open at three in the morning?"

"If you eliminate every gas station or dive bar, you can count them on your fingers and toes."

The first sip warmed my chest and ignited my brain, a much-needed second wind. Or was this my third?

With more people walking up to the counter, we signaled to each other it was time to leave. We got into Casper's car, and he pulled away from the curb, quickly passing the consulates from Tunisia and Algeria, which reminded me how much of an international city Lyon was.

"Gotta admit, Zane, I'm a bit surprised," Casper said as he wove through the streets, one hand on the steering wheel, the other on his coffee cup.

"About?"

"You showing up."

"I told you I would."

He threw me a side-glance. "Supplies are in back."

Sticking an arm between the two seats, I found two boxes, flipped one open, and saw what looked like kitchenware. Pots? "We planning to challenge the goons to a cookoff?"

"Something like that."

I chuckled. "Seriously, are the real supplies in the trunk?"

"If you're looking for a huge cache of weapons, you won't find them."

I actually had, just a few hours ago. I wondered where that truck full of weapons was headed. I'd soon find out, if we could successfully rescue Bailey and her son. "I'm not sure why your superiors aren't giving you the support you need to do your job."

"Not needed. In fact, extra personnel would only slow us down."

I shook my head.

He chuckled. "My plan is all about tricking them into thinking a bunch of guns are going off. Draw the security team away from the house to investigate the ruckus. We need to reduce the opposition numbers if we're to have any chance at rescuing the assets."

"Bailey and her son."

He nodded while chugging coffee.

"You still haven't explained the pots."

"Check out the other box."

I opened box number two, pulled out a plastic bag, and rummaged through it. "Black Cats?"

"Firecrackers. Yes sir."

I started piecing the plan together. "Set off the firecrackers in the pots."

"Absolutely, but not all at once. We'll get their attention with a couple of rounds of live fire, then set off the first batch deep in the woods behind the house. Hopefully, that will draw them out. Then, once we locate Bailey and her son, we'll leave through the front. We'll have a couple of pots in the bushes and let those rip on our way out. One pot in each set will use slow-burning fuses."

"To elongate the make-believe assault."

"Rightio."

"And that's it?"

"We'll each carry pistols. I have an extra M9 that you can carry, although you hopefully won't need it."

"About that…"

"Yeah?"

"Before I go there, any other tools I need to know about?"

He pulled out a brown paper bag from under his seat. "I did bring one toy that will allow us to immobilize anyone downstairs. Ever heard of a flash-bang?"

I hid my smile. "I think I've read about them."

"Cool. So, you want the pistol … or does it scare you too much?"

I pulled my Sig Sauer out from behind my back. "I'm more comfortable using this instead."

His eyes didn't blink, and the car nearly veered off the road.

"Just focus on driving. I've got a story to share with you."

24

Surrounded by tall trees in the forest near the Campanella villa, Casper shut off the BMW's engine—it kicked and sputtered a few seconds before finally dying. He stared into the darkness, not uttering a word. He was still trying to process the story I'd just told him, one that included a few necessary partial truths.

"Look, Casper, I really don't think we have anything to worry about. I'm positive no one saw me."

He nodded, scanned the area. Still processing, I supposed.

I continued. "As I told you, I just had this impulse to make sure Bailey was alive and—"

"You have a thing for her."

I shrugged. "It's not a thing. I'm just trying to do the *right* thing." I felt a pang of guilt for the lie, and my feelings. They really made no sense; I could barely stomach the visions of Anna's bloodied body, the loss that represented. My family was everything, and that *everything* had changed in the worst ways possible not too many weeks ago. But it still was the most important thing in the world to me—to hold on to what was left of it, rebuild it somehow. Now this with Bailey? Had to be some type of weird grieving stage on my part. As for Bailey and the looks she'd given me... I could only imagine they were more fear than any sort of attraction.

But I couldn't be sure.

Dammit!

"And you couldn't have waited just a few hours to see her?" Casper pressed.

Another shrug. "When you put it that way, I can see how irrational it was."

"You could have sunk our whole mission, Zane. Then what the hell would I do?"

I heard air hissing through his teeth. If I were in his shoes, I would have been equally pissed. Straddling this line of partial truths wasn't comfortable for me, but it was imperative that Casper understand what I needed from him.

"Look, Casper, once we get Bailey and her son safely away from this place, I'll need to quickly—"

"Tell me more about what you saw... You know, the men and the weapons."

So I did, leaving out any mention of my old college track teammate, Charlie Atwater.

"How did you know about this Interpol official, what he looked like and all?"

I shrugged.

"You're no photographer."

"Actually, I am."

He shook his head. "That might be a hobby or something..." He snapped his fingers then pointed at me. "That's your cover, isn't it, *Zane Ellington*—if that's your real name. Who sent you here? What's your objective? Tell me, dammit."

He got out of the car, so I followed suit. We stared at each other over the roof. Actually, his stare was more of a glare.

"Casper, that has nothing to do with you."

"The hell it doesn't. And I'm not going a step farther until you tell me everything."

I was afraid of this type of emphatic response. No way I could share everything about my life. The symbolic gun Simon was holding against my head. The urgency behind getting Bailey to tell me about Amadou and the weapons deal that had gone down right before my eyes. I had one shot at sharing just enough information to sound believable.

"Okay, here's the straight-up truth. I have a friend who will remain unnamed, and he has a connection with Interpol." I paused for a second. Casper didn't say I was full of shit, so I continued. "Interpol has something akin to the Internal Affairs division of a police department. And they have suspicions that Amadou is running with the wrong crowd. I've been asked to find out what, if anything, Amadou is mixed up in."

"Hold up." He lifted a hand.

I realized right then that I would have to proceed with this operation even if Casper bailed on me. My revelations might have completely blindsided him. He could respond by trying to neutralize me. I slowly reached around to my waist, feeling the steel butt of my Sig.

"Zane, or whoever you are…"

"That's my real name. Want to see my ID?"

"Could be a fake."

"But I'm not."

"I've got eyes, dumbass."

"Look, I'm standing right here, still hoping you'll be my partner on this operation."

"Partner, my ass." He spat into the woods, shaking his head. "Partners trust each other to speak the truth, and not just when it's convenient."

"Yeah, trust. It's a double-edged sword, ain't it?"

He shot me a look of derision. "Whatever. Just a while ago, you said you did your little recon act last night because you had a thing for Bailey, and—"

"You're twisting my words."

"And now you say it's because you're trying to get dirt on this Amadou guy. So, you're basically a bald-faced liar. I'm just not sure which one to call bullshit on."

"Both are true. My original intent was to see if Bailey was alive. Amadou showing up, and the weapons, and the murder... I never expected to see any of that. I'm telling you this because once we get Bailey and her son safely away from this place, I need to quiz her on what she knows."

He huffed out a breath and gazed into the woods. When he turned back, he said, "I'll have to interrogate her about the Neo-Nazi group and their connection to the Army officer."

"Of course."

He went back to his forest-gazing. My guess? He was biding time to figure out if he could trust me. "So, what's your real background?"

"If I told you that, I'd have to kill you." I laughed. Thankfully, he followed suit.

"You're not going to tell me, are you?" he said.

"I like to take cool pictures. Let's just leave it that. Are you good? Because I'm ready to do this thing."

He released a long breath and chuckled. "Some might say I'm naïve to trust you, but ... yeah, I'm good."

25

With a large garbage bag slung over my shoulder, we trudged through the second section of the forest until we could see the creek and, beyond that, the main house.

"Looks to be all quiet," Casper said.

"The late-night champagne toasts probably didn't hurt."

We waited a few minutes to see if guards would make an appearance on the front side of the house. They didn't, so we proceeded cautiously across the field until we reached the creek. Casper pointed to a tree about fifty feet away.

"You cover me from behind that tree while I hide our firecracker pots behind those bushes by the front door."

"Roger that." I grinned, but he didn't match it.

He was just about to take off when he stopped in his tracks. "I just assumed that you actually know how to use that Sig. Am I wrong?"

"I can hold my own. But if I were a betting man, I'd probably pick you over me in a shooting match."

He grunted something then headed for the house—pots and firecrackers in hand. I found my position at the tree, my gun at the ready, hoping no guard would show himself. We needed the engagement to begin on our terms, or the operation would be a nasty bust.

Casper finished the task and jogged back. "Okay, follow me."

We hightailed it to the outer rim of the woods and arced around the house until we reached the back yard.

"Still no sign of guards or dogs," he said.

"I think they drank lots of bubbly."

"The dogs got drunk too?" he asked, his face all serious.

I quirked a brow.

"Just kidding, man," he said, swatting my shoulder.

We unpacked the remaining supplies, trekked deeper into the woods, and set up the last of the firecrackers. Finally, we laid down a long fuse that ran up to the legs of the trampoline.

"Let's head to four o'clock," Casper said. "From there, I'll fire the entry shots. We wait until people start to stir and then light up the firecrackers. See how many roaches scurry away."

We could only hope that the "roaches" didn't have a spare rocket launcher at their disposal.

Casper found a branch on which to prop his gun and looked through the scope. "First floor, second window from left." He pushed out a purposeful breath and fired two shots. I heard glass breaking and brought up the monocular to confirm.

"I already see movement," I said. A second later, a light in that same room came on.

"First floor, third window from right," Casper said. Another long breath, and he pulled the trigger, followed almost immediately by the ping of breaking glass.

Like clockwork, a light came on. A man stumbled into the room.

"Here, put these in your ear." Casper handed me earbuds, but our eyes stayed on the house. Two more lights came on, and there was movement throughout the first floor.

"Should we light the fuse?" My shirt clung to the line of sweat down the middle of my back.

Casper held up a finger as he shifted closer to the fuse. More people stirred in the house. A back door opened, and a large figure stepped outside, long rifle in hand. As Casper lit the fuse, a second man rushed outside.

Not wanting to start the fight just yet, we remained very still. My breaths were shallow as I braced for the sound of the Black Cats.

Casper nudged my arm. "The moment they take off for the woods, I'll run to the house. You stay here, cover me, and look out for anyone else roving the area. Someone might come around from the front. After I throw the flash-bang, you join me, and we conduct a quick search for our two assets."

I gave him a thumbs-up a split second before the deafening bursts of the firecrackers commenced. One of the men on the back porch literally jumped in the air. He shoved his buddy out of the way, opened the back door, and appeared to yell something inside the house. Another man ran outside and the three of them—all armed—ran behind a tree, lifted their rifles, and fired blindly into the dark forest.

Pop, pop, pop, pop, pop.

A damn war zone.

Meanwhile, the intense bursts from the Black Cats continued.

The men went on the offensive, hurried past our location toward the back woods. Yelling, cursing in Italian. Emotionally charged to seek vengeance from those who dared to shoot at their villa.

The moment the three gunmen stepped into the woods, Casper took off for the back door of the main house. I was on my feet, gun out, head on a swivel. The thunder of the Black Cats still rolling.

A flash of light through the back window.

Boom!

I ran toward the back door, vigilant. Didn't want to miss someone pulling around either side of the house.

"All clear for now," I said to Casper at the door.

He led the way into a small hallway that spilled into a kitchen. From there, we hit a living area. Numerous paintings on the walls, but no people rushing about. My head never stopped rotating. My senses on full alert. I had to ensure we wouldn't get ambushed from behind. As Casper scurried through the expansive room, I swung my sights to each entrance—all five of them. Good to go.

Then Casper dropped to the floor.

Shot?

"Casper!" Four quick steps around an L-shaped leather sofa. A man on the ground, roiling, holding his ears and yelling. A victim of the flash-bang. I jumped over him.

Casper pushed up to his feet. I checked the man on the floor for weapons. None.

Moving on to the staircase, we hustled up the steps, Casper leading the way. At the second-floor landing, a shot pierced the air, coming from behind us. Chunks of wall plaster exploded in our faces.

"Down!" Casper shoved me to the side, fired off three quick rounds. The man at the bottom of the stairs tottered into a table. Framed pictures and a lamp crashed to the floor.

We hooked a right down the first hall, and Casper opened the first door. Stepped in, looked around.

"Clear," he said before moving on to the next door. I kept my gun at the ready, eyes sweeping the hallway for anything that moved.

Casper was in and out of the second room in no time—a quick head-shake told me it was empty. A sense of dread ran through me. Had Bailey and her son been moved to another site?

I was about to relay my concerns when I saw a door at the far end of the hall crack open.

"We've got visitors," I said to Casper as he brushed by me on way to the next door.

"Do what ya gotta do, but don't get shot," he said before disappearing into the next room.

I backed into the same room as Casper but kept my focus on the partially open door down the hall. Would someone burst through the door, spraying bullets everywhere? Were they waiting to see if I'd inspect the room and then shoot me at point-blank range? Another possibility broke through the noise and tension. I turned back to Casper.

"Bailey and her son might be in that room with the door cracked open," I said.

He'd just shut the door to an armoire. "Two more rooms on this end, then we'll inspect it. All in about twenty seconds. We're running out of time. The goons will be back from the woods soon."

When he stepped into the hallway, a flash lit up the hall a nanosecond before the crackle of rapid gunfire. Casper and I dropped to the floor, scrambled back inside the room.

"You hit?" My hands instinctively touched my head and chest.

"I'm good. You?"

"Fine."

Casper got to his knees, peeked in the hall, stuck his gun out the door, and fired off four rounds.

Silence, then my ears perked up. A sound, muffled and barely audible. *Probably nothing, Jack.*

"Can't just sit here and wait this out," Casper said as I started to search the room. "Get ready to cover me."

"Hold up." I opened the closet door and rifled through hanging clothes.

Casper said, "Dude, I already checked the room."

I left the closet and stood in the middle of the room. I was just about to let it go and rush out the door when my nose twitched. My whole life, this had only happened for one reason: the smell of Anna's perfume.

"They're here somewhere." I opened the closet again, searched for a hidden door. More gunfire in the hallway.

"Dammit, Zane, get your ass out here or we're all gonna die."

My nose twitched again, and I almost sneezed—right in front of the armoire. Whipping the door open, I yanked clothes off hangers and tossed them aside. Bailey and her son were nowhere to be found. I pawed at the back of the wooden armoire.

"Zane!"

But the nose knows. I searched every inch...and then I felt a bump in the wood. I stuck my nails into the crevice and peeled back a rear section of the armoire.

A woman crouched next to a little boy.

"Don't be scared. We're here to rescue you."

Fear in their eyes. I backed away. The woman pushed out of the hole and into the room, her son clinging to her side. He was shaking.

"What the hell?" Casper's eyes were saucers.

I ran to the door. "Come on." I waved at Bailey and her son.

"Are you the person from the back yard?" she asked.

I nodded and flicked my fingers. "We need to hurry."

Gunfire ripped through the air, and the little boy screamed.

"Two more shooters at the steps. We're stuck." Casper fired two return shots.

Bailey grabbed my forearm. "I know another way."

26

Mother and her son shoved earbuds into place, and Casper gave the signal. Hurling himself into the hallway on his knees, he released a flurry of shots at the partially open door at the end of the hall. Then he swung and released some lead toward the top of the staircase. I shuffled into the high-risk zone with Bailey and her son tucked in just behind me. I fired my Sig three times as we made our way up the hall to the next room. Mom and son scampered inside. I grabbed the backup flash-bang from my pocket, pulled the pin, and tossed it down the hall.

"Let's roll!" I shouted.

Casper whirled around, took three steps, and dove through the open door. I flung myself into the room, midair when the flash-bang exploded. My body slammed to the floor, my head filled with a sharp ringing. Disoriented.

Up to my knees, Bailey was at a spiral staircase in the corner of the room, urging her son to move quicker down the steps. Casper pulled at my shirt. I jumped up, ran to the staircase. A flurry of sounds—screaming, gunshots, all mixed together. Bailey struggled to keep her son moving. Only two steps from the top, he looked up at his mom, his red face coated with tears.

"Faster, faster, faster!" Casper said.

Bailey tried to pick her son up, but he was squirming, upset.

"Let me." I pushed past Bailey, scooped up her son, and bolted down the spiral staircase. "Which way to the front?"

Bailey stumbled down the last couple of steps. She was about to fall. I grabbed her hand to help, but quickly pulled it back. I didn't understand why, but there was no time to ponder. "Left," she said. "Go left down this hall."

I spun around. Casper at the top of the staircase. He took aim, fired two more rounds. "Dammit, they're coming out of the woodwork!" he shouted.

With Bailey's son firmly in my grip, I darted down the hall to a T, where I turned back to Bailey for guidance. She yelled something, but even with the ringing subsiding in my ears, I couldn't hear her. She jabbed her arm to the right.

I raced around the corner. Gunman. He'd just walked out of a room. Before I could pull back, he fired a quick shot. Plaster exploded just over my shoulder. Bailey's son screamed. I ducked, covering his head. Off balance, I raised my gun and pumped out three rounds. The second bullet hit the goon in the knee. He yelped, and his gun flew out of his hands. I kicked it away and hustled past him, racing into the living room. The front door was just beyond a foyer with a massive chandelier. "Almost there," I said.

The little boy looked up at me, then burrowed his head into my shoulder. Even with all the activity, the chaos, I could feel him quaking in my arms. Two, three, four more gunshots rang out somewhere in the house. I spun around, backpedaled. Bailey was just standing there, looking over her shoulder. Perhaps in shock.

"Can't stop running!" I said.

She took one last look in the adjoining room and hurried in my direction.

"Mommy!" The boy stretched his arms over my shoulder.

"It's okay. Let's get you to a safe spot, and you and your mommy can hold each other."

With a bead on the front door, I ran into the foyer...so fast I slipped on the tile floor. I dropped a hand down to catch myself from falling.

Movement above me. I torqued my body in that direction. The barrel of my gun clipped a table leg, and the weapon skittered three feet away from me. A guard with a broadening smile took direct aim at us. All I could do was roll on top of the kid to protect him. My body tensed to take the gunshot.

A blur off to the side.

"Bailey!" I reached out for her.

A glass flew out of her hand and smashed into the man's head. He wobbled, and I lunged for my gun. Grabbed it, fired. Hit the guy's midsection. He brought both hands to his stomach and dropped to his knees, blood oozing between his fingers.

"Run, save my son. I'm right behind you!" Bailey said.

I hurried out the front door, pulled the pots from the bushes, lit the fuse, and started to run.

A scream stopped me.

Bailey was still inside the house.

I took two steps back toward the front door when gunshots echoed from the interior. A second later, the Black Cats I'd just ignited started firing. So many competing noises. Gasoline on the chaos.

A count of three, and Bailey finally raced outside. I whirled around and ran like hell, holding fast to the boy. At forty feet, I glanced over my shoulder.

Bailey's pace had slowed—she was walking backward, her eyes on the house.

What now?

"Dammit!" I ran back to her. "Come on. We've got to run."

"They've got your partner. They jumped him."

I became paralyzed. My instincts told me to hand the boy to Bailey and go back inside to rescue Casper. But thankfully, my brain was speaking loud and clear. I'd be entering a sure death trap if I went back in. And there was no way Bailey and her son would be able to find their way off the property without my guidance and protection. As much as I hated it—in fact, felt like a total ass for abandoning someone who'd saved my life—we had to keep moving.

"Let's go!" I grabbed her hand, and we ran. We raced like deer through the creek and the woods until we reached the car.

Finally on the road with no one on our tail, my thoughts scrambled to come up with a plan to rescue my partner, Cletus Jacobsen.

27

After driving about two kilometers, Bailey spoke for the first time.

"Do you have any water for my son?" Mother and child were huddled together in the passenger's seat. She gently stroked the side of her son's head. He was calm now, his eyes closed, but he was smacking his dry lips.

I shook my head. "We can stop at a store and get some."

"Thank you for putting your life on the line, for rescuing us," she said.

I glanced at her, then back to the road. "You're welcome."

"You're upset about your partner."

I opened my mouth, but no words came out. All I could think about was having left my partner behind. *Who does that shit, Jack?*

I made the right choice. I did.

Did you?

I wondered what Casper was thinking about it all.

Bailey continued. "I'm just so sorry about…everything. And

it's all because of the poor decisions I've made in life, my inability to properly judge people."

"Please don't apologize. It's not necessary," I insisted.

She fell silent, and I was grateful for that. I was shaken. I needed to quiet the insanity. I needed space in my brain to assess our current situation, to consider next steps.

I likely had a few more hours until Simon would request confirmation of Amadou's kidnapping, so there was still some sand in the top half of the hourglass. But how much, exactly? Working on an impossibly tight deadline was one thing, but working on a timetable where the end was a complete unknown was torturous.

When I saw the glowing signage of a convenience store, I pulled in and purchased some bottled water. Bailey's son chugged half of a bottle while she gently rubbed his back.

"Your son. I don't even know his name."

"Joshua. Named after my father, God rest his soul. Your name?"

"Jack." I almost bit my tongue in two when I realized I'd accidentally divulged my real name. "It's Jack Zane. Most people call me Zane."

"So, tell me why you and your friend…"

"Casper."

Joshua sat up. "Like the ghost, Mommy."

"Shhh. Try to rest, Joshua," she told him. He lay back down on her lap and shut his eyes. She turned back to me and said, "Who paid you to find us, rescue us? I don't have any friends or family with money."

"It's not about money. I mean, we didn't get paid."

She tilted her head as she stared at my profile. I could feel her eyes on me. Was she confused? Concerned that we might want payment in some other way?

"You have nothing to worry about. Casper is a good dude, and

I have—" I cut myself off. I'd almost said that I had this wonderful family waiting for me back home. But that was no longer the case. My little family had been shattered. I rolled down the window and let the breeze hit my face. I felt a cool tear on my cheek and swiped it away before it was noticed. I cleared my throat and started again. "I'll figure out a way to get Casper back. I'll take care of that. But when he's out, he's going to have questions for you."

"About?"

I wondered how much I should divulge. Casper was running a field operation for an Army investigation. While I'd doubted some of his story—especially the lack of resources—I understood the significance of what Casper was trying to accomplish. "Casper is an MP—that's Military Police—at a US Army base in Germany. Stuttgart."

"Okay," was all she said.

I continued. "And they're concerned about possible ties between an Army officer and a local Neo-Nazi group."

She didn't respond verbally, but out of the corner of my eye, I could see her bring a hand to her head.

I said, "I didn't mean to stress you out any more. You've been through hell."

"You have no idea," she said in a voice so low I barely heard her.

Our eyes met for a brief second. No more words.

I went back to focusing on the road, and we entered the Lyon city limits.

The boy was softly snoring as Bailey rubbed his back. She said, "Jack, I was part of that Neo-Nazi group. My son and I both were for the last two years. But it was forced on us. We were basically being held captive."

"You're American, right?"

She nodded. "Used to have a reasonably quiet life just outside of Knoxville."

I perked up. "My wife and I met at the University of Tennessee."

"Oh, you're married." Her eyes shifted to my left hand, which had no ring on it.

Simon's rules. Out of the blue, anger flooded my entire being. I wanted my damn ring back. Then, as I'd done a thousand times recently, I tamped down my rage for Maddie's sake. *Stick to the program, then tell them to suck it when I'm done.*

"Anna died a while back." I kept it simple. Just saying those few words was painful enough.

She sighed. "Emmett was incredibly caring to me during a really hard time in my life."

"Emmett is...?"

"My..." She drank some water and wiped her mouth. "My boyfriend. Former boyfriend. He took advantage of me when..." Her words trailed off, and I wondered if she would continue.

She didn't.

"You don't have to tell me right now," I said. "Casper, though, will want to hear all of the—"

"I used to be a court reporter in Knox County. I developed carpal tunnel syndrome. So severe, they decided to do surgery. But when they opened me up, they found a rare form of cancer. Very aggressive. Doctors said I had maybe a few months. I had a choice to make. Go through all the typical forms of treatment and hope to beat the cancer or amputate my forearm."

She lifted her left arm—a prosthetic.

Now I understood why she had pulled her arm out of my grasp back at the Campanella compound.

"That was a courageous decision," I said.

She looked at the sleeping Joshua as she continued rubbing his back. "I did it for him. He needed his mother more than I needed my hand."

Through my window, atop the tallest hill in Lyon, brilliant gold lights illuminated the Basilica. I thought about Bailey's situation, so much like my own—where you had to make the tough decisions for the welfare of your child.

She reached out and touched my ring finger where a digit had been amputated. The most visible reminder of my first mission. "Your son may never know it, at least not for a while, but what you did was incredibly selfless."

She chuckled softly, but I had a feeling it was not from amusement. "After my surgery, Emmett was my physical therapist. He pushed me to do some amazing things, and..." She released a jittery breath. "And I guess I felt like I owed him my life. I put him on a pedestal. He...he took advantage of it."

I glanced over at her; her cheeks had turned pink.

"How did you end up in the villa, held captive by the Campanellas?"

"Emmett convinced us to take a trip to Germany—he has dual citizenship. I saw some red flags when we got there, but I pushed them aside. When we missed our flight to return home, I started to get worried. Then his personality changed...or maybe I was finally seeing the real Emmett. He got new tattoos that were full of hate, and people started hanging around our place who made me feel uncomfortable. It turned into an absolute nightmare. I had to get out. I had to get this little guy out. I couldn't let him grow up to be like...like that awful man."

"So you tried to escape?" I snuck a quick glance her way. Her cheeks were damp with tears.

"Yes, we tried. They caught us. Emmett was furious but distracted. His Campanella buddies agreed to hold us for the time being. I just think the old guy, Dominic, had a thing for me." She shuddered. "And that's how we ended up at that house."

"I'm so sorry for what you experienced. But your strength, Bailey, is inspiring."

"I don't feel strong. Actually, I feel pretty stupid."

"You did the right thing, the difficult thing. And now you're safe with your child."

"But your friend is now a prisoner because of me."

I reached over and tapped her knee. "We don't know that for sure yet. Please don't beat yourself up."

We pulled to a stop in the lot next to my apartment building. I'd have to sneak them inside, but at least they'd be safe until I figured out a way to rescue Casper.

Rescue Casper—I had no idea where to start.

Bailey grabbed my arm as I opened the car door.

"Jack, there's something I need to tell you. Something I heard from Emmett and his twisted followers."

"I'm listening." My phone dinged with a text. She started to talk, but I held up my hand as I read the message.

"Something wrong?" she asked.

"Just got a text from Casper's phone. It's the Campanellas. They want to do a trade: Casper for you."

28

While Joshua rested on the bed in my apartment, his mother paced nonstop. We'd received a second text from the Campanellas saying they wanted the trade to take place at La Basilique of Notre-Dame de Fourvière. Nine a.m. sharp. The more Bailey and I batted around ideas for our next move, the more she became worked up.

"I can't take being the cause of so much pain. Look at the trauma I've put my own son through, all because of my stupid, stupid decisions." She stomped her foot as she said those last few words, her Southern accent obvious to me for the first time.

"You think any of us have been perfect parents?" I countered. "If anyone was keeping a tally of all my mistakes…well, let's just say Santa would not be leaving me any gifts."

She paused, leaning against the back of the couch, and we locked gazes. It took a few seconds, but her face softened, and she even offered a small smile. "You're too kind, Jack."

"Zane."

She continued without acknowledging the correction. "You're

trying to keep this histrionic woman from totally losing it. After being a captive for so long, I guess I just need to vent. I'm so sorry you're getting the brunt of it."

"Don't apologize. I get it. I do. If I were in your shoes, venting would be just the opening act."

When her eyes didn't blink, I wondered if I'd given her the wrong impression. "Hey, no need to worry. I'm no vigilante or anything."

She crossed her arms. "Oh, I've dreamed of doing some awful things to Emmett. You mentioned your daughter. How old is she?"

"Maddie is five." The moment the words left my mouth I realized I'd just revealed another secret, maybe the most treasured secret of my entire life. What was it about this woman that had me so easily dropping my usual defense mechanisms?

Chill, Jack. This woman is bonding with you. She's not some covert agent sent to find your daughter.

"Just one year younger than my Joshua. Pictures?"

I grinned and pulled out my phone. We scrolled through a few photos of my girl.

"Beautiful. Her snaggle-tooth smile is heartwarming. I can see such a free spirit."

I beamed with pride and ached with pain at the same time, a strange sensation. "So, back to Casper. I think—"

She lifted her hand. "I'll go. I'll trade places with Casper. No other option that I can see."

Damn, she was headstrong. I walked over to the kitchen and opened the fridge. Two Heinekens. I flashed back to the two beers Casper and I had shared on the night he'd saved my life. Would I finally be able to return the favor?

But I knew the answer was more complicated than a straight, "Hell yeah!" First, how could I save him without sacrificing Bailey's life? Second, would all this focus on Casper and Bailey put me at risk with Simon? Could I accomplish it all—save Casper,

Bailey, Joshua...*and* kidnap Amadou—before the grim reaper came calling?

"I sure could use a beer, but I see morning light peeking through the shades," Bailey said.

I closed the fridge.

She opened the pantry. "Do you have anything Joshua could eat when he wakes up?"

My thoughts shot back to her earlier comment. "You never told me what you heard from Emmett and his followers. Something twisted?"

She closed her eyes briefly. "It's beyond twisted. They want to commit acts of terrorism—to kill as many people as possible, to support their weirdo views about a pure race. I just can't believe I was with that man."

"Any specific target?"

"Not that I heard."

Many thoughts pinged my mind right then, but one took the lead. *Get Casper out.* I walked toward the door.

"Hey, Jack—"

"Zane."

"I hope you're not running out to buy groceries."

"Actually, that was going to be my second errand."

"What's your first?"

"You still insist on being part of this so-called swap with Casper?"

She nodded. "I have to be."

"Then I'm going to the only place where I can find the device I'll need to make it happen."

29

Even on my second visit, the main sanctuary in La Basilique of Notre-Dame de Fourvière was probably the most stunning thing I'd ever seen. As I'd learned from the brochure, the materials used to create this architectural marvel were some of the most precious in the world: white marble from Carrara, pink granite from northern Italy, blue marble from Savoy, green onyx, silver and gold pieces, as well as ebony and ivory.

Of the sanctuary's many designs—spectacular stained-glass windows and intricately painted mosaics—the altar drew my eye more than anything else. A passing tour guide described the scene as Mary releasing Adam and Eve from their chains and setting them free from Hell. And I wanted to do the same for Casper, Bailey, and Joshua.

But I was no Mary.

I checked the time on my phone. Five minutes until the handoff. There were only three other people in the main sanctuary, all elderly women. The priest had left the sanctuary, and the tour guide was out front. I just hoped like hell that when the parties showed up, all other bystanders would stay clear. I actually said a prayer there would be no collateral damage. On the other hand, I couldn't sit idly by while the Campanella clan ran off with Bailey. God only knew what that Emmett person would do once the Campanellas handed her back to him.

I pulled the strings to my hoodie so my face wasn't so visible, then turned to gaze at the colorful mural on the side wall, one of the massive stone columns just to my left. From this position, I could use my peripheral vision to monitor people entering the main door.

We'd been told via text that Bailey had to come alone. No cops, no vigilantes, no Joshua, no me. Bailey was willing to do as they asked, but I would have none of it. Me being here was not up for debate, risks and all.

Movement at the front door, and as planned, Bailey entered at two minutes before nine. Without overtly looking at me, she sat on the left side of the sanctuary, sixth row.

Bailey was a strong woman; that much was obvious. But she carried a lot of guilt, and I recognized the same in myself. For her to insist on taking part in this operation was nothing short of courageous, and I'd told her that, even as I pleaded with her not to do it. To give me a chance to think of another plan to free Casper. She'd countered that there was no other way. There would be no second chance. The Campanellas were ruthless. They would likely kill Casper and then come hunting for her.

Bailey's commitment to this operation was manifested in many ways, but none more so than her allowing Miss Patty, whom she had never met, to care for Joshua. Miss Patty was delighted to assist.

"I'd be honored to help your cause," she'd said to me before smiling at Bailey. The two ladies hugged, and Missy Patty wrapped an arm around Joshua and started telling him about the history of Lyon.

Someone coughed, and I turned in that direction. Four men strolled through a side door on the far wall. One of them was Casper, with a hat pulled low over his face. He walked with a noticeable limp. I was surprised to see the Campanellas entering the church via that side door. Must have pulled some strings with their holy connections. I'd heard plenty of stories about certain priests aiding mafia families. How far would the priests in this church go to abet the Campanellas in this crime?

I ambled down the side aisle, one eye still on the murals, the other eye scanning the expansive church. A few more tourists had entered the sanctuary, including four people who had shuffled into the back pews on Bailey's side. My hands in my pockets, I touched the side of the flash-bang I'd picked up at Casper's apartment—where I also verified the pantry guy was still alive. I had to assume the Campanellas weren't yet aware that one of their own was being held by Casper. Best-case scenario, they would have insisted on including him in the terms of the swap. Worst-case scenario, they could have taken the "eye for an eye" approach and killed Casper without asking questions.

Casper and his three escorts scooted into row six on the right side. When Casper's butt hit the wooden pew, the punk next to him swung a sharp elbow into his ribs. He'd tried to do so subtly, but the impact was obvious. Casper grimaced and slowly started to fall over. Something told me this wasn't the first time Casper's ribs had been on the receiving end of an assault. The ruffian grabbed him by the shirt, pulled him back up, and patted his shoulder as if they were a couple of pals just messing around.

"You sonofa..." I whispered before catching myself. Alerting the Campanellas to my presence would sink our hopes for rescuing Casper, not to mention putting Bailey in grave danger. As much as I was inspired to live for my daughter, Bailey also had a son whose life solely depended upon a solo parent.

Now came the moment of truth. Bailey and Casper were to rise from their seats at the same time. When passing each other in the middle aisle, per our plan, Bailey was to suddenly pull Casper to her side and onto the floor between pews. I would then yank the pin on the flash-bang and toss it into the laps of the Campanella clan.

Like any plan, on paper it sounded plausible. In reality, a hundred things could go wrong. I stayed in the moment, my eyes focused on Casper being nudged or signaled by his handlers.

There it was.

Bailey put a hand on the back of her pew and started to rise. A man scooted in next to her—probably a random tourist, but I was suspicious of everyone. He kept his head bowed as he moved to his knees, presumably to pray. I glanced back over at Casper—he hadn't shifted from his seated position. The man to his right still had a hand on his shoulder. The tourist sitting next to Bailey must have spooked him.

Two options. I could approach the tourist myself, say that I ran security for the church, and ask him to step outside. Or we could all just wait him out. My concern was patience—not my own, but from the Campanella side.

With my eyes volleying between all the players, a third option took root. I could walk directly toward Casper, pull him behind me, and throw the flash-bang at the feet of the mobsters. But I feared our proximity to the stun grenade would incapacitate us.

The guy to Casper's right started to turn his head. A second later, the man next to Bailey shifted in his seat, pivoted right, and stuck a gun into the base of her head.

The man had been a plant.

"Stop!" I took just one step before a blur came around the pillar and a gun was shoved into my side.

"Don't move, asshole." It was Salvadore, the younger Campanella. The one I'd knifed in the leg. "We meet again. And this time, you'll be the one who suffers."

30

"Life is all about options," Anna would sometimes tell our daughter during a teaching moment. And right now, there were no options that would keep us all alive. Individually, there might be an opportunity to make it out unscathed. But together...the three of us literally didn't have a prayer.

And then I heard Maddie's sweet little voice whisper in my ear, "*Goonies never say die.*"

"What are you smiling about?" Salvadore's hot breath billowed against my neck.

"You'll soon find out." I seethed. Of course, I had nothing to back it up.

"What? You cocky sonofabitch, you think you can—"

"Shhh." Biaggio, from his position next to Bailey, narrowed his eyes at Salvadore.

The two brothers stared at each other a long second before shifting their sights to the thugs sitting next to Casper, then back to each other.

Who was in charge? No sign of their father, Dominic. Had they thought this far ahead in their little scheme? Of course, this "little scheme" had been good enough to fool me.

A door opened to the side of the altar, and a priest walked into the sanctuary. His eyes glanced our way—it was impossible for him not to see the gun in Salvadore's hand—but he continued walking down the aisle toward the main door, one hand gently cradling a Bible.

Salvadore chuckled. "Like I always told you, Biaggio, it's great to be the son of Dominic."

Biaggio ignored his brother and motioned for all of us to exit the building. When I took one step, Salvadore jerked me backward. "You try anything, and your brain will be sprayed all over that mural you were ogling."

Casper and the squad of hoodlums walked out first, followed by Bailey and Biaggio, with Salvadore and me pulling up the rear. Remarkably, everyone in Camp Campanella kept their guns hidden, so bystanders would not be alerted. The sun's bright glare blinded me as I stepped outside.

"Hey, Zane, funny meeting you here again!"

Karma? I turned just before she barreled into me, grabbing me by the neck. I lost my balance and tumbled into Salvadore. His gun slipped away from my side. I twisted and torqued my body, doing anything to stay upright

"I'm such a klutz!" She released her familiar snort-laugh as I tripped over her legs.

Somehow, I stopped myself before falling down the steep stairs. Salvadore wasn't as fortunate. He stumbled down the first couple of steps—his injured leg not helping the situation. Ultimately, he lost his footing completely and fell forward on top of his brother.

Someone said, "Gun!" which was quickly followed by a cacophony of screams and shouts in a variety of languages. People running everywhere. Mayhem.

I rolled away from the entanglement with Karma, spied Salvadore's gun on the fourth step, and dove for it. While I was midair, something or someone slammed into my chest. Knocked the air out of my lungs twice, once on the initial hit and again when I slammed into the unforgiving ground. I couldn't find the loose gun, but I did see Casper hobbling away in the other direction. Evading his captors.

Biaggio barreled toward me, but Bailey swung her foot out, tripping him. The weapon flew from his hand.

"Get the gun!" I said to Bailey.

Biaggio body-checked her. She went flying. But she used it to her advantage. She continued the momentum and lunged for his brother's gun, just a few feet away. Biaggio, quick on his feet, kicked her hand just before she could grab the weapon. She screamed. The gun skittered down the steps. I'd tracked it the whole way. But so had Biaggio.

He was already racing down the steps after it.

I had to reach the gun before Biaggio. Our only hope for ensuring our freedom. With Biaggio ten feet in front of me, I planted my launch foot and jumped. Midflight, a dark object whirled past me, clocking Biaggio in the side of his head. He grunted from the impact of the hardback book and tumbled awkwardly down the steps. I scooped up the gun and found Bailey on one side of me and Karma on the other.

"Run toward Evan!" Karma pointed at her boyfriend.

Without debate, we took off. The thug who still had his gun lifted it in our direction was aiming at Bailey. I started to throw myself on top of her, protect her from an almost certain execution, but the priest broke from the crowd with his hand raised, as if calling on a higher power to end this fight before someone was killed. I grabbed Casper, and we all ran out of the esplanade before a shot was fired.

Goonies never say die.

31

"Answered prayers." Miss Patty crossed herself, but other than that, she showed little emotion. I'd never been so happy to see Miss Patty's stoic facial expression. That is, until she started asking questions I didn't want to address.

"Who was the fight against?"

"How did you survive?"

"Where have you been?"

"Casper, what happened to you?"

Finally, she stopped with the queries and studied each of our faces, waiting for answers.

We were all huddled in Miss Patty's living room. The three of us hadn't had a chance to debrief; we'd been split into two cars to make it back here. I focused on the question directed to Casper. I turned to him. "Yeah, man. What did they do to you?"

Casper carefully lifted his hat to where we could see his entire face—it was almost unrecognizable. Bailey gasped, but Karma and Evan had little reaction.

I started to ponder why that was, but Casper spoke.

"I'm ready for my big break in Hollywood as a lead stunt man," he said, ending with a wet cough while holding his side. He went on to tell us about the torture sessions, where Biaggio and Salvadore took turns pummeling him with brass knuckles. They'd said their goal was to make us think that they'd replaced Casper with a complete stranger during the swap.

Joshua, who'd been tossing a small ball against the wall, chased after an errant throw and crashed into Casper, who released an elongated groan.

Bailey gently chided her son and then walked him into Miss Patty's kitchen to get a drink.

"I don't like to complain, but BS—my nickname for the two brothers—worked my ribs over pretty damn good," Casper said. "They said they were pretending to be Rocky, their favorite Italian American."

"I want to be a boxer when I grow up," Joshua said, walking back into the room with a glass of water.

"Joshua?"

He looked to his mother, who arched an eyebrow. Then he handed Casper the water. "You need this more than me."

"Thank you." As Casper started to chug, Joshua said, "Oh, and I'm sorry for not paying attention to you since you look like you've been in a fight with a shark."

"Joshua!"

"I'm sorry, it's just that—"

Casper interjected, "It's okay, Bailey. Hey, Zane, we could change my nickname from Casper to the Great White Shark, right?"

"Cutting jokes when you look like the Hunchback of Notre Dame. Nice," I said, causing Bailey to shake her head at me. But she did it with a half-smile, something I'd yet to see from her. I hoped she and her son had far more smiles than frowns in their future.

Miss Patty moved closer to Casper. "You might have internal bleeding. Who did this to you?"

Casper shifted his eyes to me. I did the same to Karma and Evan. "You don't have to hide anything from us," Karma said. "I come across as being rather oblivious most of the time." She paused and glanced at her boyfriend. "Don't say anything, okay?"

"I didn't say a damn thing."

Lightly punching his shoulder, she snort-giggled and turned to me. "Sometimes, my training kicks in, and I just react."

"Training? You threw the bible at Biaggio?"

"The bald guy, yep. Only weapon I could get my hands on. And if you ask me, he's organized crime. They all are. We stumbled into something pretty heavy, am I right?"

Bailey started to explain, but I cut in, concerned who might be directing Karma and Evan. "Hold up. What training?"

"Oh, sorry. Robert was relentless in teaching me how to read a crowd, find the real danger, and then take action to neutralize the adversary."

Alarmed but also excited that I might have just heard an actual name from someone on the inside at Simon, I was about to turn up the pressure a notch.

"Robert is her dad," Evan said. "She just calls him Robert to annoy him."

Karma gave us a round wave. "I know I can be a pain in the arse, and I don't really care."

"What's this training your father gave you, then?"

"He's retired Secret Service. Wow, the stories I could tell—" She covered her mouth like a little kid who'd just said a bad word. Evan rolled his eyes.

Miss Patty grabbed her purse off the table and marched to the door. "We need to go. Now."

"Wait, wait." I raised both hands. "Casper needs medical

attention."

"And he will get it."

"We're not calling the cops on those assholes?" Evan asked.

Miss Patty's face coiled into a hard knot. "Can't trust the police. Too many on the payroll."

"Whose payroll?" I asked.

"There are three main crime families fighting for control, but the Campanellas yield the most power, the most influence," she said with a hand on the door.

"Where is this place?"

"I will take you. All of you. But you cannot tell anyone." She eyeballed each of us in turn, and we nodded accordingly. "You will be safe, and Casper will get medical help while we assess the long-term situation."

I was good with the plan, even if the details were murky. Plus, I knew I had to take the next step with Amadou, and this would free me from worrying about the rest of the crew while I did my thing.

"You two going?" I asked Karma and Evan on the way out.

"We have a target on our backs now," Evan said with a shrug. "Not sure we have a choice at the moment."

Karma smacked him on the back, while looking at me. "Robert always said you can't just wish things to change on their own. You've got to recognize the pros and cons, and then take action. We're in."

A felony action was next on my list. Just after I quizzed Bailey one more time.

32

I took a second bite of sweetbread as I replayed what Bailey had just told me. She'd spoken so quickly it had all run together.

"So, you overheard Dominic talking to Amadou on the phone about—"

I was interrupted by Joshua, who'd just run up with a black-and-white photo in his little hand. It had been given to him by Paul Newman and Joanne Woodward, the fake identities of our hosts in this safe room of some ancient building.

"Look, Mommy, the one holding the gun is Mr. Paul's father. Mr. Paul said he was a gorilla. But he doesn't look like one to me."

Running her fingers through Joshua's hair, Bailey smiled. "Mr. Paul's father was a freedom fighter in World War II. I don't remember the name of their group..."

"The Maquis," Paul said as he walked into the room, relying heavily on his cane. "Your mom was right—they were French resistance fighters during the Nazi occupation of France. 'Maquisards' was their full name. Many of those young men initially were trying to avoid being forced to serve in the STO, which were nothing more than German forced labor camps. Eventually, they became more organized into an active resistance force."

"Was your father a hero?" Joshua asked, wide-eyed.

Paul crossed his hands on top of his cane. "I'm proud of my father, but many people were heroes during those times, Joshua."

Joanne appeared from behind Paul's broad shoulders. "Is Mr. Paul boring you with old war stories?"

"I kind of like it," Joshua said.

I studied the stone room, a basement under a small apartment building in Old Lyon. "I wonder if this room was ever used back in the war."

Joanne patted her husband's shoulder and said to him, "They're here, so I suppose we can tell them."

Paul was about to speak when there was a knock on the door, causing Joshua to flinch.

"It's okay," Joanne said. "Two quick knocks, a pause, then a third knock. That's Doc. He'll see to Casper's wounds." She unlocked the door and led Doc over to Casper, who was sitting on a cot. The two began to speak while Doc unpacked his satchel. Joanne rejoined our group just as Paul started to explain the history of this safe room.

"This room is an off-shoot from one of the original traboules built in the fourth century."

"Traboule?" Bailey asked.

"Actually, from all our research and walking around, I know that one," Karma said, arching her chin. "The word 'traboule' is a corruption from a Latin term, 'trans-ambulare.' They are mostly secret passageways through Lyon. Some say there are as many as four hundred in the city."

"Whoa. That's so cool," Joshua said. "Are there ghosts in here?"

"Maybe." Karma gave a slow nod after seeing Bailey subtly shake her head. "Well, Joshua, actually…no. But it was all about water. The original inhabitants of this area had created these traboules to get quick access to the Saone River. Silk trade workers in the nineteenth century used these passageways to carry their heavy loads from their workshops to the textile merchants at the bottom of the hill."

Paul lifted his pointer finger. "And during the Second World War, some of the traboules—including this very room—were used by the resistance for secret meetings."

There was a loud groan from across the room, and all heads turned to Casper and Doc, who said, "Just using some antiseptic. Would someone like to help me with the cleanup?"

Karma raised her hand. "Evan and I will help."

While the focus was on Casper, I pulled Bailey aside.

"I need to leave. But before I do, I need to confirm what you heard about Pierre Amadou. Tell me again."

"I was in the bathroom doing my makeup—that creep, Dominic, always liked me to dress up so he could ogle me."

"Did he ever…?"

"He tried—once. I kicked him the nuts, and he never tried again," she said, smirking.

"So, you were doing your makeup and…?"

"I heard Dominic mention weapons."

"In what context?"

"Can't say. But it got my attention. I moved closer to the bathroom room door—it was cracked open just a tad—and that's when they started talking about money. It sound like Dominic and his family were getting some sort of brokering fee."

"How much? Actually, it doesn't matter. What about Amadou? What's his role in the weapons deal?"

"Hard to say exactly. The thing I remember most is his loud, booming voice."

"You could hear it over the phone?"

She nodded while raking some of her curls out of her face. "I won't forget that voice for a long time. I haven't met the guy, but honestly, his voice shook me. I don't like to say I'm scared of anyone, not even those Campanella bullies. But Amadou is…different. Like he has this power over…"

"Dominic?"

"Anyone," she said. "Over anyone who gets in his way."

Joanne walked over with more sweetbread, and I tried to figure out how this new intel might impact my mission to kidnap Amadou.

"Are you worried about the Campanellas?"

Paul's voice jarred me for a second. I didn't know he'd been watching me. "Not really. Not at the moment, anyway."

"I saw you sighing, and I just… Well, you seem like something is weighing on you. I don't need to know what it is. But my wife always told me that a burden will always be a burden until you do something about it." He chuckled with a sparkle in his eye. "Joanne is as sweet as that bread there. But she's also got a backbone that can't be broken. I guess that's why we're in this business."

Feeling even more urgency than before, I nodded. "We're very thankful you're in this, uh, business."

"Just carrying on the tradition from my father, I suppose."

Casper released a higher-pitched moan, and I made my way over to the cot. Casper was wincing as Doc applied more antiseptic. "So, Doc, you still planning on cutting off his middle appendage?" I asked.

Casper shot up in his cot. "Ain't no one cutting off any appendage!"

"Just joking, dude. Calm your jets."

Casper took a sip of water from a cup that Karma was holding, then lay back down. "You come over here just to bust my balls?"

The next step of my journey would likely lead to the end of my stay in France. "Just want to say how much I've appreciated teaming up with you."

Casper held his gaze an extra beat. I couldn't afford for him to start pinging me with questions about my real intentions, and thankfully, he didn't. He held out his hand, and we shook. "It's been my honor, Zane. You do what you gotta do. Maybe we'll see each other down the road."

"Maybe so."

I conveyed my thanks to Miss Patty, Paul, and Joanne, and reached the door at the same time as Bailey. "Where are you going?" she asked.

I opened my mouth but didn't immediately speak. For some reason, I found it difficult to lie to her. Probably because our life situations were so similar.

"I know it has something to do with this Amadou person. When will I see you again?"

"I'm not sure."

She took me in her arms and squeezed. On the release, she touched my cheek, then planted a kiss there. "May God watch over your soul." And then I was gone.

33

I counted to five, then used the wheel to pull myself up in the front seat of my Peugeot. There was a police car driving away from me at the end of Amadou's street. I wondered if it was just a casual drive-by or an aftereffect of the church debacle?

My brain had been churning on countless threads after leaving Miss Patty's underground safe house. Amadou and my mission to abduct him... The harrowing battle at the church... So many threads, including the fact that I, thankfully, hadn't heard from Simon.

Then a new thread took hold. I couldn't pinpoint a direct connection between the clash at the old church and Amadou. From everything I'd seen with my own two eyes at the Campanella compound, and hearing what Bailey had to say about Amadou, his role appeared to be focused more on the weapons, not Bailey and her son—and therefore, not Casper or me or anyone involved in their rescue.

To a degree, Amadou was still a mystery. And apparently a

threat to Simon. As the head of Interpol's Cybercrime Intelligence Unit, he played a pivotal role in uncovering who was behind three mammoth ransomware attacks.

I asked myself this question: could there be a connection between the illegal weapons deal and the ransomware attacks, or maybe someone within Simon? I pondered that question for all of ten seconds, but not more. Time was of the essence. The answers would eventually come once I had Amadou in my custody at the designated house near Grenoble. For now, I had to focus on this operation.

I opened a flap on my box of tools and pulled out the Taser, two zip-ties, and the pistol. The flash-bang was sitting at my feet. While my anxiety was on the rise, luck was on my side. I'd already stopped at my perch on the hill to confirm that Amadou was at home. His blue Audi sedan was parked in its normal spot, and through the glare of the expansive kitchen window, I could see him mugging down with his wife. A memory of Anna and me in a full-body hug in our kitchen back in Donelson engulfed me like a tsunami.

And once again, I shoved that beautiful memory into a distant mental compartment.

I blew out a hard breath and got out of my car, walked across the street. My gait became a march, my chest and shoulders more pronounced. Given what I'd seen and heard about Amadou, if he ended up getting hurt during the abduction, I wouldn't cry over it. But his wife was another matter. It might be a naïve if not hopeful notion, but it was hard for me to believe she knew about Amadou's side gig with the weapons, not to mention him murdering that kid at the Campanella villa.

I reached the wooden fence and paused. There were voices. Happy voices. I peered between two slats. Standing on the patio near the kitchen door was Amadou's wife in a snug pencil skirt, smiling. She spoke to her husband, who was outside of my view.

Maybe she was saying she needed to run a few errands. That would make my job much easier if she left the property.

I pulled back from the fence and counted down from twenty, psyching myself up for what was to come.

…nineteen.

…eighteen.

I peered between the slats again and nearly choked on my own spit. I blinked a few times, looked again. It had not been a mirage. Mrs. Amadou was kissing a tall black man—but it wasn't her husband.

What the hell had I stumbled into now?

My phone buzzed. With one eye still on the couple, I yanked the device from of my pocket. A text from Simon.

Amadou is still free!!!

They had found out. I was too late.

My eyes went straight to my forearm. Had Simon already sent the message to the vial to release the deadly drugs? After a few seconds, I realized I wasn't breathing.

My legs turned to rubber, and I dropped to the ground. Dug my nails into my forearm. Normal breathing turned into panting, oxygen flooding my brain. As I tried to think of a way to combat this invisible force, I recalled what Simon had told me about the electro-vial: if any attempt was made to extract the device from my body, then orders would automatically be sent to release the deadly concoction into my system, killing me within seconds.

There was no alternative path. Simon would end my life and think nothing of it. The fact that I had a daughter who was already forced to live her young life without her mother would have no bearing on Simon's decision to kill me.

My darling little Maddie. "I'm so, so sorry sweet girl."

I pushed out my breaths, some type of hissing sound, as regret consumed my body. I cursed myself for my curiosity about Amadou's connection to the illegal weapons deal. I cursed myself for taking the risk to free Bailey and Joshua. And I cursed myself for thinking I could test fate and rescue Casper even as morning dawned on a new day, hours after my deadline to abduct Amadou had passed. I had been naïve to think that doing the right thing would somehow protect me.

I could blame Simon for so many cruel and horrific things, but it was my bone-headed decisions that would cause my daughter to lose her last living parent before she'd even turned six years old.

"Dammit!" As I pounded my fist into the ground, another idea came to mind, though it had almost no chance at working. I needed to give Simon an excuse, a partial truth. I began to type the text:

I was in gunfight with 6 men. Amadou escaped but I'm in process of hunting him d—

A phone call came in, halting my typing. Because it was Simon.

"Hey, I was just about to send you a text. I wanted you to know that I was in a—"

"Stop. I don't want to hear it." The voice matched the same one in the only other direct verbal communication I'd ever had with him. A carbon copy of the phlegmy, mangled voice of Gollum, the wide-eyed creature from *The Hobbit*.

The man was calling to gloat, to hear me struggle with my last breaths. It'd be just like him. I was tired of the whole charade. "What do you want?" I asked.

"We don't have time to squabble over your excuses for failing to execute the plan."

"Do you know what I've had to deal with?"

"Shut up and listen. Amadaou's passport was just used to enter Cairo, Egypt."

That gave me pause. "Egypt. In Africa."

"You have thirty minutes to reach the airport. You will be sent instructions to board a private aircraft. You will fly to Cairo, find Amadou, and—"

"Kidnap Amadou. I know."

"No. Observe him. Learn his purpose for being there."

"Then what?"

"Provide updates as usual. You'll receive further instruction as appropriate."

A rush of adrenaline lifted me off my feet, and I scampered to my car. "Okay, I'm on my way."

"Know this, Jack. Just because your mission has been altered doesn't mean we have forgotten your failure. We will deal with that after you finish this leg of your journey with us."

The call ended. As I started my car and threw the gear into drive, I turned my head to the left. Amadou's wife was staring right at me. And then, as if she were flaunting her sexual power, she kissed the mystery man again.

34

Cairo, Egypt

The pilot said not a word through the entire flight, not even to buckle up or stow my tray. But he took me from point A to point B—Lyon to Cairo—in less time than I could finish my review the trove of data sent to me by Simon. Mainly because I didn't intend on finishing the dossier.

The information was nearly worthless, most of it nothing more than what you might find on American chamber of commerce websites. In fact, when I did my first cursory read-through, I questioned if Simon had sent the wrong files. Maybe they had another operative in the field, and this data dump was intended for him or her.

"Another operative." *Interesting*. It was a theory about Simon that had never before crossed my mind. I chewed on that as I waited in the customs line with my Zane Ellington passport. Was I being shadowed? Was I just one of many Simon operatives, as would be the case for a foreign intelligence agency? But Simon was not China, India, Italy, the US, nor any other government entity. Did they have ties to one of those countries? Possibly.

Given this bizarre, other-worldly experience, I knew there was nothing that power-hungry people wouldn't do to secure the edge needed to take down the competition and pad their own pockets. Nothing.

Since I couldn't do anything at the moment to either prove or disprove my theory of shadow agents, I considered my phone conversation with the Gollum impersonator. I appreciated the second chance I'd been granted by Simon, albeit done so for their own greedy purposes. I was a tool in their toolbox, one they could wield in any way they so chose. And even though they had previously said I needed to complete two more missions after this one, that could have been a ruse. The moment Amadou was in my custody, they could send the signal to the electro-vial and end me.

I'd scratched my forearm repeatedly during the first ten minutes of the flight. But then I told myself not to focus on how or when my life could end. Doing so served no purpose. I had to believe I would survive. End of story.

A blue light flashed above a nearby door. A man emerged a moment later, his face knotted with tension. Customs employees in each of the booths were receiving some new information or instructions. A few lifted their arms in exasperation. People all around me started pointing and talking in every language except English. I surmised they were having computer problems. The last thing I needed—a delay.

Beyond this expansive room, peopled rushed down an adjacent hallway. Was the entire customs office suffering technology woes?

Great. Just fantastic. I put a hand to my head, imagining how many hours I'd be delayed. Hours? It could be days. I reminded myself that while Cairo was one of the largest cities in the world, the country of Egypt was still considered a developing nation. It might be foolish to expect an IT department to jump in and solve the issue within minutes.

Just as people in line started to sit on the floor, the clerk in the booth waved his hand for the next person to approach him. He was joined by a second clerk. The customs officials running the other booths followed suit, and the lines started moving. In less than an hour, I was at the front of the line and could see that the computer systems were indeed not running. All documentation was being done via paper and pen. They asked me a few basic questions, which I answered with the right amount of sincerity and respect, and they stamped my passport and hurried me along.

Feeling invigorated by the unexpected quick process, I marched outside and was hit with an invisible force of heat that nearly knocked me off my feet. I sent the notification for a nearby Uber driver, found some shade, and waited on a white sedan.

It didn't take long for my presence to solicit dozens of shouts from cab drivers parked along the curb, most of whom seemed to be speaking in their native Arab or in French. I ignored them and waited for my Uber. One of the cab drivers got out of his car and approached me. I couldn't help but roll my eyes.

"I will not be offended by your rudeness, not if you bless me with your presence in my chariot." The bearded man, who was wearing a Yankees cap backward, took a slight bow and extended his arm toward his yellow cab.

"That's okay, thanks."

I saw the white sedan approaching, so I held up my hand while moving to the curb. But the driver never stopped, despite my waving and whistling. Worse, the annoying cabbie in the Yankees cap was standing a foot from me with a big smile on his face.

"Are you ready for your chariot now?" He strummed his fingers together.

My phone buzzed, and I checked the text. Simon had sent the

name of the hotel where Amadou was staying. "How long will it take to get to the Fairmont Nile City?"

"For most cab drivers, probably seventy-five to ninety minutes."

"I don't have that kind of time. I'll find—"

"But for me, twenty-nine minutes."

Jack Whitfield the small-business owner would have questioned the dramatic difference, but I didn't have time to solicit other estimates. "You're hired. Let's roll."

When he laid rubber, he peered into the rearview and grinned, his pearly whites on full display. Grateful for whatever he was willing to do to quicken the pace, I held up a thumb and nodded. He laughed.

"Would you like for me to save you a future embarrassment?"

"Sure," I said while taking in the endless sea of buildings.

"Thumbs-up in the Middle East is the same thing as shooting the bird in America."

I eyed him doubtfully in the rearview mirror.

He nodded. "And I won't even charge you extra for that knowledge."

"Thanks." I felt like an idiot for not knowing this important tidbit. And angry at Simon for not supplying me the intel to allow me to assimilate and not stand out in a foreign land. Shooting someone the bird would definitely get me noticed.

"So, do you plan to visit many of our great tourist sites?"

"Well, it's possible that—"

"Might I suggest the Great Pyramids of Giza just west of the city. Nestled nearby is the Great Sphinx, the limestone statue that is part man, part lion. For lively nightlife and outstanding cuisine, you can visit the Zamalek neighborhood on Gezira Island, which is just across from the Fairmont hotel in the middle of the Nile. The Khan El-Khalili bazaar is the place to go for spices and souvenirs, if you have someone special back home." When he turned to look at me, the car veered into the next lane of traffic.

"Look out!" My hand smacked the roof.

He pulled the car back into his own lane. "No worries. Now, I don't provide this idea to everyone. But if you're into something a little more adventurous—where you will see some of the poorest areas of the city—you can stroll in the daytime through a Cario neighborhood that used to house only corpses dating back to the seventh century. It is called the City of the Dead."

His large eyes filled the rearview.

"Just need to get to the hotel," I said, cutting off his marketing spiel.

As we approached an intersection at the airport exit, there was a throng of cars and trucks in the middle of the intersection, more piling up behind them. Men—not women—were outside their vehicles, many arguing.

"What's going on?" I asked.

"This is not unlike most intersections in Cairo." He looked to the left, then the right. "Driving in this ancient city is pure chaos, and it takes special skills to reach your destination without getting into a wreck."

He was trying to sell me on his tremendous driving acumen. And it was annoying as hell. I had to get him focused. Money talks. Leaning closer to the front, I said, "I'll tell you what. If you can—"

"Look out! Man has a gun. Get down!" He shoved me back against my seat.

An angry man was standing outside of his vehicle, waving his pistol around. I dropped to the floorboard. Horns blared and people yelled as smells of oil lingered in the stale air.

Defenseless—I'd not been able to travel with my Sig—and untrusting of anyone in this completely unknown land, I wondered if I'd be the next corpse added to the City of the Dead.

35

I heard a metal ping just after a gun fired. My driver went postal. He had the window rolled down and was shaking a fist at the person with the gun, who was now being subdued by three other men.

"Dude, we don't have time to deal with this crap. Can we get moving?"

He gave a thumbs-up signal—I knew what that meant—then he slammed the gear in reverse and hit the gas, weaving around traffic like a professional stuntman. He spun us around and gunned it for about a hundred yards before turning down a side road with less traffic.

"Impressive."

He shook his head and mumbled something in Arab, then, "To be honest, we have very few traffic lights in Cairo, but that one by the airport was out. I heard others shouting something about all the traffic lights not working. I need to call my cousin."

"Why?"

NEVER SAY DIE

He held up a finger, tapped an earbud, and began speaking in Arabic to someone on the other end of the line. The conversation was fast-paced and concluded about twenty seconds later.

"What did your cousin tell you?"

"Not good."

"What's not good?"

Stroking his beard with one hand, the other draped over the steering wheel, he didn't respond.

"Did you hear me?"

"Oh, sorry." He blew out an exasperated breath. "My cousin says the computer systems are down."

"At the airport too," I said. "Something was going on with the computers."

He nodded. "My cousin said most of the government infrastructure is paralyzed, at the city and federal level. Airports, ports, government offices, just about everything. The chaos on the streets—which is pretty normal—is now bleeding into many other places. But I will figure out a way to get you to the hotel. I always keep my promises, Mister, uh…"

"Just call me Zane."

"Very well."

"Your name is?"

"Uni."

"Uni," I repeated. "Cool name."

Reaching under the front seat, he pulled what looked like a homemade cigarette from a pouch and lit it up. After Uni had taken a couple of puffs, I realized it wasn't a cigarette.

"Is weed legal in Egypt?"

He blew a perfect smoke ring. "I'd be thrown in jail, the trial would be a sham, and I'd get at least a three-year sentence in a prison that isn't fit for dogs." He blew three more rings, each one successively larger.

"And yet you still smoke."

He glanced at me in the mirror. "I was born to smoke."

Skeptical of the hyperbole, I shook my head.

"No, seriously. The name Uni means smoke. Blame it on my parents."

Leaning forward, I waved the growing fog away from my face. "I can't go to prison, Uni. So, either lose it or I'm finding a new ride."

He took one more puff and tossed the joint out the window.

The minutes passed, and Uni must have made about twenty turns, some down narrow alleys.

I watched the people, those haggling for better deals at bazaars, men gathered in streetside cafés for what looked like lively debates, and the youngsters. Kids would approach our cab whenever we slowed or stopped, some of whom could barely reach the window. Dirt and sand coated their faces; their hands were calloused like those of a forty-year-old dock worker. I wondered how many lived on their own, with no parents and no roof. I emptied my pockets of the Egyptian pounds I'd picked up at the airport and tossed them out the window. The kids went after the money like flies to honey. As Uni sped away, for the first time since my family had been wrecked, I was thankful that Maddie was safe with her aunt in Dallas.

The hopeful phrase that Maddie had repeated—*Goonies never say die*—stuck in my mind. Part of me wished I could convey that same message to the kids of this land.

"Mr. Zane, you might want to look to the west."

While the back of the Fairmont was up on the left, my sights gravitated toward the mesmerizing sunset just behind a massive pyramid beyond the city. It almost didn't seem real.

"Magical," I said.

"Well, sir, I think you'll find this fantasy world to be quite magical."

The squeaking of brakes as Uni pulled to a stop. He stuffed his business card in my hand, and I walked inside the hotel to look for a real-life killer.

36

Fairmont at Nile City
Cairo, Egypt

The eye candy was everywhere, including women, which was remarkable considering I was standing in a Muslim country. But it was the soothing music and mild vanilla scent that caused me to take in a deep breath when I entered the lobby of the Fairmont Hotel.

While I was mildly anxious about checking in—the Simon data juggernaut had already let me down once—the process went smoothly.

"No luggage, sir?" the blue-suited clerk asked.

"Ever heard of Allen Iverson from the NBA?"

"Basketball," he said with a proud nod.

"He used to buy new clothes in every city he traveled to. That's how I roll as well."

He handed me a brochure with a list of every restaurant, bar, spa, and high-end shop in the hotel itself and the surrounding area. Perfect. Amadou seemed to appreciate, if not salivate over, all things luxury. This list would be a good starting point.

"Thank you. This is very helpful," I said to the clerk. But he didn't hear me. Another man in a blue suit was whispering in his ear.

"I do apologize, Mr. Ellington," he said once he was free.

"Everything okay?"

He smiled. "Now it is. The cyberattack on many of the country's government systems has ended. Everything is back to working smoothly."

A cyberattack...and apparently not of the ransomware variety, since a two-hour payoff window was unrealistic. With Amadou being responsible for Interpol's three key ransomware investigations, was it possible that the same culprit was behind this Egyptian cyberattack? I chided myself for not considering that while I had been standing in line at customs.

"Please let us know if we can do anything for you during your stay, Mr. Ellington."

I thanked the clerk and headed for the first-floor lounge for a drink and a think. Where should I focus my search for Amadou? I sat at the far end of the bar near a wall so I could see straight through to the lobby and front entrance.

The bartender flipped a napkin in front of me. "Your order, sir?"

"Long flight, so I need a large water and a Heineken."

He grimaced. "Beer. That is not our strong suit."

"You seriously don't have any beer?"

"A few local flavors only."

"Okay, what do you recommend?"

"I shall make you a drink you will not soon forget," he said. Big grin. *Wink, wink.* He served me a glass of water and walked off to create the eighth wonder of the world. Perusing the establishments listed in the brochure the clerk had given me, I wondered if I should have kept Uni on retainer—to get me where I needed to go, when I needed to go. For all I knew, his next fare had taken him back to the airport.

My eyes drifted to the spectacular view of the Nile River through the expansive windows. Uni had mentioned the Zamalek neighborhood on Gezira Island, and I could see it from my spot at the bar. Beyond that, a smattering of five-star hotels and office buildings with dramatic architecture. From this perspective, with the skyscrapers and water, it reminded me of Hong Kong. But this land was far different, starting with the socio-economic landscape.

Back to the list. I had two options: sit here until I spotted Amadou or be proactive and try to find him.

I dialed Uni's number just as the bartender dropped off a drink that had a small flame floating on the top.

"Something told me you would call me back," Uni said with no salutation.

"You're clairvoyant."

"What is that? I am curious about your American idioms."

"I am too, sometimes. I need to get to several restaurants and bars this evening. How quickly can you get here?"

"You want to go bar-hopping. Do you have a drinking partner, perhaps a lovely lady that you have met at the hotel?" he asked, adding a devious little chuckle.

"Just me. Are you close by?"

"Eh, I am actually about to make a pickup. Give me thirty minutes, tops."

Not the answer I wanted to hear, but this would give me time to do a quick run-through of all the hotel's bars and restaurants before Uni arrived. "Okay, I'll do a couple of things here at the hotel and then meet you…"

Amadou had just strolled through the front doors of the hotel. He glanced in my general direction, then walked toward the bank of elevators.

"Mr. Zane, are you still there?"

"Yeah, Uni, I gotta go." I ended the call and stood, my eyes still on Amadou.

"Sir, did I not meet your expectations with the Flame Thrower?" the bartender asked.

I picked up the tumbler and sipped the drink. It was velvety smooth, with brandy and then a little kick at the end. "Very creative. I like it."

He offered a head-bow. "Thank you, sir. It looks like you are in a rush."

"I am. Business matters. I look forward to trying out another one of your specialty drinks at another time."

"Yes sir. Thank you."

"Please charge this to my room and add a fifty-percent gratuity for yourself." I gave him the room number and waved goodbye.

His smile could have powered half of Cairo.

At a casual pace but with long strides, I hustled toward the elevators, arriving just as the door to Amadou's elevator had closed. Three other people were in there with Amadou. I stood back and watched to see which floors the car would stop at.

It first stopped on floor three. No bars or restaurants on that floor. It stopped again one floor later—again, only guest rooms.

"Are you going up?" A woman who wore a rather formal dress for this time of day—slinky with green sequins—held the door open in the elevator to the left.

"No, thank you."

She ran her eyes up and down my body. "What a shame." And then she disappeared behind the shutting doors.

What was that all about?

Amadou's elevator continued its ascent, finally stopping at floor twelve. Another stop at fourteen. It stayed on that floor for a few beats, then started to descend. The hotel's Bab El Nil

Restaurant was located on fourteen. I snagged the next available elevator and punched the button for fourteen. If Amadou wasn't in the restaurant, I was fairly confident his room was on either three, four, or twelve. I'd start to narrow it down by researching which rooms were most luxurious.

When I exited the elevator, I stood at one end of a long entrance hall into the restaurant, one wall pink, the other a funky purple. The floors were painted black and white in uneven horizontal stripes. Riding the tail of the steady stream of folks sauntering into the restaurant, I craned my neck looking for Amadou. Didn't see him. Yet.

Once I reached the maître d's lectern, in the shape of a small piano, he asked me for a reservation number.

"Right, so… I misplaced it."

He arched an eyebrow.

"Give me a second, I might have it in an email." His skeptical expression didn't relent. "Actually, I think it was a text?" His raised eyebrow seemed to drop a tad.

Thumbing through my text messages, I tried to think of a way to get past the gatekeeper.

"He's mine."

I looked up just as the woman in the slinky green dress caressed my face.

"Mine? I mean, y-yours?" I felt the heat rising in my cheeks.

She grabbed my wrist and led me into the restaurant.

"Thank you," I said, once we were clear of the others.

She smiled, her lips were like ripe plums. "Oh, you'll be paying me back later."

37

The woman in the green dress knew her way around Bab El Nil. The waitstaff smiled or nodded as we passed. The establishment was made up of four main dining and/or bar areas, each with a slightly different décor—background music, lighting, view, and menu—all of which could be labeled opulent or opulent light. Inside two of the large dining areas, there were three glass-enclosed rooms for the elite who didn't want to use the same oxygen as the rest of the patrons.

"You sit in here." The woman pulled me toward the glass room with purple chairs and sofas.

"I'm sorry, but I'd like go to the main bar." I started to walk away, but her grip around my wrist was solid. Amadou waltzed by with two other men and disappeared around the corner into the dining area next door.

"Not yet. Not until I'm done with you."

I chuckled, but her face was an odd combination of serious and sultry. Wanting no part of either, I twisted my arm to escape her grip and attempted to walk around her. But she quickly recovered, grabbing me with both hands and whirling me around. I landed in a fabric chair that was white, until a purple spotlight splashed across my space. I looked up to find six spotlights, all white or purple.

"I'm sorry, but I need to—"

A second later, fast-paced drum music came on just as two other women in similar green dresses joined the first one.

"I don't have time for—"

The woman who had rescued me at the lectern placed her hands on my shoulders and pushed me back into my seat, finishing with her face next to my ear. "My name is Zahra. It means *flower*. Maybe you will want to deflower me after our dance."

She stood up, pulled at part of her dress, and it ripped away from her body, revealing a tiny bikini. Her colleagues did the same, then the three of them started belly dancing. The music volume increased, and more spotlights splashed across the space. I was basically on center stage for their routine. All the men around me started clapping lightly, their tongues hanging out of their mouths. This was starting to remind me of my bachelor party, when I was young and somewhat naïve.

Now, I was neither.

Zahra and her two colleagues knew how to shake their goods. That was quite obvious when her gyrating hips bounced within inches of my face. The two other women had me boxed in on the other side. I thought about just pushing past them, but I got the sense that Zhara would create a scene, which would lead to me being kicked out of the restaurant or Amadou taking notice of me. Neither were good options.

The song dragged on for far too long. Must have been a dance-club version. Finally, a loud round of applause signaled the end of the belly-dance routine.

"I need a drink," I muttered to myself as I pushed up from the chair.

"Where is my American hunk going?" From behind me, Zhara draped her arms and breasts over my head and blew into my ear while massaging my chest.

"I'm good." I finally got to my feet and pushed my way to the main bar.

"Drink, sir?" The bartender was clearly holding back a grin.

"You know how to make a Flame Thrower?"

"Our specialty. Coming right up."

He handed me a basket of pita bread, and I took a bite while slowly rotating my gaze toward the dining room to the left. Mostly full, the room contained elevated bar tables in between clusters of gold and purple couches and stuffed chairs. Amadou sat in the far corner, near a window. Two other men were sitting with him, all with drinks in hand. By the hardened looks on their faces, it appeared to be a serious discussion.

I pulled out my phone and scrolled randomly so I'd look preoccupied. I then aimed my phone toward Amadou and took three quick pictures. Two were completely blurred. The third had cut off half of Amadou. But that didn't matter; it had picked up a decent picture of the two other men. I forwarded the picture to Simon with a text:

Located Amadou. Need intel on 2 other men

The bartender arrived with my drink. I pocketed my phone and took a healthy chug. I started coughing almost immediately—this wasn't the same smooth drink I'd imbibed downstairs.

Someone ran a hand along by back. I didn't even have to look to know who it was. The woman was relentless. Grabbing a napkin to squelch the cough, I prepared to give Zhara a strong warning to find another schmuck to harass. But when I turned around, it was Uni and his bushy beard.

"Caught you," he said with a flick of his eyebrows.

"Nothing to catch. And what are you doing here?"

His eyes darted around the area before landing back on me. "You called me, remember? Or has one of the lovely belly dancers erased that part of your memory?" He giggled like a little kid and strummed his fingertips together.

Apparently, the belly-dancer seduction operation was common knowledge. "Funny. You see me laughing, right?"

He smirked and reached over for a piece of pita bread.

The bartended approached with a scowl on his face and spoke in Arabic. It sounded as though he was admonishing Uni. I waved a hand so he could see me. "He's with me."

"He needs to buy a drink if he plans to stay."

Uni ordered a Sprite, and the bartender left us alone. "Thank you, Mr. Zane. Sometimes they see people like me—people who don't look like they have money—as not being worthy of even entering this hotel."

"That's ridiculous. How did you avoid getting stopped downstairs?"

His face lit up. "I have a cousin who works the front desk."

I gave him a skeptical eye. "Another cousin?"

He shrugged. "I have a large extended family."

Before I could inquire further about his large and connected family, Amadou and his two friends walked right past us toward the exit. "I need to get going," I said to Uni.

"You are following those men," he said as we started walking out at a casual pace.

"Maybe. But they can't know that."

"I know how to pretend to not notice. Comes with the job of being a cab driver." He took out his phone and acted like he was reading something of great interest. After running into an empty table, he put away his phone.

Uni and I paused near the restaurant entrance behind a throng of people waiting to be seated, allowing me to observe Amadou and his two associates, who were by the elevators. When they got into the middle car and the doors closed, I made a beeline for the elevators and punched the down button.

"Come on, come on," I said.

"Should we take the steps?" Uni asked.

The elevator dinged its arrival.

"No need."

After verifying that Amadou's elevator went all the way down to the first floor without stopping, Uni and I jumped in and started the descent.

"Who is this man to you?" Uni asked.

"It's just business."

He nodded, but I doubted that I'd mollified his curiosity. We passed the third floor, and my phone buzzed with a text. Simon had intel on the two men from the photo: they were high-ranking officials in the Egyptian Supreme Cybersecurity Council, or the ESCC for short.

"Hmm." While staring at my reflection in the mirrored walls of the elevator, I tried to logically fit together the data points. Egypt had apparently suffered a rather severe but short-lived cyberattack, one that shut down most of its government systems, impacting everything from traffic lights, customs operations, and according to Uni's cousin, even airports and ports. A few moments ago, I witnessed Amadou meeting with top cyber officials from the lead cybersecurity government agency. If Amadou's meeting had taken place a week or even a day after the cyberattack, then I wouldn't have questioned the timing. But now...

Another ding, and the elevator doors parted. When I rounded the corner from the small hall of elevators, Amadou was exiting the building.

"You park out front?" I was striding ahead of Uni toward the exit.

"Illegally, but yes. You want to follow that man in the Armani shoes?"

"Yes, and we can't lose him. Got it?" I turned and momentarily walked backward to make sure he "got it."

He pointed over my shoulder. "I found him."

"Huh?" I swung my head around, and Amadou was practically on top of me, pulling his hand out from inside his jacket.

I was next on his kill list.

38

In less time than it took me to blink, my instincts had created a counterattack plan. A good thing, since my regular brain was still processing how I'd bungled this tail before we'd even left the hotel.

Ducking low to gain leverage, I was about to swing my elbow upward to stun Amadou when he brought a cell phone—not a pistol—out of his jacket and to his ear. He spoke in rapid-fire French. I dropped all the way to the floor and re-tied my shoes. Amadou continued walking past me like I didn't exist.

"That was close, Mr. Zane," Uni said, helping me up.

"Too close."

"What now, boss?"

I glanced at Uni, wishing I didn't have a tagalong partner. But it was a necessary evil at this point. "I'm not your boss."

"Well, the meter is running in my cab."

This guy had balls. "You'll get paid." I focused again on Amadou, who was turning down the hall for the elevators. "I wonder if he's going back up to the restaurant."

"Heh. Maybe he wants his own personal lap dance with the beautiful woman in green."

"I didn't get a lap dance."

"So you say."

A gaggle of men wearing what looked like bowling shirts poured into the lobby.

"Excuse me." I gently pushed through the men, but by the time I made it to the elevators, Amadou was nowhere to be found.

"Got a guess on which of the three elevators he took?" I asked Uni when he caught up to me.

"Maybe number four." He pointed behind me to the end of the hallway where a door I'd not noticed before was cracked open.

I pushed it open to find a long, narrow hallway that went both left and right. No sign of Amadou in either direction. With wires and pipes at about ten feet high, the space had bare concrete floors and concrete blocks for walls.

"Oh! Should we ask my cousin if we can have access to the bowels of the hotel?" Uni retreated back a step.

"No time. Just follow me." For no reason in particular, I chose to go right. Picked up the pace, now jogging. The hallway ended with a left-hand turn. Voices up ahead. Followed the sounds to an open door that emptied into a kitchen with employees and an office area where two men were seated behind a bank of monitors. Security.

I kept moving. Two more turns, and Uni panting behind me.

Up ahead, an exit to the building. I bolted through the door and saw a black-and-white cab pulling out of the small alley.

"Is your man in the car?" Uni asked, breathless.

"I think so. We need to get to your cab. Let's hustle."

Uni led the way back through the maze. Past the elevators, through the lobby, out the front doors. "Over here." Uni waved me on. He jumped into the driver's seat, me in the front passenger's seat, and he punched the gas with my door still open. It ricocheted off my shin.

"Fuck!"

"Sorry."

Wincing with pain, I pointed to a black-and-white cab up ahead. "Is that Amadou's car?"

"Is that his name?"

"You didn't hear that."

"Whatever you say."

Our car accelerated so fast that people in front of the hotel scattered. I braced myself while Uni dodged one hotel employee, hopped a curb for about twenty feet, and headed straight for the black-and-white cab.

"Look out!"

My warning was too late. He rammed the back end of the cab. The customer sitting in the back whirled around in his seat. The driver got out and pumped his fist at us. Wrong cab.

"I am so sorry." Uni spoke as if they could hear him. He backed up, then gunned it.

I was now a part of a hit-and-run. Just add it to my growing list of bad deeds and felonies. "Where did he go?" I scanned the nighttime landscape, which was illuminated by bright lights from the hotel, streets, and neighboring businesses.

Uni acted like he didn't hear me while patting the dashboard. "I'm proud to say my car seems to have survived that minor accident, and we can proceed on your quest to find this Amadou person."

Couldn't he just forget the name? "But where's the black-and-white cab that took him? We've got to find that cab."

As if on cue, a black-and-white cab motored under the cone of a streetlight.

"There!"

"I am on it." Uni executed a U-turn and pressed the gas pedal to the floor.

We moved a hundred feet and another black-and-white cab passed right by us going in the opposite direction. "You see that?"

"I see that one, plus three more." He pointed out the window while slowing down. "This might be like finding a needle in a sewing kit."

"Haystack."

"My mother always referenced a sewing kit."

I leaned forward and squinted through the flash of lights, struggling to confirm which, if any, of the black-and-white cabs was the one that held Amadou.

"Which way, boss?" Uni threw his hands up as his car petered to a stop along the curb.

"Don't stop, Uni. Just catch up to the cab in front of us. That might be the one."

"Oh good. Glad you are confident."

I wasn't, but we couldn't just sit there and wish. "Go, go, go."

And he did. Moving south on Nile Corniche, our speed increased gradually, and he began to weave in and out traffic as though he were playing a video game. I still had my eye on the black-and-white cab in front of us, even as my peripheral vision picked up other cabs of the same color scheme.

"Quick question: what's the difference between the yellow cabs like yours and the black-and-white ones? Other than the color, of course."

A motorcycle cut in front of us. Uni jabbed the brakes, swung the wheel to the right, and unleashed a torrent of what sounded like Arabic curse words at the man on the bike. "To answer your question, yellow cabs are higher end."

Had Amadou taken a lower-end cab on purpose? Hell, I would have expected him to be chauffeured or driving a luxury rental car.

"I have almost caught up." Uni's shoulders scrunched higher as he hovered over the wheel.

"Just don't tag his bumper."

"Sure thing, boss."

The traffic opened up a bit on the straightaway, and the car's engine whined louder as Uni increased the speed. The Nile was to our right—gold, red, and white lights shimmering off a black slate that stretched as far as the eye could see. Hulking in the middle of the Nile for a few hundred yards was Gezira Island. It was fully developed and just as crowded as inner-city Cairo.

Uni yelled, "They are taking a U-turn," a second before slamming on the brakes. The car released a hideous squeal and then started to shake violently.

"Is your car going to fall apart?" My voice had a jackhammer quality to it.

"Hopefully not today."

The black-and-white cab shot forward, heading north, but the glare from all the car lights made it impossible to see if the Interpol official was inside or not.

"Dammit! Let's catch up. If this isn't the car, then—"

"We are shit out of luck."

Uni was catching on.

I wondered if the black-and-white cab was heading back to the Fairmont—we were moving in that direction. But a breath later, the car's brake lights came on as it took an exit ramp. When we followed suit, I picked up a quick view into the back seat.

"I'd bet money that we have our man," I said, shaking a finger straight ahead.

"We're coming to get you, Amadou!" Uni was white-knuckling the steering wheel.

"Forget the name, and you need to keep your distance."

"Too late. I am going to jail." He smacked his Yankees cap off the dash.

"What the hell is wrong with you?"

He pointed over his shoulder. I turned to see a police car with flashing red and blue lights closing in on us.

I barked out a few expletives. If we stopped, we'd surely lose Amadou. I didn't even want to think about what Simon would do to me.

"I am going to jail for a very long time." Uni tossed his cap to the floor.

"What for? Why would you say that?"

He mumbled something I couldn't understand.

"Uni, what's going on? We're only going to get a speeding ticket, right?"

"I have sinned. But these people…they have nothing better to do than harass us. Most of the world has finally opened their eyes and changed their ways. But no, not here in Egypt. We will build another pyramid before we legalize cannabis."

I briefly shut my eyes, shaking my head. "What are you saying?"

His eyes popped open, and he pointed to the roof.

"You have an idea?"

Reaching under his seat, he pulled out a worn paper bag and looked inside. "Not the right one." He leaned over and searched the area under his seat again.

"Cops are almost on top of us, Uni. What's your plan?"

He pulled out a second bag, looked inside, and smiled. He scooped out a what looked like small, black Chinese stars. "What do you have there? And what are you going to do with them?"

Without saying a word, he tossed a handful of the black widgets out the window. They exploded when they hit the pavement, and the police car swerved violently. It lost control and crashed into a telephone pole.

Yelping with excitement, Uni punched the gas.

39

I looked over my shoulder at least a dozen times. Didn't look like the cops had called for backup or anything. The coast was clear. *Unbelievable.*

We'd caught up to Amadou's cab and were now tailing him on the El Helal Exchange at a comfortable distance in moderate traffic—just enough to stay concealed. And I finally took a deep breath, my first since spotting Amadou at the Fairmont.

"How much weed do you have, Uni?"

A slight tilt of his head, but his determined eyes remained fixed on the road.

"Uni, I'm here with you in this car. You said you could go to jail for a long time. Which means I could go to jail for a long time. Actually, since I'm a foreigner, they might make an example out of me and throw away the key."

"I am sure they would have a backup key." He flashed his teeth and returned his gaze to the road.

I shook my head. "The weed, Uni. Give me the details."

He sat back and ran a hand across his face. "I am an entrepreneur," he said, struggling slightly with the multisyllable word.

"And so...?"

"I made a pickup just before your call to go back to the Fairmont." He stopped again, as if he'd just filled in all the holes. He hadn't, but he would.

"Uni..." I gave him the eye, the same one that Mama—my grandmother who'd raised me—would flash whenever she was about to scold me, which was often.

"Your death stare is working. Okay, I will give you a behind-the-scenes view into Just Chill, Incorporated."

"That's the name of your company?"

"You like?" he said with an eager smile.

"I only want to know how much weed is in this car."

"Just ten kilos on this trip."

I smacked the center console. "Ten kilos? That's over twenty pounds."

"Twenty-two pounds. See? Not very much."

I jabbed my fingers into my hair and pulled. This mission bullshit was a constant nightmare of epic proportions.

"I do not like to take chances," Uni continued. "I usually make fewer hauls with more product. It is not like I have a death wish."

At least he was trying to think in a shrewd manner.

"Where did you stash the damn weed?"

"I have a compartment next to the engine."

"If we pull off the road to remove it, then we'll lose the cab. But next time we stop, you need to dump it."

He winced and began to protest, but Amadou's cab made a hard right off the Exchange. Uni stopped complaining and took the same turn. We entered an area with very few lights and many homes nestled close together. They were no bigger than my garage back home, and in far worse shape.

"We have now entered the City of the Dead. Full of death, but also full of Ashwiyats."

"And those are?"

"You might call them shantytowns. Two-thirds of the Cairo people live in Ashwiyats. As strange as this might seem, we are a hopeful people. We look for opportunities to create a better life for ourselves and our families."

Just Chill was apparently Uni's opportunity for a better life. We followed Amadou's cab in silence. The conditions surrounding us were horrific. The buildings were dilapidated, some covered with graffiti. Kids picked through piles of garbage along the road—as did the dogs. The whole scene reminded me of videos taken after aerial bombings in war-torn countries like Syria and Lebanon.

But a larger question remained: for someone who maintained a hedonistic lifestyle, why was Pierre Amadou traveling into the Cairo slums—at night, no less?

The black-and-white cab continued rolling east through the City of the Dead until there was a sign for Mansheya Nasir. "Do rich people come out here to buy drugs?"

The whites of Uni's unblinking eyes glowed in the dark. "People are forced to use many avenues to pay for their basic needs—all the citizens of Egypt cannot utilize the Nile to make a living. Drugs are sold, yes. But if people know you have them in your home or are carrying them, then you will be the target of thieves. And they will use knives or guns. So, it is not wise, not in this environment. Also, some women sell their bodies."

"This is a Muslim country. Won't those women face harsh punishment if they're caught?"

Uni offered a reluctant nod.

I'd witnessed Amadou's wife making out with another man in Lyon. Amadou could be on his way to rendezvous with his own side love interest. Maybe he and his wife had some type of open-marriage arrangement. I'd heard of crazier things, especially since I'd been thrown into the mosh pit with Simon.

"They turned into a small parking lot next to that building." Uni pointed off to the left.

There were cars and chunks of concrete and rebar, but I couldn't delineate a formal parking lot. Uni followed in the same general direction and parked just beyond a pile of debris.

"Can you see anything?" I twisted in my seat but had lost sight of Amadou's cab.

Uni stuck his head out the window. "Oh."

"What is it? What do you see?"

He brought his head back inside. "I think I strained something in my neck."

"But what did you see?"

"The same man from the Fairmont walking away from that cab, down a narrow alley between those two buildings."

Without a word, I slipped out of the car and walked along the street toward the building complex. I got a few looks, but no one screamed. A small victory. Uni shuffled up next to me.

"I shall be your escort just to make sure you are not accosted. Or worse."

As much as I wanted to work solo, I couldn't argue his point. "What's our plan if someone tries to question me?"

"Play stupid and let me bullshit him in Arabic."

Sounded like the smart play. We circled the massive pile of debris—a rotten egg smell was pervasive—until we reached the black-and-white cab. The driver was slouched down in the seat with a hat over his face.

And Amadou was entering a door off the alley.

I followed him. Uni followed me. No words were spoken.

Bricks and pieces of concrete littered our pathway, which severely sloped downward. This slowed our progress somewhat, but I had a bead on that door.

Uni broke our silence. "You saw him?"

"You didn't?"

"I did not. I was paying attention to the men behind us carrying chains."

I whipped my head around but saw no one holding chains or preparing to pounce on us.

Uni shrugged. "I guess they did not follow us."

Unarmed, I was not adequately prepared for a violent confrontation. I had only my recent experiences and my legs. Not sure how far those would get me in a chain fight in the City of the Dead. "Sixth door down on the left," I said. "That's where he is."

"Whatever you say, boss."

I glanced at Uni, but his attention was focused on trying to avoid the debris and stay upright. Having successfully negotiated the slope, we turned down the adjoining alley, which bordered the backside of the apartment building.

Using my hand like a security gate, I stopped Uni in his tracks.

"You see something?" he asked.

I lowered myself and duck-walked to a small wall near a set of windows of the sixth apartment. There was a flash of movement in between cracked blinds. I raised my head above the brick wall and peered inside, Uni right next to me.

"I see Amadou," I whispered, shifting around a bit until I got a better view. A man in a traditional green thawb walked up to the window and looked outside. Uni and I both froze. Then the man turned and kept talking. Another Arab man, this one shorter and with a gray beard, stood in the background next to Amadou. I promptly pulled out my phone and took ten pictures, then fired off a quick text to Simon with the pictures saying I needed IDs ASAP.

"Now what?" Uni said.

While frustrated I didn't have a weapon on me, Simon's latest instruction was to observe, not kidnap Amadou. "We sit and watch."

Uni peered behind us for a quick second.

"You worried about our safety?" I asked.

He nodded. "The longer we stay, the more people might wonder about our purpose. They trust no one because they have no reason to trust people, especially outsiders."

"But what about you? They would trust you, right?"

"Usually. But I am with you," he said in a flat tone.

The identities of the men with Amadou would offer some insight as to his purpose in Cairo. Something told me it wasn't simply to speak with cybersecurity officials.

"Let's give it a few minutes." I stared at my phone, willing Simon to respond in quick order.

A young boy walked past. He glanced at us but kept most of his focus on working his yo-yo. What the hell was he doing roaming around such a dangerous neighborhood all alone in the middle of the night? Couldn't be more than twelve years old.

A blur passed by the window. "Is that a fourth person?" I asked and took another peek inside.

Uni was already on it. "Non-Arab. Western Europe or American. Wearing casual clothes. Seems a little out of place."

I looked at Uni. "You picked all that up in a second?"

"He stood out. I do not think he's with the two Arabs in the room."

I kept my eyes on the window, hoping the mystery person would show himself so I could snap another picture and send it off Simon.

Uni started sniffing. "Ah, I can feel the pangs of hunger coming on," he said.

I picked up a waft of something homemade. "What is it, you think?"

"Someone is in the process of making ful medames, which is basically mashed fava beans. They slow-cook all night in a metal jug. The meal is often served with tomatoes, radishes, and spring onions. My mother makes the best ful medames. Maybe I can have you over some time."

"Maybe." I heard a rumbling noise coming from…Uni? "Is your stomach growling?" Before he could respond, there was another flash of the unknown person by the window. The man paused, his back to us.

My phone buzzed. A message from Simon.

Person in green thawb runs Big Dig Gold Mining. Man with gray beard is likely a partner, but still running background check.

With Uni looking over my shoulder, I didn't need to share the message. There was really no reason to hide such basic information.

"A gold-mining outfit," I repeated while staring at the back of the unknown man in the window.

Amadou came into view, and he placed his hand on the mystery man's shoulder. The man took a drink from a cantina, but it spilled down his chin. He lurched, and his face became visible.

40

**Mansheya Nasir
Cairo, Egypt**

"Charlie Atwater." My old Tennessee track teammate. I'd last seen Charlie at the Campanella compound near Lyon, inspecting weapons. But what was he doing in this Egyptian shantytown?

Uni tugged on my shirt.

"What?"

"Why did you say that name? You know that gringo?"

"You're not Spanish."

"So you know him."

I nodded, thought about Amadou at the compound, standing in the midst of blinding headlights and murdering the young man who was screwing around with the rocket launcher. "Those weapons," I said aloud, my stomach already knotting up.

"Whose weapons?" Uni asked.

Uni had nailed the key question, even though he didn't know

any details. Where had those weapons been headed? Who was the seller? Who was the buyer? And what roles in this dangerous game did Amadou and Charlie play?

I shook my head and looked up at the sky.

"You are looking for inspiration, Mr. Zane?"

"Answers. I'm looking for answers."

"Charlie Atwater and weapons. Those are the two clues you have given me, Mr. Zane. Perhaps if you were to provide more information, I could offer you an educated response."

I ignored the comment. Picked up a handful of dusty rocks and bounced around a couple of thoughts. While I was curious, if not worried, about Charlie's presence in both Lyon and here in this rundown apartment in Cairo, it didn't seem like he'd been kidnapped or was being held at gunpoint. I had direct experience with coercion, though—thanks to Simon. Perhaps Charlie was also being blackmailed in some way. If so, was Simon the puppeteer? No, that would be too crazy. Too coincidental. It had to be another group or country. Or maybe my entire train of thought had no merit.

I wondered out loud, "If I could get five minutes alone with Charlie, would he help me out?"

Uni nodded. "If he is a trusted friend, he will help you."

My thumb ran across jagged edges of one of the rocks, and I let it drop to the ground. There was a time when Charlie had viewed me as a good friend, but that was so long ago.

I was willing to take a shot at it, but in a dangerous location at night without a weapon…

No. It would be far too risky.

"We need to follow Charlie whenever he leaves that apartment. That's our plan, Uni."

"I like that plan. Just remember the meter is still running."

I knew Uni's priorities, and now that I'd seen the harsh reality of Egypt beyond the flashy five-star hotels, I respected his desire to make money.

"Might want to relax some," I said. "Could be a while before this meeting breaks up."

Resting on one knee, I stayed in observation mode. Amadou was doing a lot of nodding as the two Arab men took turns speaking. Charlie stood nearby, drink in hand, with only spotty engagement.

Pierre Amadou and Charlie Atwater. The Cameroon-born head of Interpol's Cybercrime Intelligence Unit operating out of Lyon, France, and a country boy from the Smoky Mountains of Tennessee who just so happened to have great hops. Two men from opposite sides of the world with very different backgrounds were connected. But how?

"Business partners?" I said aloud.

Uni glanced my way with raised eyebrows but refrained from asking questions. He knew I had zero answers.

I tried to come up with a narrative that would explain why Pierre Amadou and Charlie Atwater had crossed paths. One prominent theory was difficult to dismiss: Charlie was some type of illegal weapons dealer. How he'd worked his way into that role was the million-dollar question. As much as I wanted to talk to him about Amadou, about everything, I doubted that was a realistic expectation. Even if they weren't best buddies outside of their business relationship, money could create rock-solid bonds.

But money could also create mistrust. That might be the angle I'd take with Charlie. If I got the chance to talk to him.

The boy with the yo-yo walked by us again, his eyes lingering on us more than the last time. I checked the apartment again. Could the two Arab men both be part of the gold-mining company? That was the assumption Simon had made.

"Gold mining and weapons," I muttered while fumbling with another small stone.

"Gold," Uni said with a nod and a flick of eyebrows.

"I thought gold was something more likely to be found in South Africa. Or is that diamonds? This is an area about which I have zero knowledge."

He raised his forefinger and smiled. "I have a cousin…"

"This is like a Conan O'Brien standup routine."

"Conan the Barbarian?"

"Forget it. So, you have a cousin…"

"Very worldly man. Works in the Egyptian consulate in Tripoli."

"Libya."

He nodded. "Mahmoud said there are three countries that mine the most gold: China, Australia, and South Africa. So, you were right."

"Lucky guess."

"Mahmoud also said there was some gold to be found in the Middle East. Here in Egypt, I believe he said, the gold-mining efforts are focused in the Eastern Desert."

We'd just identified a possible link: weapons for gold. But there were still dozens of holes in this story. From where had the weapons originated? Who would receive the weapons? And for what purpose would they be used?

"Look, Uni, I think we might have something, although it's still pretty foggy," I said, keeping my eyes on the window. "You don't know all the players. Hell, I only know one personally, and the other only from a distance. But once I talk to Charlie, I hope I can get the info I need to piece this puzzle together. By the way, you will be paid for every second of your time. It's only fair."

No response from Uni, and that was surprising, especially since it involved money. I glanced his way, but he was staring at something behind me.

"Is there a problem?"

He didn't respond, and I started to turn…

Metal object to the head.

I crumbled to the dirt and pawed at the pantleg of my attacker. My fingers fumbled with the material just as my mind slipped into oblivion.

41

Sounds of people yelling pierced through a dark haze, jarring me awake. Peeling my eyes open through a thunderous headache, I saw an old box TV with rabbit ears and a fuzzy picture of three, possibly four men dancing around and screaming something in Arabic.

I pressed my eyes shut and opened them again. I was in a room with a low ceiling and green paint flaking off the walls. My hands were tied around a beam at my back. I tugged at the knot. It didn't budge.

More screaming. That wasn't from the old-fashioned TV set.

I rotated my head. A door partially open. Shadows skipped across the floor, a heavily stained and scarred concrete.

"Uni," I muttered through parched lips. He had seen the attacker. And he had done nothing to stop the person or even warn me. "That sonofa…"

I clenched my jaw and pondered the idea of Uni being connected to this weapons/gold-mining scheme. I'd noticed a sparkle in his eye when he shared his knowledge about the business of gold mining. His cousin Mahmoud was most likely fictional. For that matter, his entire clan of cousins might be nothing more than make-believe.

Money. It had to all boil down to him receiving some type of payout to drag me along, learn about my operational goals, and then, at the right opportunity, signal the all-clear for one of their henchmen to knock me out.

A doorknob rattled, and a man in the adjoining room spoke in a quiet tone. Barely detecting a slight twang, I tried to place the voice.

"Charlie?"

The door swung open with a loud creak and in walked...not Charlie. It was one of the men who'd been meeting with Charlie and Amadou. The gray-bearded man sized me up, then waltzed over to a water cooler next to a folding metal chair. He poured water into a plastic cup and approached me.

"Water?" He held the cup inches from my mouth.

"Yes, please."

He dropped the cup and lifted a pistol. Pressed the barrel against the bottom of my chin. "Tell me who sent you." His eyes flickered like a light bulb about to pop.

"No one. I'm just a tourist."

"You are lying. I know it, and you know it. You will tell me who sent you."

"I'm being serious." The moment I uttered those words, I braced for the blow that came a second later. The gun popped off the bridge of my nose. Blood spurted everywhere. Even into my eyes, which freaked the shit out of me.

"Tell me who sent you!"

This guy wasn't going to stop until he got the answer he wanted. I couldn't tell him the truth—he'd laugh and pound me again. My only hope was to play the delay game, even if that meant spinning a tale that might eventually burn me for good.

"I lost all my money, and I heard you guys talking about gold. I'm pretty desperate, so I was wanting to figure out how to get in that game." I'd taken a gamble that this man also worked for the gold-mining company, Big Dig.

His eyes narrowed in the middle of wrinkled flesh as though he were debating the validity of my story. "Where... Where did you hear us talking about gold?"

"When I was walking by outside."

"Why were you in this neighborhood? This is not a neighborhood for tourists."

My chest suddenly felt like it had been wrapped in rebar. I'd chosen this path, and now I had to provide a convincing story. One chance to save myself from torture, possibly worse. "Look, I have some addiction issues."

"Addiction?" He shook his head.

"I can't go a day without coke. Cocaine. I try other shit, but nothing makes me feel like coke does, ya know? Not even alcohol. Yeah, so...I heard I could score some snow if I just came out here and strolled around.

He lowered the gun and walked over to the TV, gazed at the program, but his eyes didn't follow the movement on the screen. A minute passed, and he poured himself a cup of water and downed it, wiping his face on his sleeve. I was thankful he'd taken the time to think over my story. It showed he was rational, which could only help my cause. Avoid further abuse. Secure my freedom. Maybe.

One step at a time.

He ambled in my direction, his pistol pointing at the floor. "I have experience with people like you. People who think that because they got a college degree in the US, they are savvy in all the ways of the world. That they are automatically smarter than everyone else who walks this planet."

He cleared his throat and began to swing his pistol around. I watched the gun with enough intensity to put me in a trance.

"I have seen people lie about the dumbest things. I have also seen people lie about things that led to people being slaughtered," he continued. "I know when someone is lying. It is a skill I have acquired, a necessary one for me to stay alive, for our cause to move forward. And you, my American friend...you are lying. And they are not innocent lies. Like many others, you are a professional liar. And that means only one thing: you are a spy. And you—"

"No! Not true. You have it all wrong. I'm just a stupid addict who needs a fix. That's all I need. You gotta believe me."

He chuckled, and not in a friendly way. "You are a spy. You were sent here by the American CIA to learn more about our plans. Somehow, there was leak. I will find that person and behead them and not have a single bit of guilt. The only question—"

"Man, please, just look into my eyes. They're coated with blood, but you'll see that I'm an addict just looking for my next fix."

"So, if I had a pile of cocaine in the next room, you would snort it?" he asked while crossing his arms.

He was bluffing. He had to be. Well, I hoped he was. "If you had coke in the other room, I'd probably kill everyone in this building to get to it. That's how messed up I am. This isn't normal. I know I need help. I'm not proud of what I've become. A sad, scummy addict." My nose twitched as my eyes gleamed with moisture.

I'd just put on the performance of my life.

He nodded, turned his back to me, and strolled to the far side of the room. My eyes landed on the TV power cord that was plugged into the one outlet on the wall. I felt like I'd traveled back in time about sixty years.

The man flipped around, took in a deep breath, and stared at me. Then he lunged, slamming into my chest. Growling, he put the pistol against my forehead. "Your sentence is death."

"Tariq!"

I looked up.

Charlie Fucking Atwater.

42

My first response was relief—even with a gun pressed against my head. I'd known Charlie since I was eighteen. Even through all his addiction issues, I knew he'd ultimately do the right thing, make the right decision.

But this wasn't Charlie from college. I didn't know this Charlie, the one who cavorted with a murderer—Amadou. The one associated with illegal weapons deals.

Still, I went with positivity. "Hey, Charlie. Glad to see you, man." I searched his face for an acknowledgment of our past bond.

Charlie barely looked at me. Stuffing his hands in the front pockets of his designer khakis, he gave a subtle chin-nod to Tariq. "Not needed. I know this guy."

Tariq lowered the gun, and my shoulders relaxed. "Thanks," I said to Charlie. But Tariq wasn't done with me.

"This man is a spy." Tariq waved the gun in my face. "He lies like a professional. I know it in my bones. I have experience in these things, as you know."

Charlie shook his head but did not reply.

Not the kind of staunch defense I was hoping for.

"I want to interrogate him some more," Tariq said. "Make him tell me who sent him and what information he has passed along. Is he CIA? Or maybe he was sent by someone else who wants to obstruct our cause?"

The more Tariq spoke, the more I wondered about this cause of his. What was it, exactly? Something big enough that he was worried about the CIA or other intelligence agencies. I hoped he would inadvertently spill the beans, almost as much as I wanted to get the hell out of there.

"I understand you know this man," Tariq continued, "but I need a little time, that is all. And then we will know what obstacles we might face. Just give me ten more minutes with this man."

I looked to Charlie, hoping to catch his eye. Again, he would not meet my gaze, nor did he speak on my behalf. Tariq huffed out a sigh, rolled his shoulders. Charlie seemed to be studying the flakes of paint on the wall. Was he trying to come up with a response? Was he debating whether or not to let Tariq beat the truth out of me?

My heart thumped so hard it shook my entire body, and a new thought found its way to my frontal lobe: Tariq, who by virtue of calling out the CIA, had to be part of some military or terrorist group. According to Simon's message, he was probably a higher-up with the gold-mining company. Unless Big Dig was some type of front. Regardless, Tariq was seeking permission from Charlie—*that* was noteworthy. But my old college buddy didn't act like someone who held the power. Quite the opposite, in fact.

"Mr. Atwater," Tariq said with disgust in his voice. "We run the risk of this entire operation failing if we do not take this opportunity to uncover any unknown enemies. For all we know, a battalion of foreign mercenaries could be on their way to our headquarters right now to destroy us."

Charlie walked over to me, and Tariq moved out of the way. Charlie stared directly into my eyes for a good ten seconds. "He's not working for the CIA."

"But how do you that?" Tariq said. "We cannot afford to be wrong."

"I just know."

"But, sir, I cannot sit by and allow—"

"Colonel," a voice boomed from the adjoining room. "You wanted to share logistical details with me, correct?

The door opened, and there stood Pierre Amadou, arms crossed and feet shoulder-width apart. But it was his stone-cold expression that told me this guy was a force.

Tariq glared at me, then shoved past Charlie to follow Amadou into the room. Before the door closed, I spotted four computers sitting on a large meeting table, two flat-screen monitors hanging on the wall. The space looked like a modern-day war room.

Amadou slammed the door shut so hard I flinched. Charlie, though, stood there as if we'd just happened to run into each other at the office water cooler.

"You going to untie me?" I asked.

He scoffed. "Jack, Jack, Jack." Shaking his head, Charlie had now instantly switched his persona to that of a cocky salesman. "How did you get from Knoxville, Tennessee, all the way to BFE?" He tried to hold back a laugh, but it was a poor attempt.

This was the Charlie that I loathed. But I couldn't rail on him. *Maybe later*, I thought to myself—to keep my temper under control.

"Honestly, it's really just like I told your buddy, Tariq. I've had some issues in my life lately. I traveled to Egypt on business, but my deal fell through. More bad luck. Look, I've got some addiction issues. I've lost a lot of money, and... Well, anyway, I was told by someone at the hotel that I could score some coke out here."

He pinched his nose as if he'd smelled something foul. "For starters, it's hard for me to believe that the All-American guy, Jack Whitfield, has any flaws, and especially not addiction issues. You were perfect in college. Got the perfect girl, and then nearly made the Olympic team."

"*Nearly*. Nearly made the Olympic team."

"You pulled your hamstring in the javelin event, if memory serves me correctly."

"You see? All wasn't perfect."

"Right, right," he said as his voice and his eye contact faded. He stared at the wall for so long I thought he'd fallen into some type of catatonic state. A loud voice from the adjoining room snapped him back to life. "To be honest, Jack, I could have very easily let Tariq tear you apart. But I wanted to give you the chance to give me straight answers."

"Thanks. And now you know." I gestured toward my binds, signaling that he could untie me now.

"But I'm not sure I can believe you, Jack. Or should I call you *Zane*?"

How did he know?

Uni. *That rat bastard.* Uni the traitor. "Oh, that? It's no big deal, Charlie. Obviously, you've traveled a lot. People are always trying to scam you, steal your identity. I just like to stay ahead of the game."

"That's the Jack, or Zane, that I know. Always a step ahead. Never behind the eight ball. Which is why I'm curious about this supposed cocaine problem."

"Supposed problem? You don't think I know my own body?"

"To stay alive, I think you'd say or do anything."

I shook my head.

"What are you upset about?" he asked.

"You're basically threatening my life, Charlie. Do you not remember how I supported you back in college?"

He shrugged but looked away.

"Everyone else gossiped about you, but I refused. I could see how all the talk just added to the anxiety you felt. I hated that for you. I just wanted to see you get better."

"I, uh…" He rocked forward, eyes diverted.

I didn't fill the dead air with further commentary. I wanted him to feel my disappointment at how he was treating an old friend.

He sighed. "Okay, I have to admit you were good to me, Jack. Better than anyone. You understood me. You listened to me. So, thank you for that. It really did mean the world to me."

He strolled over to the TV and stared at the screen. I wondered what was going through his mind.

"Charlie, how did you end up here, with these dangerous men in this rundown neighborhood in Cairo?"

He lowered the volume on the TV, walked over to the water cooler. His back to me the whole time.

"Hey, man, just like in college, it's never too late to change course. I can help you, Charlie. Whatever is going on, I can help you."

He finally turned to face me, arched a quizzical eyebrow. "I thought you were just an addict looking to score a little blow."

I shrugged. "I want my freedom. But I can also see you're not comfortable with all this. Whatever *this* is."

He shrugged. "A little late for life changes at this point."

"What's your role here, Charlie? Do you work for someone else? Are you some kind of independent contractor? Tell me, man."

He pushed out a long breath and pinched the corners of his eyes, which were surrounded by dark circles and stress lines.

"Hey, forget my questions. Just untie me, and let's figure out a way for us to escape. You and me, like a couple of Tennessee Volunteers."

The door swung open, and Uni walked in. Someone from the

other room called out for Charlie.

"I'll be back," Charlie said, and left the room.

"What are you doing in here?" I said to the man I'd mistakenly trusted. "I don't want to see you or talk to you, asshole."

Uni came to a stop one foot in front of me, shaking his head, hands on his hips. I didn't know what he was trying to prove, but I was having none of it. "Let me be, Uni. Get the hell away from my face."

He smirked. "You are a liar, Zane."

I was seething with such intensity I couldn't speak. I just shook my head. He studied me, and it looked like he might vomit. If he stayed where he was, I might beat him to it.

"You, like all smug Americans, make me sick to my stomach. Do you hear me? Sick!" He jabbed his finger into my chest.

"Cut me loose, and let's see how long that finger remains attached to your hand."

"American policy has harmed my people for decades. To you, we are nothing more than pawns in your game. One in which we have no voice. And even after we go through difficult times, the American intelligence agencies still try to mettle in our affairs by sending over people like yourself. I have tried to understand the psyche of the American spy. Self-righteous and yet complacent," he said as he slowly circled the beam I was tied to. "I knew that the moment you got into my car."

"You begged me to get into your car. You don't remember that?"

"I coerced you. I manipulated you. Why? Because I knew right away you had no respect for the people of this country, for the religion of Islam."

"You're full of shit, Uni. I don't have anything against the people. I feel sorry for how they're forced to live in such horrible conditions. But as long as weasels like you are running around—"

He came around the pillar and swung his fist. Just before impact, he stopped himself. "I don't want your disgraceful American blood on my hands. But I cannot wait until the gentleman in the other room cuts off your head. I will personally mail it back to the CIA."

Uni held his piercing gaze for a few long seconds, then walked out the door.

I was alone. But his warning was still ringing in my ears.

43

Focusing on taking measured breaths to keep my nerves under the red line, I attempted to assess my surroundings for a way to escape. The assessment was brief. I was in a room with one door. And that door led to a room where Amadou, Tariq, Charlie, and others were assembled to...do what? Oversee some type of military operation?

Military operations need weapons. Weapons like rocket launchers.

My breath caught in the back of my throat. Was Tariq the leader of this military operation? What was the endgame?

A thunderclap practically shook me. But it wasn't the natural kind of thunderclap. It was the jarring clap of laughter from Pierre Amadou. As his laughter continued, he sounds less like a human—not a sane human, at least. There was this maniacal vibration that hung in the air like pollution cloaking a city, choking its residents.

Creepy stuff, but I had to stay focused on freeing myself. I ignored all the extraneous sounds, maniacal and otherwise, and conducted another survey of the room, this time searching for potential weapons. The folding chair could do some minor damage; same for the water cooler. But my best bet was the TV, specifically the antenna. I could snap off one of the rabbit ears, creating a sharp, sturdy instrument that could be used as a weapon. I would have to be close to my target. But if I was, I could neutralize anyone who got in my way.

I huffed out breath. I was in dreamland. I was still tied up, and even if I could escape, where would I go?

There were times when I hated the extra voice in my head.

My brain stopped working the problem when I realized everything had gone silent. No laughter, no yelling, no clamoring of any kind—inside or outside this building. Had they left me here alone? Considering the fact that Uni was foaming at the mouth for Tariq to decapitate me, I was okay with being left alone.

But was I actually alone?

Knowing I might have only minutes before my potential murderer walked through the door, I wrenched my wrists back and forth, trying to loosen the ropes. I pushed aside any thoughts about protecting my skin and directed every ounce of energy into my working my arms, shoulders, and hands. Sweat poured off my face, and my wrists burned like they were being held over a fire.

"Come on, come on," I grunted. The ropes were loosening. Progress, but it was slow.

Amadou's voice coming from the adjoining room again, and I stopped moving. He wasn't yelling. In fact, his tone was one of a leader speaking to his followers.

"We cannot have any mistakes, Colonel." And then his voice faded to where I couldn't hear his exact words. I got the sense he was circling the meeting table, hands clasped behind his back. I strained to hear more but was only able to pick up an occasional word. *Strategy... Goal... Rebellion...*

"A rebellion," I said to myself. Were they plotting a coup

against the Egyptian government? If that's where this was headed, Amadou's involvement seemed much bigger than that of a weapons supplier. Of course, I'd yet to confirm that he had masterminded any type of illegal weapons deal. But it was obvious that, for whatever reason, he was playing a significant role in this mystery operation—one that I was having a hard time trying to connect to his day job.

I wiggled my fingers to keep the blood flowing. In doing so, my hand bumped my phone, which was still in my back pocket. These bozos had forgotten to remove my phone.

I toyed with the idea of trying to adroitly pull the phone out and fire off an emergency-alert text to Simon. But just the thought of having to rely on those bastards to save my life turned my stomach.

I heard chairs scooting across the floor. The meeting was breaking up. Tariq would likely walk through the door at any moment. Would he be carrying a machete? I'd seen pictures of ISIS terrorists holding the decapitated head of one of their victims. Reflexively, I swallowed.

Amadou cleared his throat, and there was silence. I didn't hear anything, not even a murmur of a car driving by or a dog barking in the distance. Then he muttered a single sentence. Only one word, the last one, was loud enough for me to hear it.

Benghazi.

As in Libya? I racked my brain to figure out how Benghazi fit into the larger puzzle.

"In twenty hours," Amadou continued with authority, "we will destroy their world. And then we can claim what is rightfully ours."

Twenty hours.

A man cursed in English. It was Charlie, and he was very angry. "I will not stand by any longer and watch you murder hundreds if not thousands of innocent people. Not for all the money in the world. I won't participate in this…this slaughter. I don't care what country you're talking about."

As if in response to those words, gunshots sounded from outside the building. I was in the middle of a war zone.

44

People screamed, some close by, others at a distance, but the rapid-fire gunshots didn't let up. Unable to move my position laterally, my butt hit the floor in quick order.

I was an easy target in my current state. I tugged on the ropes again. Same result: stabbing pain from the lack of skin around my wrists and no noticeable progress on freeing myself. But I didn't stop. I thrashed my arms and wrists to the point of exhaustion.

My fingers brushed over a thin metal object on the floor. Twisting my head around, I did a double-take. My eyes weren't lying.

A razor blade.

A moment later, a bullet blazed through the door and hit the wall behind me. Six feet from the ground—the perfect height to pierce my skull if I'd been standing. No clue who was raiding the place, but I probably wouldn't be viewed as a friendly. In fact, I could count my Egyptian friends on less than one hand: two bartenders and Zhara the belly dancer.

I picked up the blade and put all my strength into sawing at the rope between my wrists. One, maybe two minutes passed, but the rope was still intact. I looked back and saw loose threads dangling to the side, the rope about halfway cut. I touched the blade with my forefinger—the sharpness was closer to a butter knife than an actual razor. Now I knew why the blade was on the floor.

"Goonie never say die," I said, pumping myself up.

I sawed at those ropes like a maniac.

Multiple doors slammed shut. Had someone just entered the building or exited?

I kept sawing, rocking up and down to add even more energy to each slice.

With a pool of sweat surrounding me, I looked back at my progress: a single strand remained. After three more saws, it finally broke. I quickly pulled the rope off my wrists, which were oozing blood. It didn't even faze me. Now it was all about escaping with my limbs intact. And that meant dodging anyone with a gun, especially the head hunter, Colonel Tariq.

The gunfire had dialed back to about one shot a minute.

I rushed to the door while keeping my head no higher than the doorknob. Peeking through the crack, I saw a room not only void of people, but also computers and monitors. Amadou and team had taken the laptops with them.

I needed a weapon, something I could use to protect myself. I poked around the room, but only a single extension cord remained. Not much of a weapon. Then I remembered the rabbit ears.

I raced over to the TV and grabbed one of the rabbit ears. Violently bent and twisted the piece of metal until it snapped in two. The edge was sharp enough to puncture skin. "If you get close enough." I shoved the miniature harpoon in my back pocket.

When I wheeled around, my eyes picked up a different color on the wall behind the beam. I hurried to the far side of the room. Particle board covered a space about two feet high and three feet wide, starting at ground level.

I tugged on the board, and it gave a couple of inches. Gripped it with both hands. Dropped to the floor, straddled the board, and pulled back until the board screeched away from the wall.

And there was a small, cracked window.

I kicked out the glass and peeked outside. A mound of debris and rank garbage to the left of me. Beyond that, a dog trotted between two buildings. Laundry hanging on wires stretched from one side to the other.

The window had to be a safer route than through the door. I scooted my feet and legs through the small opening. Jagged edges of glass scraped my legs, but I didn't hesitate, knowing I was exposed during this transition. Wiggling my torso, I squeezed through the window, huddled behind the massive pile of garbage. Panting like I'd run a marathon. Which way to go now?

I tried to get my bearings. The buildings around me looked familiar. Then again, most buildings in this area had the same basic composition: three or four stories high with concrete exteriors—scarred and painted a sad tan color; clothes hanging over wires; and debris piled up everywhere. Somehow, I needed to find my way back to the hotel.

I wondered if they'd actually make the effort to come find me. If so, Uni knew where I was staying. Just thinking his name made my blood boil.

No sign of people, so I darted out into the open. Jogged around the corner of the building, hoping to spot the main road. It wasn't visible. Just another building like the one that had been my prison for the last few hours. There were a few people on their balconies, some looking directly at me. I couldn't imagine they had been part of the gunfight. Most of the people in this City of the Dead were just trying to survive another day.

I was focused on surviving the next hour.

Amadou and his team. Had they escaped? Or were they lying

in some ditch with bullet holes in their foreheads? Simon would be asking for an update soon enough, but I couldn't focus on others right now. I had to protect myself, find a safe place to hide until daylight. I felt a surge of energy and picked up my pace.

A popping sound, and concrete from a building exploded just above my head.

I dove for cover behind some rubble piled just a couple of feet high. I lay flat on my chest and looked around for the shooter. Only empty balconies, a few with outdoor lights, many without. Behind me, forty feet to the end of the building and hopefully to safety. But someone could take me down in a snap—a sniper's wet dream.

I had two options. Wait out the shooter from this undesirable location or make a run for it, using a zigzag method.

Up to my knees. A final scan, and the countdown began... "Three, two—"

A boy appeared from around the rubble. I waved for him to get low, but he didn't seem to get it. He had a yo-yo in his hand—the yo-yo boy from earlier. I lunged for his arm to pull him down, but he jumped back.

"You've got to get down, or you'll be shot," I said in a pleading voice. I doubted he understood English, but certainly he could understand my tone and body language.

He shook his head, waved at me to follow him. Lacking other amenable options, I hustled alongside him. We approached an apartment door, and just before we entered the building, he turned to look at me. "Stay with me if you want to live."

And I did. I could only hope it wasn't a trap.

45

Stumbling over loose chunks of concrete, I fell forward, my shoulder slamming into a doorframe, the space in front of me pitch black. "Where did you go?" For all I knew, the kid could be standing behind a row of determined men with guns trained on me.

"I am here," he said. "Keep moving so you do not get shot."

Didn't need to be told twice. I held my arms out in front of me and sort of felt my way through the room. It was as though I'd been blindfolded. "Which way did you go? I can't see a thing."

"Must keep it dark. If person with rifle sees light, he will shoot."

The kid was a survivor. "How much—" My shin struck something immovable and sharp. A chunk of concrete maybe? "Errr," I said through gritted teeth.

"Be careful, but please hurry. They might be following us."

"Right." I worked my way around the impediment, shuffling forward in small steps. Another ten feet or so, and my eyes began to adjust to the darkness. I could see the kid, who was waving me onward. He seemed to have no issue traversing this minefield. "Are you leading me to a place to hide or what?"

"You just have to trust me. Hurry up."

"But where are—"

He turned left and vanished down a hallway. I tracked behind him, kicking rubbish along the way.

A light pierced the darkness. The kid was holding a lighter in front of his face. Three seconds, and the flame disappeared.

"There could be gas in this apartment, so we cannot take too many chances," he said.

Gas? "I'm good with taking no chances."

"Come on. Just a little more." He turned into a room. I caught up a few seconds later.

"Where did you go?"

He stuck his head out from around a side wall and lit the flame again. "Here I am."

"I see you, just put out the flame, will ya?" When I made it around the corner, he was trying to open a window, but it seemed to be stuck. "Let me try." I had to put my legs into it, but the window opened, revealing a path that led to a road.

Once we were both outside, he pointed straight ahead. "Go down that road about two kilometers. You will see a masjid on the right side. Go to the back door and knock five times. Quick knocks. Bashir will help you."

I shook my head in bewilderment. "What is all this? Who do you know?"

"Just go!" He shoved me in the direction he'd indicated.

"But what is a masjid?"

"A mosque. Just go. Please. You must be safe."

I had so many questions, but reaching a safe haven overrode my need for answers at the moment. "Thank you."

"Go!"

I started to walk backward. "But what about you?"

"I know how to stay safe."

"How?"

"I do not tell my secrets." With the nimbleness of a cat, the boy scampered back into the building.

I marched along the path with my eyes wide open. The boy had put his life on the line to help me. Why? What had compelled him to do that when it would have been easier, and far safer, to run away from the gunfire and protect himself? God only knew if the kid even had family to look after him.

I had to admire his moxie. Then again, he could be leading me to my death. Who would want me captured or killed?

"Who wouldn't, big guy?" I muttered as I cleared some exposed rebar.

46

Amadou had been talking about some type of military action planned for Benghazi, Libya, within twenty hours. For the first time, I finally grasped what he was involved in. But the most alarming comment had come from Charlie: *"I will not stand by any longer and watch you murder hundreds if not thousands of innocent people. Not for all the money in the world. I won't participate in this...this slaughter. I don't care what country you're talking about."*

How did Charlie get involved in this coup? Was he even still alive?

All the chaos had broken out just after he'd made his declaration that he wanted no part of Amadou's military strike. I had no idea if Charlie had the necessary skills to protect himself. Which led to my next thought: who the hell had started the gunfight?

That question bounced around in my mind as I reached the road, only a few streetlights sprinkled amongst the dark landscape.

Part of me wanted to take off in a sprint. Two kilometers was about 1.2 miles. Even at my advanced age of thirty-six, I'd been able to run a mile in just under six minutes. With my life on the line and my adrenaline pumping, I was confident I could cover the 1.2 miles in no more than seven minutes.

But this short trek wasn't just about speed. It was about not attracting attention to myself. I stayed closer to the buildings than the road, cautious, my senses on high alert.

I passed what looked like a car repair shop. Graffiti on the windows. Car parts scattered across the lot near a rusty truck. I considered pausing to search for better weapons than my broken antenna. Thought better of it. The priority was reaching safety.

A few minutes passed, and I turned to assess how far I'd come—a little more than a half mile. "It's all downhill from here, boys," I said, repeating the phrase my track coach used to yell at us over his bullhorn.

My foot kicked a piece of metal, and it clanged against a trash can. I paused a second, then did a three-sixty. All clear. I released a breath and started to turn around.

A figure exploded from the darkness. Two beady eyes, four active legs, and a menacing set of white teeth. Before I could bolt out of my stance, a powerful bark shook the air.

"Dammit!" I slipped on trash, used my hand to keep from falling, and ran like hell. Hardly any light. I was moving too quickly for the conditions, but what were the options?

To make matters worse, the surprise attack had screwed up my breathing. Panting like *I* was the dog, my lungs burned from overload. A quick glance over my shoulder. The four-legged beast was north of a hundred pounds, paws the size of my hands. I had nothing against dogs, but he was pissed. Probably had very little food. Forced to survive on the streets. A kill-or-be-killed mentality.

I lifted my knees with each step to ensure I cleared all the hazards, but the wild dog was barreling toward me at a speed I couldn't match in my fastest days when I wore orange and white for the Volunteers. My breathing became even more erratic. I frantically searched for a way to escape this beast before his jaw locked around my throat. Besides random trash, there was nothing in the vicinity other than discarded road-building materials: rebar, huge pipes, bags of sands. I longed to find a bag of trash with food in it. I could toss it in the dog's direction, allowing me to make it to the mosque unscathed.

He was almost on top of me—I could hear him, sense him right there. I hurdled a lead pipe, dove headfirst over a pallet of sandbags. On the way down, a blur caught my eye. I turned my head just in time to see the wild dog flying through the air and another four-legged creature leaping out of the pipe.

As the two beasts fought, I scampered down the street. The growling and high-pitched shrills ceased when I was about a hundred feet out. I turned to see the dog standing proudly under a beam of light as the other beast—what looked like some type of jackal or wolf—limped away into the darkness. The dog then started to paw at the trash. He'd saved me from serious injury. I just wished I could have rewarded with him a thick, juicy steak.

I walked on to the weed-filled lawn of the mosque. No lights on in the building. No indication there were people inside. Heeding the boy's instructions, I walked to the back, found the door, and knocked five times.

No one answered the door.

"Now what?" I released a loud sigh. But my frustration was quickly replaced with unease. Again, I questioned the motivation of the kid. Why would he help me, an obvious foreigner? Like many people living in these conditions, he had to have a jaded attitude toward the world, especially toward someone who would be seen as privileged. Or by some, an enemy to Islam.

I took a step back and studied the stucco building. All windows were dark. No one was walking the grounds. At the far corner was a small shed. I could hide in there for a few hours until daylight, then somehow catch a ride back to the hotel.

The air was heavy and still as I made my way toward the shed. Not a soul in sight, but I felt oddly conspicuous, as though eyes were on me. A truck engine roared from the abyss, and I turned to see headlights blinding me. Was that Tariq or some other enemy on patrol? I backpedaled toward the shed, hoping to find a shovel or some other tool to protect myself. Not that I recommended bringing a shovel to a gunfight, but I'd feel a whole lot better with something more than a broken antenna.

I whirled around, sprinted toward the shed. Waited for the rev of the engines indicating they were coming to run me down. Heard none.

I risked a glance over my shoulder. The truck had turned left in front of the mosque, motoring leisurely away from me. I released a breath. Without wasting another second, I hurried to the shed and pulled on the door. Locked. The entire plastic structure looked rickety, leaning to one side. At the corner of the shed, a small gap at the joint of the two pieces of plastic. Wedging the tips of my fingers into the small crevice, I tugged on one of the pieces. The whole shed shook, but it didn't pull apart.

Probably for the best. I moved to the main door and gave the locking mechanism a solid kick. And then another.

The door popped open, and I peered inside. Scant moonlight revealed numerous tools on the walls. Random equipment and spare parts on the floor, including a hedge trimmer. That might work as a defensive weapon. In the back, there was a large air compressor. A hiding place. I stepped inside.

Movement from behind me. A hand snaked around my neck and covered my mouth.

"Do not make a sound."

47

My defense instincts kicked into gear. I looked to the right. A pruner within reach. I could throw an elbow to the ribs, followed by a headbutt. Grab the pruner. Pray the man didn't have a gun, or a partner, or a partner with a gun.

"I am Bashir. You must be quiet," he whispered.

I tried to speak, but his hand remained, so I tapped his arm, and he finally pulled his hand away, but only a few inches. "I won't scream as long as you don't try to kill me," I said.

"Why would I do that?" He released me and took a step back.

I turned to face the man. "I've been through a few things in the last several hours. And I just hope that—"

Lifting a flat hand straight up as though he were going to recite an oath, he hushed me while leaning backward and looking outside. The whites of his eyes were like beacons in the darkness.

"See anyone?" I asked.

He didn't respond, so I waited a moment before inching out and looking for myself. I saw no one, but his unease had me concerned.

"Okay." He faced me. "We need to move quickly, but we have to make sure no one is following us."

"Move where?"

"You will find out when we get there."

I was starting to get annoyed with the lack of information-sharing. "Why should I trust you?"

He shrugged. "Do you want to get shot?"

"Of course not. But I need to know who you're working with, why the kid with the yo-yo helped me, and what this is all about."

He sighed and rubbed his eyes. "It is late, and I am tired. But if you want, I can stand here and give you all the details you wish—at least, all the details I know. You might be aware of what happened already, but there was an all-out battle about two kilometers down the road."

I tapped my chest and started to talk, but he talked over me.

"I cannot be certain who was involved. But I have seen a truck of armed men rolling through this section of the city. It appears they are looking for someone."

Was that someone...me? Who were the armed men affiliated with, anyway? If Amadou and team were still on the run, was their coup in Benghazi still a go? Too many life-or-death questions, and I had zero answers.

"Is your curiosity satisfied?" Bashir asked. "Or do I have to keep talking to you while gunmen roam our neighborhood?"

"Talk later. Is your hideout close by?"

"Follow me." He made a beeline toward the next lot.

He hadn't answered my question, similar to the kid. Maybe they were related. Still, I was thankful to be alive.

A small strip center up ahead. We walked around the back of it, a route that was more hazardous than my earlier hike. Shit everywhere.

At the end of the strip center, Bashir stopped and peeked

around the corner. Since I was taller by a good six inches, I peeked around the edge from above his position. Two headlights and the rumble of a loud engine.

"Need to be careful. We shall see if this is the truck with the gunmen," he said.

The headlights grew larger. The vehicle came into view at the cross street. Men standing in the truck bed. At least two were holding rifles.

Bashir mumbled something I'd heard Uni say—it had to be an Arabic expletive. I hoped that the similarities with Uni ended with a propensity for cursing.

"Where do you think they're going?"

That question was answered a moment later—the truck barreled into the front parking lot of the strip center. Bashir and I pulled back. "No way they saw us, right?"

He muttered more curse words. "Change of plans. Let us hope they do not have night-vision goggles." Bashir ran toward the metal fence behind the building and squeezed through a small opening. Before I could make it to the other side of the fence, a spotlight swept across me. Men started yelling from the side of the strip center.

More Bashir cursing, then, "Run!"

Sharp metal points scraped at my skin as I shoved myself through the opening and caught up to Bashir.

"This way," he said, veering left.

After a hundred feet, we crossed a small road and ran into a wooded park. "They'll find us in here," I said.

"We will not be staying." Bashir hurried up a small hill and stopped. I was about ten feet below him.

"What are you doing? They might see us from the road."

"I hope they do."

"Are you insane?"

He stayed put, waiting, watching.

"Dude, we can't stay here. Where is your hideout?"

"Get up here next to me."

"Why?"

"Just do it."

I jogged up next to him, then looked over my shoulder. There were three men racing across the road. "Is this some type of setup?"

"Yes. For the gunmen."

"Fuck that." I started to walk down the other side of the hill, but Bashir grabbed me by the wrist. I jerked out of his grip, seething with pain.

He said, "Ah, you are injured. Your wounds will be addressed."

"When?"

"Soon. Very soon." He glanced over his shoulder. "They might be able to see us now. Come up here with me."

Reluctantly, I did so. And ...

He shoved me.

What the hell is this? I shoved him back.

"Good, keep it up," he said, and I was starting to catch on. After three more rounds of shoving, one of the gunmen broke through a cluster of trees.

"Okay, now let's run." Bashir tore down the hill, me close on his heels. But we never made it to the bottom. Halfway down, he cut across the hill, pumping his arms and legs like pistons. I could see his strategy. We were circling back to the front side of the park by staying under the apex of the hilltop. We exited the park, ran across two streets, and slipped down a narrow alley before barreling through a door of a building.

"Resting?" I asked, huffing a bit.

"No. This is home." He flipped on a light. On the other side of a kitchen, there was a woman praying in an adjoining room.

"That is Mama. She will take care of your wounds."

I took another look at Bashir. Spotty facial hair, as if he were still going through puberty. Yet, despite his youth, he'd just risked his life to lead me to safety.

"How old are you?"

"Old enough to help the cause."

"What cause, Bashir? I'm really confused about everything that's happened in the last several hours."

"All in due time." He brought his hands together. Then his mother walked into the room—never looking me in the eye—opened a cabinet and pulled out a black bag. "Mama will tend to your wounds while I make us some food."

"But I have questions. And right now, you're the only one who can answer them."

As he pulled out a skillet, he looked back at me. "In due time."

48

Mama—my grandmother—had raised me not to curse. There was a tree in her back yard that produced plenty of switches to keep me in line. For the most part, it worked. And that verbal muscle memory was still mostly evident as an adult—though admittedly I'd been slipping quite a bit lately.

But Bashir's mother had just taken me to the edge of the cursing cliff, and it took every ounce of self-control to keep from unleashing a string of F-bombs.

"Most men, even the ones who believe they are brave and macho, do more than cringe when I clean out wounds like these. Most curse, and some even cry," Mama said as she dressed the wounds on my wrists. "Then they beg for me not to tell anyone."

"And do you?"

While she wore a traditional hijab, her face was visible, and a small grin began to take form. "I have friends, and we exchange stories."

"Here, try some of these." Bashir set a plate of something that smelled very appetizing on the table next to me. "They are called tamiya. Fava bean fritters. Quite tasty."

"My son, the master chef," Mama said.

I took a bite. "Outstanding. Is that your profession...chef?"

"Not yet. I hope to be admitted to culinary school in the fall. First, I must pass an entrance exam."

Mama fished for something in her black bag. "No, Bashir. First, you must study. Then you will not only pass the exam, you will have a grade that are you proud of, that gives you confidence. And after you pay your dues in five-star restaurants across the globe, you can open your own restaurant—as long as you cook Egyptian food."

Bashir smirked. "Yes, Mama."

He brought me what looked like tea. Not my first choice to quench my thirst, but I didn't want to be rude to someone who had put so much effort into helping me. "That's sweet," I said after my first sip.

"It is karkadeh, which is made by boiling dried red hibiscus flowers. I added an adequate amount of sugar."

"It's very good. You're talented, Bashir."

Smiling briefly, he went back to cleaning the kitchen. I finally had my wits about me to check my phone for texts from Simon. There was one. When I read the message, I sat straighter.

"Please don't move," Mama said.

"Sorry." With my pulse thumping the side of my neck, I replied with the requested update.

Amadou connected to possible coup in Libya and gold-mining company. He might be leader.

I drank more karkadeh tea and watched my phone for a reply. Bashir approached me. "Need to go on patrol. I should not be gone long."

"Patrol? Where? Why?"

He walked to the door.

"Bashir, you never told me what this all about, why you and that boy with the yo-yo are helping me."

He glanced over his shoulder. "All in due time." And then he left the apartment.

I leaned back, shaking my head.

"All done." Mama threw away the gauze pads she'd used to tend to my wounds, then began to repack her black bag.

"You know, don't you? You know what your son is involved in."

"I have an idea, but it is his life. I have raised him with certain values. I am here to support him and provide guidance." Her eyes remained on the task of packing up her bag.

"But you're his mother. You have a right to know."

She paused and lifted her eyes to me. "I recognize that you are not aware of our traditions. I am a woman in a man's world. I have accepted that. Bashir does not take advantage of the power he has over me. That is another reason why I love him."

I nodded, scratching my face, puzzled if not concerned that I still didn't have a clue about the purpose behind this network of people helping me. Yes, they had led me to safety. But were they purely innocent players? I'd read about the Middle East political landscape; I knew there were countless factions supporting a myriad of causes, for better or for worse.

A loud thud against the front door. Mama grabbed my upper arm. "Someone must have seen you come inside our home. Quick, you must hide. I have a place."

"Mama, I need help." It was Bashir calling out from the other side of the door.

"I'll get it for you," I walked over, opened the door. Slow and easy.

Bashir was holding up a wounded man covered in blood.

"Charlie!"

"You know this man?" Bashir asked.

"Get him inside," Mama ordered.

Charlie's legs gave out, and I jumped in to grab half of his body. Bashir and I carried him over to the table as Mama unpacked her medical bag and pulled out a stethoscope. Charlie's eyes were closed, and he groaned and wiggled around. Smacking his lips.

"Please keep him still," Mama said as she rested the stethoscope on his chest.

"Blood is everywhere," Bashir said. "Not sure where the wounds are."

"Charlie, can you hear me?" I moved closer to his face. His eyes remained closed, and he moaned even louder.

When Mama ripped open Charlie's shirt, I could see the bullet hole in his chest. "An exit wound," she said. "He was shot in the back at least once."

"Can you save him?"

Mama bit her lip. "We need to get him to the local hospital."

"But, Mama, you know it is not possible. They will refuse to provide treatment. And then they will make phone calls," Bashir said with a solemn shake of his head.

I wasn't ready to give up. "Is that the only wound?"

Mama had pulled out a pair of medical scissors and started to cut back more of the tattered shirt.

"Here, on his side," Bashir said.

Mama inspected the hole. "Looking at the angle I am worried this bullet might have entered the lungs."

"But you can take the bullet out, right?" My voice had a quiver to it.

"I do not have the facilities or the skill. We are not equipped to do that in my home. I am sorry. We will try to make him as comfortable as possible. And then we will pray."

Bashir grabbed a thermos and poured some water into a small cup.

"Here, let me." I brought the cup to Charlie's lips. After a few seconds, he opened his mouth and drank. "Can you hear me, Charlie?"

He swallowed but kept his eyes closed. "Jack."

"Yeah, I'm here, Charlie."

"I'm sorry. Sorry about…everything."

"It's okay, Charlie. I just wish you could…"

He seemed to try to chuckle, but it morphed into a cough, and blood trickled out of his mouth. Mama wiped it up, but she had a dire look on her face.

"Jack, you still there?" He pawed at my chest until I took hold of his hand.

"I'm here for you, Charlie."

He smiled through cracked lips. "Just like old times, Jack."

"We had some good times, didn't we, Charlie?"

"Jack, I got myself into some bad shit. My job at Firewall…" He paused, wincing. "My…job put me in front of some terrible people. But I took it to the next level. Got involved in an illegal arms deal with a bunch of nutjobs who want to overthrow the Libyan government. All because…"

He winced again, this time releasing an agonized moan. The coughing resumed. Mama shook her head while using a wet washcloth to wipe his face.

"All because—" He turned to one side, and his whole body cringed from the hacking cough that just wouldn't stop. It was so violent I thought it would break ribs.

"Take it easy, man," I said. "Take it easy."

"I'm trying to tell you—" Another bout of severe coughing. His face was contorted, a deep red shade.

"It's okay, Charlie. You just need to relax and save your energy."

He released his grip but then took hold of my bandaged wrist and squeezed. "Jack, I've got to tell you. No one else gives a damn, and I can't die without someone knowing."

"Knowing what?"

"Amadou. He's the ringleader, Jack. On both fronts."

Bashir and I locked eyes. Charlie had confirmed what I'd overheard while tied to that pole. I shifted my sights back to Charlie. "This military operation in Libya is one of those fronts, right?"

He nodded and his grip on my wrist became tighter. "Not just an operation. It's a civil war, a coup. I never signed up for that."

"Did you and Amadou supply the weapons?"

A tear escaped his eye. "It's the worst decision I've ever made. I did security consulting with Interpol, for Firewall. Amadou saw it as a way to funnel money and weapons into this rebel group, as long as I found the weapons dealer."

"But why? Why is Amadou leading this coup?"

"It's about the gold. It's an untapped resource in southern Libya. While the war is going on in the northern populated areas, Amadou plans to cash in on these gold expeditions without anyone giving a damn."

"Amadou is a sick, twisted guy," I said, instantly receiving a nod from Bashir. His mother focused on wiping up Charlie's blood. My mind shot back to the time at the villa when Charlie, Amadou, and the Campanella clan had been inspecting a truckload of weapons. Those weapons, and maybe others, must have been shipped to Egypt. Maybe during the cyberattack. "Who, Charlie, who supplied the weapons?"

His breathing increased five-fold, and I thought he was going to pass out. Then he rubbed his eyes with his free hand and said, "I hate myself for all this."

"Tell me what you know, Charlie."

A hiss escaped his throat, indicating the start of another coughing fit, but he was somehow able to hold it at bay. "There's a guy who runs a Neo-Nazi outfit in Germany. An American who has his hands in all sorts of wicked shit. He can get weapons of any kind. Name is Flynn. Emmett Flynn."

Stunned, I had no words.

I fed Charlie more water, the last bit trickling down his chin. The coughing started up. Damn, he was in so much pain. "Is there anything more we can do for him?" I asked Mama.

She shook her head and continued to gently dab his face with the damp washcloth.

"How did this happen, Charlie? Who did this to you?"

"Right after all hell broke out back there, I ran for cover. But Amadou caught me, said I couldn't be trusted, then pumped the lead in me. Lots of bad people in this, Jack. Greedy sonsabitches. Even in our government."

My mind was trying to process all the shocking details that Charlie had revealed when he suddenly opened his eyes and stared right at me.

"What? What else, Charlie?"

His eyes clamped shut again as he grimaced and roiled on the table. I held tight to his hand. It was all I could do for him, and that made me feel unbearably helpless. Was this the end for Charlie?

"Hey, man," I said. "Thanks for telling me everything." With his face in knots, I wasn't sure he'd heard me. "You're a good guy, Charlie."

His lips turned up at the corner for just a second before he took in a gulp of air. "There's someone else besides Amadou. This person has power. Real power. Might be the most devious person on the planet. And I can't die without telling you—" He erupted into a coughing fit, which morphed into screams of anguish. Perspiration soaked his entire body, mixed with blood as it drained down the crevices of his face. Mama was on her third washcloth, but it too was turning crimson.

"Charlie, who is this person?" I hated pressing him, but this was critical information. I had to know. He wanted me to know. "Charlie, can you hear me?"

He tried to speak, but all that came out were more coughs and groans.

"Charlie?"

He squeezed my wrist until his bloody knuckles turned white. And then, as suddenly as a clock striking midnight, he stopped coughing, and his hand went limp in my grip. "No, Charlie, no! Don't die, man. Please…"

Tears filled my eyes as my old friend took his final breath.

49

I paced the room, my gaze constantly gravitating to the sheet that covered Charlie. Under Muslim rules, Mama had insisted on washing the body and then covering it in a sheet.

"He is in heaven, Jack," Bashir said, placing a hand on my shoulder.

He handed me a glass of water, and I gulped it down, pushing past the painful lump in my throat. Mama had led a brief service to honor Charlie and prepare for his ascent to heaven. I learned from Mama that Muslims believed there were seven levels of heaven. I just hoped Charlie would enjoy the ride.

The hours had raced by. The coup planned by Amadou and team would happen in less than two hours—if they were still active. Bashir had patrolled the area several times, each instance returning home with a report that it was not safe for me to leave yet. I'd sent off a text to Simon asking what was next. They'd been strangely silent, although I doubted that meant this mission was over by any means.

Bashir left again on a new patrol, and I helped Mama clean the house. Anything to keep my mind occupied. "Your name is Jack," she said.

No sense in convincing her otherwise. "Yes." She handed me the broom, and I started to sweep up dust in the main room.

"Jack means one who is devoted and protective," she said.

My grandmother had told me a different meaning for my name, but now wasn't the time to argue the point. "Thank you."

"Your life is complicated, Jack. I do not expect you to tell me what you have experienced. But through your devotion and desire to protect those you care about, you will find fulfillment and happiness."

I could only hope she was right. "Thank you. Again."

"Shukran," she said with a friendly nod. "That means 'thank you.'"

"Shukran," I repeated. In many respects, I was a lucky man to have run into the young boy with the yo-yo, and then Bashir and his mother. They had renewed my faith in the kindness of people. While I was still somewhat curious if or how they were connected to some greater cause, I was mostly at ease—which, in and of itself, was a strange sensation for me in such a foreign land.

But the clock was ticking. A mere ninety minutes from now, a horrible plan to overthrow a government could be taking place. And I had no way to stop it.

My phone buzzed as Bashir arrived back home following his patrol. "Any sign of the bandits?" I asked.

He walked over to the refrigerator, pulled out the mug of karkadeh tea, and chugged until it was empty. After wiping his mouth, he turned to me and proclaimed, "All clear."

"So, I can leave?"

"Now that I have directions, yes."

"Directions?" I said as my phone buzzed a second time. I pulled it out to check the text message. It had taken hours, but

Simon had finally replied with a new order.

Amadou must be stopped at all costs. If necessary, you need to eliminate him. You have until dawn tomorrow.

Heat raced up my neck, and my ears burned. They were ordering me to assassinate Pierre Amadou. A killer. An arms dealer. The de facto leader of a coup. A man who wanted to use the rebellion as a diversion so that a gold-mining expedition could make him rich, stripping Libya of another natural resource. Pierre Amadou was also a husband and a father.

"A father. Just like me," I muttered.

"I am sorry?" Bashir said.

"Nothing."

"Did you hear my instructions, Jack? They are time sensitive."

I turned my palms to the ceiling and shrugged. "Sorry. Say it again?"

"Walk out this door and go left down the alley. When you reach the end, get into a parked yellow car. Hurry before your ride leaves."

I walked to the door, stopped, and looked over my shoulder. "You never told me who you're affiliated with."

"You will learn in due time."

"How's that?"

He shook his head. "Don't be late."

After opening the door, I turned back to Bashir and his mother. "Shukran."

Unlike the time when Bashir and I had scurried through the neighborhood under the cloak of darkness, it was now dusk and the alley was filled with people. Many carried baskets of food; some held their kids by the hand. I looked for the boy with the yo-yo. I didn't see him.

While I received a few glances, most people ignored me. I moved as nonchalantly as possible, weaving through the clusters of people. I reached the road at the end of the alley, but there was no car parked nearby.

"Oh, great." I slowly rotated to ensure I hadn't missed a yellow car.

A tap on my shoulder. Turning around, I instinctively lifted my arms and readied myself for a fight.

One that I might enjoy for a change.

"You're going to regret tapping me on the shoulder, Uni." I started to circle him, looking for an opening to land my first punch. He might be carrying a weapon or have a bomb tied to his body.

"Jack, you must—"

"Shut up and let me pat you down. Arms up."

"If you must." He lifted his arms straight to the sky, and I conducted my search.

"All clean. Now are you ready to fight, or will one of your military friends put a gun to my head?"

"Get in my car."

"You're crazy."

He shook his head and moved closer to me. I instantly jumped back.

"I am behind the produce van down the block," he said.

I leaned to my right and saw a yellow trunk. My heart sunk. "The yellow car. So, Bashir is a traitor just like you?"

"No, Jack. Quite the opposite. But you are starting to draw unwanted attention to yourself, to us. Please. The car."

Weighing my options for a second, I nodded and walked with Uni to his car. He slipped into the driver's seat, but I held back and studied my surroundings, alert for anyone who seemed sketchy.

"Are you getting in the car?" He leaned across the front seat to speak to me through the open window on the passenger's side.

"Just doing a quick check." After a few seconds, I got into the car and said, "Hands on the wheel."

He did so, and for the first time, I noticed he was wearing a sling on his arm.

"What happened to you?"

"Can I bring my arms down?"

"Not yet. You might have a weapon under your seat."

Someone honked their horn, and Uni's eyes shifted this way and that. Nervous. "Jack, we need to drive, okay?"

I huffed out a breath. "Okay. Just keep both hands on the wheel."

He pulled away from the curb and blended in with traffic. "You can trust me, Jack."

I laughed. Loudly.

"I understand your cynicism. I do. But I am the one who learned you are not Zane Ellington."

"Whatever. You learned that only because you're working with the kingpin."

"*Was*. And it was a ruse."

"Yeah, well...my old friend was part of that group, something he regretted till his dying breath. Amadou is killing people just to pad his pockets. And you gave me up to that man. So, no, I do not trust you."

A smile crossed Uni's face as he tapped the brakes and slowly pulled around a man on a donkey.

"What's so damn funny?" I asked.

"I appreciate your reference to history. We can always learn from our past. However, some choose to pretend the past never took place. They just ignore it."

While I didn't want to admit it, Uni's comment carried a great deal of wisdom. But I still wasn't buying this sales job to get me to trust him. They could have intercepted my communications with Simon and knew they had to take me out before I got to Amadou. They could have sent Uni to assassinate me, whatever.

"What's this game you're playing, Uni? And what role is Bashir playing, or that boy with the yo-yo?"

He glanced at me.

"I'm not stupid, Uni. I know you're all connected in some way. Maybe you're all part of some radical group. Got into bed with Amadou because you want some of the gold. Am I right? Or maybe it's the idea of overthrowing the Libyan government? You know, just kill a few thousand to support some fucked-up cause?"

He kept driving but didn't immediately respond. A soccer ball bounced into the street. He stopped to allow a child to grab it, then continued motoring ahead. "Sounds like you have additional data, Jack. That is good. We need to share notes. But first we need to come to a mutual agreement of trust. I think your country used to call this action 'détente.'"

"Not happening, Uni. You ready to drop me off? I have a coup to stop. And one other thing to do."

"Jack, I have something to share." He maneuvered around some children playing in the street.

"Do you ever give up? You refuse to answer my questions about what you and your two assistants are involved in. What bullshit are you going to give me now? And I don't want to hear you use the word *trust* again."

An officer was directing traffic in a busy intersection. As we passed, Uni waved in a respectful way.

"You're doing a good job of fooling everyone, Uni. Everyone except me."

"You must listen."

I checked the time on my phone. Just over an hour before the start of the coup. I had to stop it from happening. Somehow, some way. I also had to find Amadou. "Dude, unless you're going to take me to Amadou, I don't want to hear it. Just drop me off."

"One minute." He raised a forefinger before wincing and grabbing at his shoulder.

I rolled my eyes.

He continued. "Jack, how did you escape from captivity?"

"Well, I—"

He tapped my arm, and I stopped talking. "I will tell you. You used a razor blade that you found on the floor."

That caught me off guard for a few beats. Then I realized it didn't mean a thing. I did not trust this man. "So what? You saw the blade on the floor when you came in to mock me. Forgot about it while you had your nose up Tariq's ass."

He shook his head. "I dropped it there. I knew you would find it, cut the ropes, and escape once I commenced the second phase of my plan."

"Second phase?"

"The gunfire. I hired those men. Although I have some regret now about who I hired."

I shook my head and turned in the seat to face him. "You hired those thugs?"

"They were to fire warning shots only, to bring Amadou and his team out of the building. And it worked. But it went too far. I realize now that the thugs were just roaming the neighborhood, looking for a fight."

I raised my hand. "They chased after Bashir and me last night."

"Thankfully, you are okay."

"I'm only safe because of Bahir. And a large dog."

He arched an eyebrow. "While I suffered an injury in the process"—he gently patted his upper arm— "it appears you survived with minimal injury."

This was getting aggravating. Should I trust him? Punch him? Jump out of the vehicle? "Uni, are you for real? What faction are you, Bahir, and the boy with?"

"Jabari is the boy's name. Bashir and Jabari are simply helping the cause."

"What cause?" I shouted. "You're acting like this cause is to protect wildlife. If you want me to trust you, then start by being honest, dammit!"

"I'm going to share something with you that is highly

confidential." He paused and looked like he'd just had a bout of indigestion.

"Okay."

"I am not a cab driver. That is my cover. I work for the GIS. The General Intelligence Service."

"For what country?"

He smiled. "Egypt. And we cannot afford for Libya to return to chaos. Lives will be lost, and refugees will flood our borders. We can barely take care of ourselves."

I blew out a slow breath. "Why didn't you tell me this early on?"

"Why did you not tell me your real name? Or that the CIA was trying to stop Amadou?"

"I'm not with the CIA."

"Whatever you say, Jack," he said with a mocking wink.

Moving on... "So, are you going to call your buddies at the GIS to bring in some backup to find Amadou? I'm assuming he's not sitting in an Egyptian cell."

He blew out a slow breath. "This is where it gets a little sticky, as you might say."

"Sticky? How?"

He reached under his seat, and I jumped. "No need to worry, my friend." He pulled out a package of gum, popped one in his mouth. Chewed loudly. "Want a piece?"

And then he blew a bubble in my face.

50

On our second pass by Church of the Blessed Virgin Mary, a few of the construction workers had started to stow their tools.

"They are preparing to leave just in time for Amadou's team to work without interruption." Uni took a left at the corner and drove south, away from the church. He'd learned of the coup leaders' new war room location from Bashir, who had several contacts in the area.

I said nothing.

"Something is on your mind. Perhaps you are surprised that we have a Christian church. In fact, ten percent of our population is Christian."

"Actually, I'm still trying to process what you told me on our way here."

Uni had shared that there were certain factions within the Egyptian government—even a few high-ranking officials within the GIS—that supported the overthrow of the Libyan government. Which is why Uni was a lone wolf, unable to request assistance with his mission. In fact, he'd been told that if he were to create a "situation,"—yes, he'd used air quotes—then his leadership would disavow any association with him.

"I am sorry for putting you in this position, Jack."

"Not your fault." I studied his face—no signs that he was jerking me around. At least none that stood out. "We need a solid plan, and we've got less than thirty minutes until the military action starts in Benghazi."

Without saying a word, Uni took a sharp left down a narrow alley. A woman had to jump back into a doorway to avoid being hit. "Look out, dude. What are you doing?"

After narrowly avoiding a trash can, Uni slowed, then turned into an open garage.

"Is this where we're going to leave the car? By the way, I hope you have a weapon you can loan me." I squeezed my way out of the car in the tight space. A gray-bearded man walked through a door and stopped in front of the car. His sour expression told me he wasn't excited to see me.

"Uni?" I kept my eyes on the man. "What's going on here?"

"I would like to introduce you to my cousin." Uni walked over to the man, draping his arm around his shoulder. "Abash, this is my good friend, Jack."

I cringed, wishing he hadn't used my name. "An actual cousin."

Abash gave me a round wave and turned to Uni. "I know you have very little time. I think I have what you need just inside."

Ten minutes later, we walked back into the garage, each wearing work boots, cargo pants with plenty of pockets, a tool belt, and a hard hat. In addition to the construction-worker clothes, Abash had supplied us with weapons. Inside a pants pocket, we each carried a Beretta 92 semi-automatic pistol—standard issue for Egyptian military. I was also able to secure one of my new favorite toys, a flash-bang. Abash had called it "a brain explosion grenade."

While the weapons gave me at least some piece of mind, we didn't pretend that we could just go in and overpower them. No telling how many we'd be up against, which is why Uni had suggested a Trojan Horse approach.

"The toolbelt is going to feel a bit heavy as you walk up to the church," Abash said. He must have seen my sagging pants. "If you want, you can remove the hammer."

"That's my backup weapon."

He nodded his approval.

He then drove us to the rear of the church. Our plan was to blend in with the dozens of construction workers on site.

Uni noted the time before we exited the vehicle. "Only ten minutes until Amadou will give the signal to start the rebellion offensive in Benghazi."

Little time for diversions or negotiations.

We stood behind the church after Abash had driven off, the fiery sun low on the horizon, creating an orange-purple sky. I nudged Uni. "You don't think these guys will notice that we haven't been working here?"

"Many are day laborers. Just lower your hat as much as possible."

He was saying that my sandy hair would be a giveaway. I didn't argue the point, just adjusted my hat to better cover my head.

A front-loader blocked the back entrance to the church, so we had to modify our planned entry point. Only one other option: walk through the front door of the church.

Halfway through the back yard, which had more weeds and sand than grass, Uni spotted a pile of lumber. He picked up a two-by-six. After wiping dirt on my face, I did the same, slinging my post on top of my shoulder. I marched behind Uni, passing a handful of workers, but no one paid us any attention. A small victory.

"I think it's working, Uni. Brilliant plan," I said.

He mumbled a response, but I couldn't hear him since he was facing forward. As we came around to the front of the church, we saw scaffolding attached to the façade. Three workers were on the top, and two were descending to the ground. While we had traversed this dicey yard without incident, I was unable to predict what we might face inside. My pulse increased with every step up the stone staircase.

"Tawaqaf!"

The booming voice came from behind me. I twisted my torso, but the post I was carrying clanged off the scaffolding. A rookie mistake. Uni lowered his post to the ground and stepped in front of me, engaging the man in a hushed but firm tone. The man, possibly a foreman or other person in charge, puffed out his massive chest but had lowered his voice to match Uni's. A relief.

But the workers coming off the scaffolding were giving me an extended stare. I lowered my hard hat to the point where I could hardly see in front of me. Trying to appear unfazed by the confrontation, I readjusted my toolbelt, reset the post on my shoulder. I worried this foreman was going to kick us off the site, or at least delay our entry to the church.

Uni nodded, turned, and picked up his post.

"You convinced him we were part of the team?"

"No way that would work. I simply told him that my cousin Abash would pay him three hundred pounds if he kept quiet."

Twenty dollars, US. "Whatever works."

"Inside," Uni said with a motion of his head.

Through the front door, there were more workers and equipment. We set down our posts and walked past two workers who were finishing up some woodwork near the back of the main sanctuary.

"No sign of Amadou or Tariq," I said, my voice low.

"Probably in one of the main offices."

"Don't have much time to search every room."

"Give me twenty seconds." Uni had a brief conversation with the two laborers and started walking toward the side aisle.

"What did you tell them?"

"That we found a passport outside, and we were hoping to find someone from France inside the church."

"And they told you where you could find Amadou?"

"They described him."

"Is he in the office?"

"Actually, in a small wedding chapel."

I scratched my head under my had hat. "No kidding."

"One worker said there was a ton of computers and stuff in the chapel. At least six men."

"I'm ready for a gunfight if that's what it takes." I tapped the pocket that held my Beretta.

He shot me a side-eye. "There are a lot of stories of Westerners having shootouts."

"I could come up with a similar generalization for those in the Middle East."

He grunted.

"Best to judge everyone individually and not with a broad brush, and then see if you can trust them," I added.

"And do you?"

"Do I what?"

"Trust me."

"If I didn't, I sure as hell wouldn't let you run around with a Beretta in your pocket."

"Same." He flashed a quick smile.

With Uni leading the march toward the front of the sanctuary, I glanced over my shoulder a few times to ensure no one would surprise us. Up ahead, under three stunning stained-glass windows, massive brass pipes ran down a wall and connected to the organ.

To the left of the choir pit, Uni opened a door. "The chapel should be down the hallway, around the corner, then on the left."

We crept along the hallway, prepared to take action if anyone popped out of a closed door or from around the corner.

"You ever shot anyone before, Jack?" Uni asked.

"Yes."

"Part of your work for the agency?"

"I told you I don't work for them."

He glanced at me. "Must be a contractor, then. Maybe working for another country? France, maybe Germany?"

I shrugged. "Have you shot anyone?"

"Yes. Killed two people. Each time it happened, it was justified. But I could not sleep for a month. Had all sorts of nightmares. Screwed with my brain."

"And you're telling me this now for what reason?"

His turn to shrug. "For us to stay alive and stop this rebellion, I will gladly have nightmares for the next two months," he said with a wry smile.

When we came to the end of the hallway, Uni paused.

"You hear something?"

"Not sure. Let's keep going."

We rounded the corner, Uni pointed up ahead, and we proceeded forward. The corridor was long with closed doors on both sides. Eyes were on us—eyes of the deceased. Pictures of religious figures, including priests, lined the walls, and every expression was either contemptuous or just plain sad. Something that might provoke further thought at a later date.

If I survived this operation. If I could stop Amadou. If Simon allowed me to live after my transgression back in Lyon.

It was quiet. One might think too quiet. Holding my breath for a second to pick up any extra noise, a shadow flashed in front of me.

It was an ambush.

51

Ever since my family had been decimated, I'd acquired a much-needed new skill—multitasking. In fact, on more than one occasion, this ability had saved my life and many others.

The shadow...

Moving on nothing more than pure instinct, I wrenched my body so that I presented a smaller target. Dropped to my knees, leaned back, and looked up. Caught a reflection in the metal disc that circled the ceiling light fixture. A man six inches shorter than me, beefy, with thick, compact arms—in the middle of a downward swing with a long object.

The pipe was less than a foot from connecting with my shoulder when I realized I had on a hard hat. Counter to logical thinking, I flipped my shoulder away from the incoming pipe, which put my head directly into its path. I braced for the impact. When the pipe smacked the hard hat, I knew the hat had been cracked. Though it had protected my head, the impact was jarring.

Crumbling to the ground, a moan escaped my lips.

Roll, roll, roll!

The next swing of the pipe struck the carpeted floor two inches from my face. By the time I blinked once, Uni lunged over my body, led by his fist. I started to push up from the floor. Timing was way off—my shoulder clipped Uni's foot. His body dropped instantly.

Up to my knees, I got my first good look at the attacker. It had to be Tariq's twin, but with numerous gaps in his grill. I patted my thigh pocket where I'd stored my Beretta, but there was no time to pull out the pistol. The man was already batting for my head. Uni stirred beneath me. I picked up a flash of yellow bouncing around nearby. His hard hat. With my sights still on Tariq's twin, I snatched the hat out of the air and flicked it at the monster's face. The maneuver only bought me a second.

That was all I needed.

I rushed the man, connected my shoulder blade with his chin. He stumbled backward, fell on his ass, moaning. Uni scrambled to his right and clocked the man on the head with his Beretta, knocking him out instantly.

I quickly put a finger to my lips, and we both froze.

"Hear anything?"

He shook his head.

"That's very odd."

He then tapped his wrist—he wore no watch—to signal we didn't have time to debate strategy. I pulled out my pistol, unlocked the safety. Leaving our hard hats behind, we moved down the hallway another forty feet. Light flickered from beneath the door to my left.

The chapel.

Uni, inches from my face, said, "We might only have one option here, Jack. Shock and awe." He quirked an eyebrow.

"You stole that from us."

"But it works."

"Let's hope it does."

I removed the flash-bang from my pocket, and Uni locked eyes with me and nodded. I held up three fingers and counted us down. Pulled the pin and kicked in the door. It snapped back so fast, it hit a charging Uni in the face. I shoved him out the way, tossed the stun grenade inside, and jumped to the side of the door, landing on top of my partner.

Explosion. Bones rattling. A slight ringing in my ears. But not enough to cover the baritone moans coming from inside the room. A small window of time to gain control of the scene. Smoke poured into the hallway. Uni and I plowed through the haze. I went low, hitting the ground with my gun raised, while Uni stayed high, shouting in Arabic.

Two men on the floor, writhing in pain. I didn't recognize either of them. Another man wearing a headset stumbled over his colleagues. I recognized that one.

Tariq.

He kept his balance while reaching for something on a desk.

"Down on the floor. Now!" I screamed.

He didn't acknowledge me. Could he even hear me?

To my left, a man bull-rushed Uni. I ran to my partner's aid but tripped over a chair and skidded to the floor. One of the groaning men pawed at my ankle. I kicked it away, and Uni started to gain control over his assailant. As I pushed up from the floor, there was a sound that stopped me dead cold: the frightened whine of a child.

I flipped around, squinted through the haze. Too much smoke. I dove back to floor and scanned the room from that perspective. My eyes landed on the child—a boy.

"Is that…?"

I scrambled to my feet, but someone grabbed the bottom of my trousers. I torqued my body, trying to pull away, fighting to stay upright. But when my thrashing arm whapped against a chair, my pistol when flying.

More whimpering from the boy.

The boy with the yo-yo. Jabari.

I kicked at the man holding my trouser leg until he released me and glanced over my shoulder. Uni struck his assailant in the head with his gun. Apparently, his go-to move. I felt around the floor for my gun but was distracted when Jabari cried out again, much louder. I'd have to find the gun later. I started to go to him but, after just two steps, was stopped in my tracks.

"Do not come any closer!" It was Amadou. And he was holding the boy like a sack of potatoes, a gun to his head. "I will shoot him. I will do it. You need to leave. Now." For someone who had previously seemed so in control, Amadou had the nervous tic of a person hooked on a very powerful drug.

Greed.

"Just let the boy go," I said in a measured tone. Amadou's eyes flicked to Uni, who drew up next to me. Uni spoke to him in Arabic. Amadou shouted back at him while pressing the gun harder into the boy's head.

Uni set his pistol on the floor. "What are you doing?" I muttered, but quickly concluded that Amadou had threatened to kill the boy if Uni didn't follow the instructions.

Amadou shouted at his men to pull it together, focus on the plan. While two guys clawed at a table, trying to stand, Tariq was already seated in front of a computer. He acknowledged Amadou's orders with a nod and a grunt, then started banging away at the keyboard.

"Everyone, just do your damn job!" Without losing his grip on the boy, Amadou peeked over his shoulder and edged his way toward the corner of the room.

"What is he doing?" I whispered to Uni.

Uni yelled something in Arabic, but that only agitated Amadou even more. He waved his gun at us, spewed vitriol in our direction.

Kept moving toward the corner of the room. Where was he going?

Then I saw it. A section of the wall was a slightly darker shade of blue than the rest of the room. Just barely.

A concealed door. I'd been finding a lot of these lately.

"He's going to escape," I said, starting to inch closer.

Amadou jabbed the gun into the boy's chin, yelling, "Stop. Go another step, and you will force me to kill this boy. His blood will be on your hands."

Uni put his hands together and pleaded with the crazy man. "Careful, Amadou. We cannot let anything happen to Jabari."

Amadou's eyes danced like pinballs. I didn't think he'd even heard Uni.

Our eyes were locked on Amadou and the gun, even as Jabari cried for help. Normally, my heart would ache for the youngster. But I separated myself from any emotions—that was the only way to logically think through how to save Jabari's life. And stop the coup. And take down Amadou.

Amadou fired off more instructions as he neared the hidden door. One of the men got to his feet, but he didn't have a weapon. Tariq was solely focused on the computer. He was likely communicating to the rebels in Benghazi to start the offensive. We had to act now. There would be no second chance.

"Uni, stop Tariq." My eyes stayed on Amadou and Jabari, but I spoke quietly, unmoving. "You might have to fight through other men, but you can't let the coup begin. Can you do that?"

"Yes. You go after Amadou, save Jabari. I owe that young boy."

Amadou must have seen Uni and I talking. With one foot out the door—and Jabari still tucked under his arm—he promised all of his men more money. Then he ordered one of his goons to grab a pistol and told us to drop to our knees. We hesitated, and the room erupted in wild screams. The zoo had awakened.

As Amadou slipped out the hidden door with Jabari, the goon

with the gun started laughing and jumping around like a schoolkid whose teacher had just left the room. The others joined in, frolicking around like drunken sailors. But not Tariq. He was in another zone. His beady eyes were fixed on the monitor. Every few seconds, he would type something and click the mouse. The lingering smoke, his wild-ass colleagues, even Uni and I—we didn't exist.

Who knew how much time we had to stop a war? A few minutes? On top of that, I couldn't let Amadou escape. I needed some type of advantage or even a diversion.

I got the latter.

The goon circled Uni and me twice, yammering something to his brethren in Arabic. Uni, with a stoic face, stared straight ahead. Had he resigned himself to defeat, possibly death? Or was he just waiting for a chance?

And then he spoke, first in Arabic, then in English. "You are traitor to your people!" he said to the goon.

The large man started to chuckle, but after a few seconds, he realized his colleagues weren't laughing. So he stopped. Uni hit him again. "Your family will disown you. Your religion will disown you. You will live in disgrace the rest of your life. And you will deserve it."

The man charged at Uni. Arms outstretched, gun in one hand, body midair. But just before he reached his target, Uni bent straight forward. The goon's eyes lit up, but he couldn't stop himself. As he started to fly over Uni, I reached out and knocked the gun from his hand, catching it before it dropped to the ground.

"Here you go." I tossed the gun to Uni and launched myself at Tariq. His computer and his body went flying. I pulled myself off the floor and yelled at Uni, "You got this!"

I raced out the door to rescue Jabari.

52

All light had seemingly been sucked away. My first step whiffed on the invisible ground. Unable to brace myself, I face-planted. Spit sand and pebbles out of my mouth, pushed myself off the ground and...

Jabari's scream sliced the air. A moment later, an engine came to life. Front or back? Had to be back, right? I bolted out of my stance so fast my feet skidded in the dirt. Finally gained traction, and I shot forward, making quick progress—for all of seven steps. On my eighth, I ran into a stack of stones.

"Dammit!" I peeled myself off the stack. I'd have to slow down in order to navigate this obstacle course in the dark. With my arms acting as feelers and my body hunched close to the ground, I dodged lumber, piles of dirt, rebar, and trash cans before rounding the corner to the rear side of the church.

No car in sight.

He had to be in the front. Without another thought, I took off around the church, this time on the other side. A single light from a nearby strip center gave me just enough visibility to traverse the hazards with little impact on my speed. But even as I made quick progress, I worried Amadou would be long gone with Jabari.

I tripped over a pile of dirt, but I hardly lost any speed. Ripped through the curve that rolled into the front yard of the church...

No car. No sign of Amadou or Jabari on foot.

I was too late.

Hunched over with hands on knees, I huffed out breaths, wondered where Amadou could have gone. He'd basically ordered the start of a coup in Libya with the hopes of ultimately lining his pockets with gold. But that gave me no clues as to his next destination.

"Not Lyon," I said while lifting up.

A pair of brake lights flashed in the distance. And then a second time. The car lurched forward, jerked to a stop.

Amadou.

The second I took off running, the ground next to me exploded, rocked me off balance. Tariq was on the steps of the church, two hands gripping a pistol.

What the hell had happened with Uni?

I swung back around. The car jolted forward once more. Was it really Amadou?

Only one way to find out. I ran toward the car. A piece of plywood just in front of me shattered. Wood splinters sprayed my face. Unable to see, I stumbled to my knees. Once the debris cleared, I looked for the car—it was on the move. No way I could outrun a car. I prayed the engine would stutter again.

I darted away from my position and ran the zigzag pattern. I mixed up my cadence while making progress down the street. A bullet zipped by my ear and smacked a telephone pole. I kept moving. Thought I heard Tariq laughing from behind me.

Another pop. This bullet hit the ground, then ricocheted off the sole of my boot. I was the target at the gun range. Moving in random spurts certainly helped, but it only took one lucky shot to end my life, taking away Maddie's last living parent.

Adrenaline shot through my body. My quickness picked up, and so did my spirit. Red flashed before my eyes—the car had lurched to a stop.

With a final burst, I abandoned the zigzag strategy. Ran straight for the car. Hoping, praying that I could avoid a shot in the back.

At thirty feet away, I had eyes on Amadou. He frantically tried to turn the engine key, smacking the steering wheel with each failed attempt.

Faster. I had to run faster.

At twenty feet, movement in the passenger seat. Jabari.

At ten feet, the car still hadn't moved.

At five feet, I planted my left foot and launched my body toward the driver's-side window.

Amadou's stunned face looking in my direction.

The engine turned over, and he punched the gas. I missed the damn window and flew across the front hood. Just before I would have flipped off the far side, I reached for the lip of the hood by the windshield. My fingers grabbed hold. My body whipped violently against the side of the car, but I held my grip.

Pain ripped through my shoulder. I didn't let go. Couldn't let go, even as my feet bounced helplessly off the road.

Amadou took advantage of my precarious situation, jerked the car left and right while increasing his speed. The car had to be moving at least thirty miles per hour. My feet tried to keep up. Impossible. My grip started to loosen. Fingers going numb. My arm too. Couldn't hold on.

Another hard swerve to the left as the car stuttered just a bit. My leg swung underneath me and in front of the tire. Just as I pulled it back, the car lurched forward and ran over my foot.

"Ahhh!" I yelled.

A voice called out for me. Opened my eyes—Jabari. The wind rushing through his dark hair. He reached out the window, tried to help me. Not possible. Not unless...

The car choked again. In an instant, our speed dropped to a crawl. A miracle. My lungs heaved out a painful breath. I got my feet underneath me. But the relief lasted for only a second. Amadou pumped the gas, and the car launched forward. I jumped on the hood, grabbed hold of the edge with both hands. Separated by a one-inch piece of glass, Amadou was only two feet from my face, the faint orange glow of the dashboard revealing the eyes of a killer.

With the feeling returning to my shoulder, I felt strong enough to survive just about any of Amadou's breakneck driving techniques. But how I could force him to stop?

A secondary issue. The vehicle was picking up speed. With one hand on the steering wheel, Amadou lifted his gun, flicked off the safety, then reached his arm out the window.

My split-second thought was to let go—a death wish, if not a surefire way to be seriously injured. Then again, so was a bullet to the head.

I maintained my grip with one hand, released the other. Swatted at the gun.

He swerved.

My legs swung off the hood, the car's front tire spinning off my front foot. With no other choice, I brought my free hand back to grip the hood's metal lip. My legs found the hood once again, but the gun was now pointed at my head. Amadou's white-tooth smile lit up the car. I braced myself to be shot.

Jabari launched himself at Amadou, pulled on his hair, pounded his face, gouged his eyes. Amadou yelped as he lost control of the car. We spun once, twice. The car hit the curb, flipped—I went flying.

Jabari screamed.

53

A toxic smell invaded my nose, jarring me from unconsciousness. Burning rubber—I couldn't mistake that pungent odor. A buzzing sound filled the air. Pushing myself up to an elbow, I blinked once. And then again. The car had flipped onto its roof, a front tire spinning against a large stone, one of many scattered around the car.

I wiped my face, slick with sweat and blood. A copious amount of blood. Although my neck felt like it had been twisted into a pretzel, no bones seemed to be broken. Somehow, I'd survived. I replayed what had just gone down. A sputtering car, an untethered Amadou flashing his gun while driving, and the bravery of Jabari.

With one of the car lights nearly blinding me, I shoved boulders to the side and moved to my knees. Then to my feet, teetering for a second. I stumbled to the front of the car. Amadou was halfway out the window, groaning in pain, covered in blood. He'd probably live. Down on my knees, I peered past him.

My heart dropped.

No Jabari.

I heard a voice. Someone yelling. I spun around to see Uni emerging from the darkness, running in my direction.

"You survived. You made it, Jack!" He pulled up next to me, then bent over, gasping for air. He looked at me then past me to the vehicle. "Amadou," he growled while taking steps toward the injured Interpol official. "You deserve to die a hundred deaths!"

I grabbed Uni's arm. "Forget him. I can't find Jabari. The car flipped, and I guess he…" I didn't want to say it out loud.

Uni ran to the other side of the car and looked inside. "Where could he have gone?" Desperation, if not fear, had already gripped his voice. "How did this happen?"

"He attacked Amadou when he was about to shoot me. He's got to be around here somewhere," I said.

"That boy has been through so much," Uni choked out, "but he only wanted to help me, to help his country. Even at this young age, he always thought he had a higher purpose."

"Don't talk in the past tense. He's here. He's going to be—" I stopped the short the moment I spotted the object twenty feet from the car. Hurrying over, I picked it up just as Uni sidled up next to me.

"His yo-yo," Uni said, his jaw hanging open.

"Jabari!" I waited for a response, any sign of life.

Nothing.

We scoured the area around the yo-yo. "See him?" I yelled, even though I knew if Uni had seen Jabari, he would have called out.

Shifting closer to Uni, I sifted through a pile of garbage on the side of the road, hoping I'd see a leg or an arm. Preferably moving.

Again, nothing.

"Dammit!" I whirled around to face the spot where I'd found the yo-yo. Tried to calculate the trajectory of where the boy might have been tossed. But it was impossible. I had no experience in this type of forensic analysis.

I looked up. Uni was walking around a dumpster. "Any sign of him?"

He shook his head and started to looked inside the bin. Groans emerged above the whistle of the spinning tires against the stone. It was Amadou, pawing at the road. He started gabbing nonsense as dogs barked somewhere off in the distance. I could only hope that a wolf would tear Amadou's flesh until he took his final heartless breath.

A gasp, then, "Jack!"

I ran toward Uni's voice. "Where are you?"

"Here."

The dumpster. I cut right, then slipped on some trash, and crashed into the metal bin, creating a bass thud. "What is it? You've got Jabari?"

When Uni finally locked eyes with me, I saw pure dread. "He's…" Uni couldn't speak as he lifted the motionless boy out of the bin. With the harsh lighting from the headlight illuminating little Jabari, his body had a ghostly green hue. "He has no pulse, Jack. He's dead." Uni took in a jittery breath. "I must say a prayer for him."

Sobbing, Uni lowered to the ground with Jabari cradled in his arms.

I didn't want to believe it was true. After all that brave young man had done for me, and I couldn't save him. A new thought began to take root, and it grew inside of me. As it sprouted, so did my bitter resentment, a hatred for those who'd caused this.

A groan from the car. I walked in that direction as another man ran up to me. Abash took hold of my shoulders, and I explained what had happened. He hurried over to Uni. When I saw Amadou groaning, clawing at the road, I remembered the message from Simon.

Amadou must be stopped at all costs. If necessary, you need to

eliminate him. You have until dawn tomorrow.
And eliminate him I would.

54

On my fourth punch—or was it my fourteenth?—I realized there was more than just Amadou and me in my hyper-focused universe.

"Jack, Jack, Jack." Uni tapped my back, then took hold of my arm, jarring me from my trance.

I glanced at Uni, then pulled my arm back to throw another punch at Amadou, the man who'd needlessly killed a little boy. But Uni jumped in front of me.

"Leave me the hell alone, Uni. He killed Jabari. Don't you want to see him suffer?"

"Jack, Abash was—"

"I don't care if you agree with me or not. This is justice. My form of justice." Another flare of anger came to life, and I shoved Uni out of the way and hurled another punch at Amadou, who tried to cover his face. But Uni didn't give up easily, and he literally tackled me to the ground.

"Get off me, dammit! Why are you protecting this maggot?"

"Jack, you cannot kill him. If you do that, especially here in

Egypt, you will be sentenced to die."

My chest lifted at a rapid rate, maybe too fast for me to think clearly. But a single image punctured through my rage. It was Maddie, running and laughing with Spots in Aunt Zeta's yard. Damn, I missed my daughter. As much as Amadou needed to suffer for all he had done—and his sins were many—I couldn't allow my single-minded fury to blur my ultimate goal: reunite with Maddie and live our lives in peace.

Pushing out from under Uni, I got to my feet, reaching for my neck as a stabbing pain shot through it. "Sorry, Uni. I just lost it. That little boy, Jabari... I don't know. This world can be so cruel. Actually, it's the people. Some people are just pure evil."

Uni gripped my shoulder, which was on fire—some type of radiating pain from my neck—and I pulled back.

"Jack, you didn't let me finish," Uni said. "Jabari...he's alive."

I turned to face him. "What did you just say?"

He pointed to the dumpster where Abash was on his knees next to Jabari. The boy was sitting up, leaning against the bin. "What... How?" I asked while walking over to the bin.

Catching up to me, Uni said, "Abash used to be a paramedic. He knows CPR."

I dropped to my knees and put a hand on Abash's back. "You are a godsend."

He smiled, his gaze focused on Jabari.

I continued. "But my greatest thanks goes to you, Jabari. I've never seen a boy—"

"I am not a boy. I am a man." He flexed his biceps.

We chuckled, although Abash still appeared concerned. "Do not overexert yourself."

"Those muscles will grow, Jabari," I said. "And someday, you can do great things like these two men, Abash and Uni."

"Tell him, Uni." Jabari started to stand, but Abash convinced him to sit and rest. "Uni, you said I was your top man, right?"

Uni smirked. "Yes, I did say that. And I meant it." He turned to me. "Jabari's name means a man known for his bravery. He tells me this all the time."

"That is why it was meant to be…for me to save you from that bad man." Jabari pointed at the car wreckage.

The kid was a hero, no doubt. "You're very courageous, Jabari," I said. "But right now, I'd like for you to take care of yourself. Do you go to school?"

His eyes shifted to Uni, who said, "I have received approval for Jabari to attend one of our premier boarding schools. But he has pushed back. Says he does not like school. Hard-headed, this one."

"But I want to be one of you, a field agent fighting against bad people like Amadou."

Uni said he had to run back to grab his car, and I took the opportunity to encourage the boy. "Jabari, if you go to school, you could be Uni's boss someday."

His face lit up. "Wow. I could wear a real suit and drive a fancy car like a Rolls Royce." He lifted his chin and mimicked the sound of a car engine, pretending to drive. Cheesing it up. Kids were good at reminding us to find joy in the simple things in life.

But my life was anything but simple right now. I wondered what my third Simon mission would be. Maybe I would be allowed to fit in a short vacation with my daughter back in Dallas.

I heard a banging noise and turned my head, the glare of the wrecked car's headlights blurring my vision. Holding up a hand to block the light, I saw Amadou up on his elbows, kicking at something inside the car.

I went to take a closer look. Amadou was trying to free himself from the wreckage, kicking at the shattered dashboard that had him pinned. His eyes were mostly swollen shut, his face a bloody mess, but he continued talking gibberish.

Uni drove up, and I said, "Hey, I don't want Amadou walking

away from this wreck. Are you going to formally arrest him? I can't afford to let him escape."

Uni hopped out and slammed his car door shut. "I will arrest him. Absolutely."

Amadou's voice cracked as he shouted a word that got my attention. I moved over to the car, where he had collapsed again. Uni came up next to me. "Did he say something about Lyon?"

"I think so." But I'd also heard something else. Maybe. I nudged Amadou. "What are you saying?"

He mumbled, his eyes fluttering for a second before closing them. I looked at Uni, who shook his head. "Jack, he's clearly delirious."

I nudged Amadou again. "What are you trying to say?"

Smacking his lips, his eyes blinked open for a second. "Lyon…terrorist…attack."

I lowered my face to within inches of Amadou's "What? What kind of attack?"

"Lyon. My beautiful Lyon." He began to cough and weep at the same time.

"Jack, could he be telling us something?" Uni asked.

I shook Amadou's shoulder. "Pierre, tell us what you know about this attack."

Panting for a moment, Amadou scraped his fingers on the road. "I made a bad deal. And now Lyon will…"

"Will what?"

"People will die."

"Where, Pierre? And who did you make this bad deal with?"

His hand reached for my arm. "That crazy Nazi, Flynn."

And then he dropped back to the road.

"Uni, we need to alert authorities in France. Put them on a terrorism alert. I think I know who—"

"This is horrible news, Jack. But officials running our government will turn a blind eye. We are a dictatorship now. An autocracy. They will not lift a finger to help a Western democracy. Not officially."

"What about unofficially?"

He turned his head in many directions. "There are a few good people in my agency."

I felt a calling to help the friends I'd left back in France. But I also knew Simon would not use their resources to assist us—after all, they had their guy. "Uni, I need your help getting back to Lyon."

"Jack, I…" His sentence faded as he scratched his chin.

"What? Did you think of something?"

"I have a cousin who works in the Egyptian consulate in France. And they have access to a plane."

"Get me on it. Whatever it takes. Please."

55

The tires of the Learjet 75 Liberty bounced off the runway at Lyon-Saint Exupéry Airport. Crunching on an ice cube, I dialed Casper's number for the third time.

Five rings, and it rolled to voicemail.

As the aircraft taxied toward the hangar where I would deplane, the bright sun splashed through the windows and bounced off the chrome accents of the luxurious interior. The type of indulgence that Pierre Amadou would not just appreciate, but very likely kill for.

Earlier, when Uni and I had discussed Amadou's fate—whether he would face charges for organizing a coup to pad his own pockets—we could foresee lots of high-paid lawyers trying to muddy the waters of fact versus fiction, dragging out the court battle for months, if not years. The drive for prosecutors, and even the public, to push for a conviction might wane over time, which would be his lawyers' strategy. Ultimately, the odds of Amadou serving any real prison time were not good at all.

Which got me thinking about my mission directive from Simon.

Amadou must be stopped at all costs. If necessary, you need to eliminate him. You have until dawn tomorrow.

I didn't want to kill Amadou in plain sight. Thankfully, Uni had one last trick up his sleeve—rather, in a hidden compartment next to his engine. His weed business really did exist, a necessary side gig since his government paycheck was lacking. Uni handcuffed Amadou's wrists to the steering wheel and planted the preponderance of his weed stash in Amadou's car.

"Amadou will not be able to squirm out of this," Uni had said with a smirk on his face. "Authorities will take a hardline stance. And he will rot in a very harsh jail."

I disembarked the aircraft. I'd been given priority status through customs, thanks to a phone call from another well-placed Uni "cousin." I hustled outside to find a ride. The curb was filled with business people, men and women jockeying for cabs in a plethora of languages. Arguments began to break out over who had dibs on a particular taxi.

I walked past the knot of onlookers and tried to find my own ride. As the air filled with vehicle exhaust, the foul smell sent my mind back to the "bad deal" Amadou had struck with Emmett Flynn, leader of a Neo-Nazi group. The heartless man who'd coerced Bailey during a vulnerable time in her life, who'd forced her and Joshua to live as captives in a gangster's home. While Amadou had not shared specific details of his agreement with Flynn, it wasn't difficult to understand at least part of the transaction: Flynn had provided Amadou's team with the illegal weapons. In some of Charlie Atwater's final words, he had stated illegal weapons were, essentially, standard business for Flynn.

But what had Amadou given Flynn in return? That was what I'd yet to uncover. And may never get the chance. I still didn't know the key facts about the terror event: when and where it would take place in Lyon. But the first priority was to find my friends and ensure they were tucked away in a safe location outside the city.

A cab driver finally took pity on me, and I gave him the address to Miss Patty's apartment building. I dialed Casper's phone one more time. And one more time, it rolled to voicemail. I tried Miss Patty's number. It too went to voicemail. That was the extent of my contacts. I had no number for Bailey or the owners of the safe house, Paul Newman and Joanne Woodward. Could the entire crew still be holed up in the basement there?

The red-tile roofs of downtown Lyon came into view, and I released a full breath. The Campanella crime family was in many ways the muscle for Flynn. They had held Bailey and Joshua captive. And during the supposed swap at the Basilica, they'd tried to abduct all of us. With force. And probably would have killed both Casper and me.

But were they terrorists?

"Doesn't make a lot of sense." I sharpened that thought. The idea of a crime family pulling off an act of terror made very little *business* sense. The Campanellas made money in many ways, but it started with the basic concept of consumers buying a product. If the Campanellas intentionally made Lyon a ghost town, then there would be no spending from which they could line their pockets.

The cab's brakes squealed as it pulled to a stop and I walked inside the building, straight to my apartment. It was empty and cleaned out. Miss Patty must have presumed I wasn't coming back.

"Where did everybody go?" I asked the walls.

Maybe my friends were on the run, aware of the pending act of terror by Flynn and his gang? There was no way for me to know for sure. Yet. Hopefully, everyone was still at the Newman-Woodward complex. I made my way to Miss Patty's place. The door was slightly ajar. I rested a hand on the wooden façade, pausing for a moment and then knocking three times. "Miss Patty, are you home?"

No response. My pulse ticked faster, and my ears became warm.

"Miss Patty, are you doing okay?" I carefully pushed the door open.

I spotted her foot, which was pointed toward the ceiling, behind the kitchen counter. She certainly wasn't standing. I rushed to her side; her arms were draped over her head. Relief surged through me when she shifted slightly.

Alive.

"Miss Patty, can you hear me?"

"Is that you, Jack?" She pulled her arms down and blinked rapidly.

"What happened? Did you have a fall?"

A pause, as if she were trying to put the pieces together…then she grabbed my hand. "They took them, Jack. All of them."

"Who?"

"Bailey, her beautiful son, Casper, and the two from Alabama."

Karma and Evan.

"I tried fighting them off, but the leader hit me with a gun. I'm so sorry." She rubbed her head and began to weep.

I helped her sit up and poured her a cup of water. She took a large gulp and released a jittery breath.

"Miss Patty, can you describe the people who took them?"

"There were three men. All had guns." She briefly closed her eyes and shook her head. "We'd just gotten back from the safe house. I'd heard through my contacts that the Campanellas had left the city. They were feeling a lot of heat after the attempted kidnapping at the Basilica."

"Right, but what did these men look like?"

"Oh, Jack. They were all skinheads. Nazi skinheads."

My greatest fear. If Flynn was planning an act of terrorism, though, why had he wasted time in kidnapping them? What role would they play in his scheme?

Miss Patty moaned as she rubbed her head, and I poured more water for her. "You need medical attention."

"I'm fine, Jack. Just need to rest."

I looked her in the eye. "Did the kidnappers say anything about where they were taking our friends or any plans they might have?"

Heavy footfalls shook the floor.

A man jumped me from behind.

56

The initial force delivered by the attacker knocked me off my knees, but it was his sheer weight that had me pinned down. Thrashing my arms and legs, I tried to squirm out from under him before he could stab, shoot, strangle, or pummel me.

Grabbing the handle of the fridge, I started pulling myself out from under the man. A quick glance over my shoulder. He was about twice my size with thinning gray hair—yelling and flailing like a wild man. Miss Patty's voice cut through the hysteria.

"Fritz, Fritz…" She spoke in another language.

"That's not French." I freed myself and jumped to my feet.

"It's Fritz, my male friend. He's German and doesn't speak very good French or English."

The man finally got to his knees. He had a deep cut just above his eye. "Did you do that when you crashed into me?"

He touched his forehead, moved closer to Miss Patty, and spoke in German.

"Oh," she said after a moment. "Jack, he thought you were one of the skinheads coming back to kill me. Fritz, you tried to save my life, you big old lug." She took him in her arms and hugged him as I scratched my head—had the old guy not seen my hair? Maybe he was too scared to notice.

After a moment, he pulled back and turned to me. "I am sorry," he said with a nod. "Skinheads did this to me." He pointed at his cut.

"When? Where?"

He spoke to Patty, who gave me the answer in English. "Just a few minutes ago, in the alley on the west side."

The alley, where I'd first been attacked by the Campanella crew. Fritz and Miss Patty began speaking in German. He seemed quite alarmed about the bruise on her head, and she had similar concerns about his cut.

I wanted to let them be, but I had more questions. "Miss Patty, Fritz, in your time around the skinheads, did you overhear anything about where they were going?"

Miss Patty shook her head and shrugged at the same time.

"What about Fritz? Did he hear anything?"

"Oh, sorry." She turned to address Fritz but stopped and asked me a question. "Is there something you're not telling me, Jack?"

I had to be honest. "We've got information that Emmett Flynn, the leader of these skinheads, is planning an act of terrorism here in Lyon. But we don't know when or where."

Her eyes bulged, but she patted her chest, gulped in some air. Apparently fortified enough to proceed, she took Fritz by the shoulders and spoke quickly in German. Between the two of them, they must have spit out a thousand German words over the next two minutes. I only knew they were done when both turned their heads in my direction.

"And?"

Fritz shifted his eyes to Miss Patty, then said. "Bombe."

"Is he saying bomb in German? He heard the skinheads say

something about using a bomb?"

Unblinking, she nodded. "That's what he overheard outside, Jack."

"How long ago?"

"Maybe thirty minutes, give or take," she said before asking Fritz in German. He confirmed with a full-bodied nod while using his hands to simulate a bomb exploding.

"Any idea on when this might take place?"

Miss Patty did the interpretation again, then she and Fritz shook their heads no.

Did I have ten minutes or six hours to stop this event? I had no idea. I paced, ending up at the door. "I know this is a bit of a flier, but do either of you have any thoughts on what the target might be?"

"Target?" Fritz shook his head while shifting his eyes between Patty and me.

"Where do they plan on setting off this bomb?" I asked in a volume far too loud for being indoors.

Fritz covered his ears for a moment and stared at Miss Patty for the interpretation. She gave it, and when he relayed the answer, she shrieked, bringing a hand to her mouth.

"What…what did he say?"

"The most iconic destination in all of Lyon. La Basilique of Notre-Dame de Fourvière." She gasped and grabbed a piece of paper from the counter, flapped it in my face. "There's a multicultural celebration at the church today. Oh no, Jack. There will be even more people at the church than ever before."

I cut between them and hurried to the door, pausing briefly as I considered my next steps. "I don't have any wheels. Do you have any taxi-driver friends?"

"Hugo," she muttered, instantly biting a nail.

Fritz looked at her, but she quickly shook her head. "My nephew. He drives a taxi when he's not being a daredevil on his motorcycle. But he's never available." She smacked Fritz's arm.

"Fritz is a taxi driver?"

"No, no," she clarified. "He's got a scooter. Parked against a tree along the sidewalk."

"Can I borrow it?"

He only shrugged, looking to Miss Patty for an explanation in German. But she was over it. She reached into his pocket and pulled out a set of keys. "The little one. That goes to the red scooter out front. Do you think those skinheads are going to put our friends inside the church before blowing it up? Oh dear. Just go, Jack. Please save them before it's too late."

57

The scooter didn't start on the first or second try. Or even the tenth. I called the inanimate object every curse word I knew, and it finally came to life. Peeled some rubber, then cut across the road. A delivery truck was almost on top of me. All I could do was throw an arm up. The truck stopped inches from my leg.

"Sorry!" I waved and whipped around the truck, hauling ass toward the cross street, where I hooked a right onto Rue Vauban. My speed increased significantly as I weaved around slower vehicles, bikes, and a few pedestrians who'd meandered onto the road. Some yelled at me as I whizzed past them. I torpedoed forward, unfazed.

I had no idea where the bomb was located, what it looked like. But did it matter? I just had to get everyone out of the church before the damn thing exploded.

A knot of cars, and I skidded to a stop. I angled my sights upward. On the far side of the Rhone and Saone rivers, the church's four towers spiraled so high they appeared to poke the clouds. Seemed the most direct route to the church was through the sky. Not an option. But with so many one-way streets, I'd be routed southward almost two kilometers before I could cross the rivers. Time I couldn't waste.

I gunned it and split between two cars, my arm slamming a side mirror. I turned left on Rue Pierre Corneille, still within the flow of traffic. But that was about to change. Passing a multitude of shops, including a jewelry store and barbershop, I hooked a right onto Lafayette. Cars were moving east. I was playing a three-thousand-pound game of Russian roulette by moving west. If I were to be hit head-on by a truck, I'd be nothing more than a bug splattered on its windshield.

I bobbed, weaved, and dodged through traffic, a man on a mission. One near-miss after another. A stark reality hit me: my odds of surviving this leg of the journey were practically nil.

* * *

The Skinhead

The man finished his inspection of the contents in the back of his sixteen-foot rental truck—just over one ton of ammonium nitrate. He hopped down, pulled the roller door closed, and locked up.

Brought his cell phone to his ear. "The timer has been set," he said in German. "I am starting the last stage of the journey."

"As planned. Very good," the person said on the other end.

The man waited for a final goodbye, a few words of encouragement to remind him of the significance of their mission to cleanse the earth of all who were not of a pure race. It never came. But that was okay with him. He'd come to terms with how he was being used to fulfill a greater good. Sometimes, it took a few good men to sacrifice their lives so the one true race could carry on. That was his mantra, one he had repeated for several days before going to sleep. Whenever sleep came. And it rarely had since the plan was conceived by Emmett one month ago, when he'd finalized a deal with the Interpol official—supply a cache of weapons in exchange for one million euros. He recalled Emmett's ecstatic response, how he'd declared this cash influx would be the seed money to take their small operation into a global movement, one terrorism event at a time.

He slid into the driver's seat and slowly pulled out of the parking lot, heading up the hill toward the church.

* * *

Jack

I changed my strategy—and that still didn't guarantee I would survive this jaunt unscathed. Shifting my scooter to the middle of the street, I stayed on the hashed line, began flashing my headlight and waving an arm. A few cars jerked to a stop; others swerved out of my path. It was working.

Until I reached the Rhone River. On the bridge, vehicles had much less room to maneuver.

A car barreled right down the center of the bridge.

"Hey!" I said.

The driver jerked the vehicle hard to the right, missing me by a mere ten feet. I kept going. There was no turning back now.

* * *

The Skinhead

As the slowest vehicle on the road, the man began to feel conspicuous. He pressed the gas pedal to the floor. The RPMs revved higher, as did the growl of the diesel engine. Still, the vehicle moved at a tortoise-like pace.

He banged his fist off the steering wheel as perspiration beaded on his bald head. There was no way in hell he would screw this up, even as doubt began to poke holes in his resolve. Like, what if the bomb went off en route? Could happen, the damn truck was so slow. They'd miss all their intended targets—the non-whites at the multicultural event at the church. His legacy would be cemented as a screwup, a laughingstock.

He picked at an eyebrow piercing, remembering Emmett's planned timing for this last stage. Fifteen minutes, which left five minutes of lag time on the back end before the detonation. He had synced his watch with the timer in the back of the truck. His watch currently read 9:16 a.m. The seconds seemed to be moving faster than normal.

Grinding his teeth, he kept his foot pressed to the floor as he made a hard right onto Rue Cleberg. While the climb was about to get even tougher, he could now hear the tower bells clearly through his open window.

He smiled.

* * *

Jack

I'd thus far survived the drive against the flow of traffic. Nothing short of a miracle. Moving east on the Alphonse Juin bridge of the Saone River, I could see the cross street up ahead.

Flashing blue and red lights emerged from traffic. Police. Four officers came into view, walking out from under a thick canopy of trees in the median. They moved into the cross street, three holding up hands, one extending his arms. That officer was aiming a gun in my direction.

I debated whether to turn around and find another way, but I quickly nixed the idea. I couldn't risk the extra time.

As more officers flooded the intersection, cars continued to spill onto the bridge. That was both a curse and a blessing. I had to keep my eyes on the cars—I was still flashing my lights and waving my arms—but a plan began to materialize. A way to get past the officers: use the cars as a screen until I was past the front line and then make a break for the labyrinth of alleys and short streets. No way they'd keep up.

A blur zipped past me, moving in my same direction. The motorcycle must have been going fifty kilometers per hour. The speed limit was twenty. Could that be…?

"Hugo?"

Stunned, I almost turned the scooter over. After righting my bike, I watched the remaining cars on the bridge either rock to a stop or careen into each other to avoid the daredevil on the motorcycle.

This was my one chance.

Opening the throttle as far as it would go, I planned to take full advantage of the diversion. All vehicles had stopped on the bridge, people emerging from their cars and walking around and pointing, mostly at the crazy guy on the motorcycle, who I assumed was Hugo. I was nothing more than a funny side note.

I followed his path, his flannel shirt flapping violently in the manufactured wind. When his brake lights flashed, our distance from each other closed in a hurry. The cops were trying to cage him in.

He fishtailed twice and evading their human net. Just as I reached the northbound lane of Quai Romain Rolland, the guy shot a look in my direction. He wore aviator shades, and his bare belly was practically resting on the motorcycle's gas tank. He gave me a thumbs-up before fishtailing once more. Smoke filled the air as the bike's back end swerved back and forth across the street. Officers jumped out of the way.

The motorcyclist's final fuck-you was an impressive wheely just before he sped away.

Officers raced to their police cars and started the pursuit. I dodged two of them when I crossed the northbound lane, hopped the curb to traverse the median, and then cut through slower traffic on the southbound side before I turned onto a tiny street.

Safety after a white-knuckle ride. I'd made it.

Time to save the world.

* * *

The Skinhead

For the fifth time in the last two minutes and forty-three seconds, the man honked the horn of his rental truck and leaned his head out the window to yell at two men holding up the entire show. They were taking forever to exchange information after their slow-motion wreck right next to a flower stand.

Flowers. He still couldn't believe his eyes. The two men—both of whom had powder-blue sweaters tied loosely around their necks—were actually smiling and laughing. Were they comparing notes on how they'd taken their eyes off the road while ogling which flowers to buy their lovers?

The man cursed the French, a regular occurrence in his world back in Germany. The French had no drive, no purpose in life. And this incident was just further evidence of that fact. Normally, he couldn't wait to get back home and share with his comrades what he'd witnessed.

"Did you beat the shit out of them?" his buddies would certainly ask.

But they wouldn't have the chance to ask. He would be dead, a martyr, lauded across the globe by those who held the same single-race beliefs.

If all went well within the next six minutes.

Sweat poured down his face. He had to make the call—get out of the truck and force the men out of the way? Or stay put and hope the discussions ended soon? He'd give them until the count of ten.

He made it only as far as five before losing patience.

Throwing open the door, he marched in the direction of the two men.

"Hey," he said, speaking in English, "move your damn cars."

They gave him an incredulous look and went back to talking. He would find very few things more fulfilling than pounding the shit out of two French men. But he had to remember that he had higher goals. Time-sensitive goals. He yelled at them and pulled out the butt of his pistol, a Ruger LCP II.

The men immediately shut their mouths.

"Move the cars. Now."

Thirty-six seconds later, the man was, once again, motoring up the hill. He still had time.

* * *

Jack

At the bottom of the hill that led to the church, I made a beeline toward the south side, the quickest way up the slope. Only a few cars on the road, so I made good time on Saint-Barthélemy. I could practically feel the lush greenery on the sloping hill as I sped alongside the Parc des Hauteurs. I reached Rue Cleberg and took a sharp right. Another hundred feet, and I followed the road left and slowed to make the final turn up the hill.

"Dammit!" The narrow road was filled with cars and trucks. Had there been a wreck? I looked for seams in the congestion. Tried to map out a path. I couldn't afford to get trapped.

There was one more route to the church—a longer route, and one that would require me to use the same wrong-way method as before. But I had little choice. I turned my scooter around and headed back to Cleberg. When I reached the cross street, ten cars were stopped at the light up the slope of Rue Roger Radisson. I hooked a right and sped by the still cars. Heads turned, and I heard a whistle from behind. Probably a traffic cop.

I revved the engine.

Dodging oncoming cars and bikes, my pulse didn't redline this time. Most importantly, nothing slowed me down as I raced up the hill. The back side of a smaller church was up ahead, where the street split into two directions, one moving up the hill and this one moving down the hill—except for me and the scooter. Not slowing down a bit, I motored around the corner. A large rental truck was barreling right for me. I hopped the curb in front of the church to avoid becoming roadkill, just before the driver of the truck made a sudden turn to the right. For a split second, the right side of the truck lifted off the road and slammed back to the ground, then motored toward the Basilica.

As I thumped my chest just to make sure my heart was still pumping, my mind replayed the latest near-crash. One image stood frozen in my eyes: on the side of the driver's neck, a red and black tattoo. The Nazi swastika.

Screeching off the curb, I split between two cars and headed straight for the rental truck, which had just stopped directly in front of the Basilica.

* * *

The Skinhead

The man threw the gear into park, huffed out a breath, and rested his sweaty head on the steering wheel. He'd made it. What had seemed like an impossible challenge would now be part of his legacy, a story that would make him a legend across the globe. The man who started this movement by making the ultimate sacrifice. His buddies would be happy. His mentor, Emmett, would forever herald his actions as the launching point for the next phase of their movement—the one that would put them on a global stage. Emmett had told him privately that once they had their own country, their own capital, they would make a statue of him, honoring his sacrifice.

With a peaceful smile, he lifted up and studied the people milling about the esplanade. Couples of different races holding hands, their kids looking like a mix of the two parents. He lost his smile. Pulled out his Ruger, extended his arm, and started to track a few passers-by.

"Nothing like a little target practice before we all go boom." He chuckled, but only for a moment. He needed to steady himself so he could hit his first target.

Metal clanged. He heard the back door roll open. "What the hell?" He looked in the side mirror but couldn't see directly behind the truck. He slid out of the cab. Marched toward the back, pistol at the ready. Someone was going to pay with their life for being so nosy.

* * *

Jack

"Ammonium nitrate." The implication of what I was seeing stole the breath from my lungs. The Oklahoma City bombing—the worst attack on US soil before 9/11—was caused by a rental truck packed with a similar substance. It had been executed by skinheads. Was Emmett Flynn connected to the OKC bombing?

All those thoughts went out the window when I saw a timer

next to a barrel. The minutes and seconds counting down....

3:18...

3:17...

I had three minutes to clear the entire area. I turned and took in the whole scene—people learning, sharing, smiling. Enjoying life. Hundreds of people.

How could I possibly clear all of them from the area in three minutes?

I hustled around the truck...

And ran straight into the driver.

He had inadvertently dropped his gun during the collision, and we lunged for it at the same time. It bounced off my fingers and skidded two yards. Before I could get to my feet, a truck drove by us, scooping up the gun in its tire tread, which launched the gun farther down the road.

"I will kill you anyway." The man jumped on top of me and started to slam my head against the road.

Lights flashed in my vision. I had to end this now. Raising my legs, I locked his head between my ankles and pulled him off me. As he fell backward, I got to my knees and put my weight behind one solid punch. It connected with his throat.

He flailed like a dead fish, and I jumped into the rental truck. I had maybe two minutes to park this truck far away from this crowd. Any crowd.

I threw the gear into drive and took off. I'd figure it out on the fly. The story of my life.

58

I crushed two trash cans while executing a U-turn. People pointed at me as I motored past the church. The blatant move had gotten their attention—they jumped out of my path. The clear road didn't last long, though. Halfway down Rue Roger Radisson, cars and pedestrians filled the street. "Move. Out of the way!" I shouted through the open window.

I got stares. Glares. But they all moved away from the street, motioning for others to do the same. That bought me about a hundred feet until I was blocked by cars at the light, which turned green the moment I'd tapped the brakes.

"Come on, come on, come on." Willing the cars to move faster. The car right in front of me lingered too long at the light, and I had no other choice but to plow into the back of the vehicle, moving it out of my way so I could turn left onto Cleberg.

A bed-and-breakfast sat on the right; other buildings and homes lined the other side of the small street. No place to dump the truck and run. I rounded the curve to merge onto Saint-

Barthélemy, heading south. I couldn't remember where that street ultimately ended. A shopping area? An open park?

Drive. Just drive.

Jamming the brakes at the last second, I turned the wheel sharply to the left. The huge truck cut across traffic—car horns blared—but I was more concerned about keeping the truck on the ground. While the truck leaned severely, somehow all wheels stayed in contact with the surface. There was a thicket of trees off to the right of the curving road. Was there enough room to tuck the truck deeper into the woods?

Below the sloping tree line, a plethora of red roofs. I had no idea how large the explosion would be. I thought of the demolished Murrah Federal Building in Oklahoma City.

"Hell no."

Traffic opened up, allowing me to pick up speed as the truck surged down the hill. I took a slight curve at twice the speed limit. The truck veered into oncoming traffic. One car caromed into the guardrail and ricocheted in the other direction, narrowly missing the truck's back end.

Up ahead, I saw nothing but wall-to-wall buildings, no place to leave the truck.

Seconds ticking by. How much time did I have left?

Just past a thicket of towering trees, my eyes picked up the Saone River farther down the hill.

Could I reach the water?

I pressed forward, the truck now officially in haul-ass mode, heading down Saint-Barthélemy.

My internal clock guessed there were about forty seconds before the explosion. I was probably off, but by how much? And in which direction?

Near the bottom of the hill, I could see where Saint-Barthélemy dead-ended at a large building before it took a ninety-degree turn to the right. I waited as long as possible, then jabbed the brake pedal so hard I lifted from my seat. The truck began to tremble, the tires locked, kicking up smoke.

I was headed straight for a brick wall.

Counter to intuition, I pulled my foot off the brake for a count of two and then started pumping the pedal again. The truck veered left and right. A woman on a bike fell onto the roadside. Two men on mopeds rammed a smaller car that had come to a complete stop. Inside the shadow of the wall, the truck finally responded. The brakes unlocked, and I executed the turn without crashing or losing too much speed. Beyond a train station and more buildings…

The water.

Maybe a few seconds left. I was on a direct path to cross the bridge, but not for long. The moment the truck's tires touched Quai de Bondy, I jerked the wheel to the right, slammed through a metal fence, and launched the rental truck toward the water.

Midflight, I kicked open the truck's door and dove away from the truck's trajectory.

59

For a fleeting moment, I saw Lyon from ten feet above the river, a split second before my head felt the full concussive impact of the detonation. I hit the water and sunk, my equilibrium in disarray, my mind struggling to stay conscious.

Water started to fill my lungs, but that was a good thing. Reflexively, I choked, jarring my mind out of a deep fog, allowing a lone signal to fire out to all body parts: swim.

I kicked my way to the surface, coughed, took in a quick breath, and pumped my arms and legs with robotic efficiency. Rocking waves added more resistance, so I pushed myself even harder. How far did I swim? A half mile? Twenty feet? I had no idea. But I swam until my body gave out. When I stopped, still coughing and snorting up water, there was shouting over my left shoulder. Huddled near the mangled railing, a growing crowd of people stood with hands over their mouths, some pointing at me, others pointing to the river where the water was most disturbed from the detonation.

I made my way to the side of the river, and a strange thing happened. A few people started clapping. Then more. And more. A man offered a hand to help me out of the water.

"Vous avez failli mourir. Vous êtes fou, mais vous êtes aussi un héros pour tout le monde à Lyon," he said through glassy eyes.

I picked up a couple of words, but nothing more. He apparently had noticed.

"Hero. You are a hero," he said, patting my shoulder.

"Merci." I sounded more cheerful than I felt. The ringing in my ears had subsided somewhat, but it felt as though a jackhammer had been implanted in my brain. A second implant to go with the electro-vial.

The familiar two-note sirens echoed throughout the city canyon, and someone in the growing crowd offered me a towel. I wiped my face. I didn't like the attention and knew I'd be forced to come up with some type of believable story for the police. My best bet was to keep it simple and short.

Beyond the people surrounding me, a white van pulled to a stop just north of the clogged intersection. Through the sun's harsh glare, I noticed a picture of a satellite dish on the side panel, along with French words, some type of company logo. But as the van rolled a few feet, I snagged a clean view of the driver. Bald with eyebrow and nose piercings. And a tat on his neck—same as the rental truck driver. Too far away to know for sure, but I'd bet it was a Nazi swastika.

I meandered through the crowd, engaging with members of the crowd, shaking hands, accepting hugs. My gregarious nature was an uncomfortable posture, but it was serving a vital purpose. It allowed me to shift closer to the van without telegraphing it.

At about twenty feet, I ran out of people to mingle with, so I bolted for the van. A man sitting in the passenger seat nudged the driver, who punched the gas. Running alongside the van for about two seconds, I could do nothing more than smack the rear panel and helplessly jog to a stop. The van spewed gray exhaust as it raced westward on Quai de Bondy. They had to be part of the terrorist plot to blow up the Basilica. I might have just missed an opportunity to catch Flynn…

And to learn where they were keeping Casper, Bailey, and the others.

If they were still alive.

A plume of smoke engulfed me a second before an engine whirred above the screech of rubber.

"Hugo?" I said.

"Need a ride?" His curly windblown hair looked like a colony of bats about to take flight.

My butt had barely hit the seat of the Yamaha when Hugo launched the bike, sending pedestrians scampering out of the way. He slid between two cars, lowered his body, and opened the throttle, reaching fifty, sixty kilometers per hour in no time.

"The white van!" I shouted through the fierce wind.

He nodded and gunned it even more as we angled the bike into a curve. Two police motorboats plowed through the river off to our right, but we raced by them as though they were static buoys. The van was moving at an accelerated speed, but it was no match for this land-based rocket.

"What's the plan?" Hugo shouted, his voice thick with a French accent.

I offered the first thought that came to mind—he didn't question it—and he moved the motorcycle closer to the rear of the van. "Just a little closer," I said.

The van's brake lights flashed, and Hugo clamped down on the cycle's brakes. We skidded, and my feet bounced off the road as he strained to keep us upright. We were on a path to ram the larger van—until Hugo locked the front brakes. Stopping on a dime, our back end lifted one, two, three feet off the ground. We were going to flip. I was about to bail. But just before reaching the apex, Hugo released the brake, and we dropped back to the road.

The van had already hit the gas and was at least fifty feet in front of us. Hugo launched the Yamaha rocket, but the cycle stalled out. He restarted the engine while muttering what I assumed were a few French curse words. Lowered his torso. We catapulted forward. Before I had time to wipe bugs from my face, Hugo had closed the gap. This time, he stayed to the left of the rear part of the van.

"Little closer," I yelled, moving to my knees on the seat. At six inches from the van, I lifted to my feet and jumped. The van's driver, though, had just swerved to the left, grazing the cycle's front wheel. My new buddy lost control just as I grabbed hold of the handlebar on the van's back door, the tips of my feet clinging to the back bumper. The motorcycle toppled over while still moving at a high rate of speed before skidding off the road and into the river.

I paused for a second. Hugo bobbed out of the river and gave me a thumbs-up sign.

Wasting not a moment longer, I climbed up the back of the van and onto the roof. Given my experience on Amadou's hood, I knew this was a vulnerable position. I scampered to the front end with a new idea in mind. Leaning forward across the front glass, I snagged a windshield wiper and tugged until it snapped off. Pushing back up to the roof, I slid toward the driver's side but didn't show myself. Not yet. I peeled off the rubber and extra plastic from the wiper until I had a pointed object.

Once I saw the dome of the bald head lean out of the driver's window, I thrust my arm downward with the same power I'd used back in the day to launch the javelin two hundred feet. My makeshift weapon stuck in the skinhead's eye. He wailed like the gutless baby he was. The van swung abruptly left and right across the narrow road. Then it hit a bump. When I saw we were headed for an inevitable crash, I leaped for the roof of a parked car. Slid straight across it. Tumbled to the road.

Metal screeched—the sound almost deafening. Shards of glass rained on top of me.

I jumped up, ran toward the back of the toppled van. Half of the driver's body was crushed under the vehicle, the wiper still jutting from his eye, blood everywhere. I yanked open a stubborn, dented back door.

Five faces.

Bailey, Joshua, Casper, Karma, and Evan all shook their heads, moaned, but ultimately smiled. Another skinhead lay motionless at their feet.

"Shot himself when the van crashed," Casper said as he stepped over the man with a hole in his forehead. "Sucks to be him."

Bailey reached out, touched my arm. "Did you get Emmett?"

"Driver or passenger?"

"Passenger."

I raced around the van and looked inside. Empty. I saw a trail of blood that vanished about thirty feet in front of the van.

Bailey pulled up next to me. "You see him?"

I shook my head, and her hopeful expression faded away. I slung my arm over her shoulders, and as six police cars rolled up.

My friends were safe.

But I knew that a roach like Emmett Flynn would eventually emerge from obscurity.

60

The celebration at the Newman-Woodward complex lasted well into the night. But only after a lengthy set of police interviews had been interrupted by Miss Patty, Fritz, and a local attorney, who used his connection to a powerful judge in Lyon to end the interrogations for the day.

Little did they know that would be my last interview in Lyon.

Paul pulled out his accordion and played lively tunes, leading to spontaneous dancing and singing, eating and drinking. But not too much drinking for me. I had to maintain a clear mind at all times.

The group's underground doctor took turns treating each of us. Miss Patty insisted. My neck was sore as hell, so he gave me some ice and a couple of aspirin.

Karma approached me as I ate some home-baked bread. "What you did out there was nothing short of Bond badass."

I couldn't hide my smile as Evan joined us. "Didn't know that was a term," I said.

She giggled, cocked her head back, and drained her glass of wine.

"She gets a little a little silly when she has too much to drink," Evan said, staying closer to Tipsy Karma than usual, a hand on her upper arm to keep her steady.

"I resent that statement," she said with a snort. When her legs gave out, Evan lifted her up. "Okay, maybe I'm a little snookered."

"Here, Jack, you really need to try this." Bailey walked over with a bowl and spoon. "It's—"

"Crème brûlée. Love that stuff." I took a few bites and smacked my lips. "Perfect."

"Hey, Mommy, what's 'snookered' mean?" Joshua walked up with a small train that Paul had given him.

She patted her son's head. "Just means someone is having a good time."

"Does that mean I'm snookered?"

The entire room erupted in laughter.

He screwed up his face. "Hey, what's so funny?"

Bailey shook her head, but Paul diverted Joshua's attention by asking him to dance to the next spirited accordion tune. Bailey joined her son on the dance floor, and his face lit up. Karma and Evan jumped in next.

"I would have never guessed this all would end in such happiness," Casper said as he sidled up next to me, nursing a Heineken. "For a while there, I thought Flynn was going to sacrifice all of us when the bomb exploded. Himself included."

"Not a chance. When he walked away after the crash, that told me everything I need to know about that guy. Flynn manipulates everyone else to do his dirty work while he just sails off free."

"Free." Casper released a reluctant sigh. There was another story behind that word. I asked if he wanted to share it with me.

He said, "Jack, I may not be a free man tomorrow when I head back to my base."

"What? You'll be a hero. Your MP team can hopefully arrest any base leaders connected to Flynn's gang."

He scratched his chin. "I'm AWOL, Jack."

I paused, accepting that I didn't know much about the real Casper.

"Here's the straight scoop. The rumors about a leader being connected to a Neo-Nazi group were true—it was actually my commanding officer. After I said something, drugs were planted in my locker. I had no choice but to run and figure it out. Now I have to pay the piper."

"If you need a good word, I bet Miss Patty's lawyer will help you out, even if it's across the German border."

"I better get his phone number, just in case."

I popped him on the back. "If you run into trouble, let me know."

"What could you do about it?"

"Just keep me in the loop."

The party died down, and everyone found chairs and talked quietly for a while. Joshua fell asleep in his mother's arms, which made me miss Maddie that much more.

"You got a rugrat too?" Casper asked, a chin-nod toward Bailey and her son.

"A little girl. She's my most precious gift."

"When you leave here, are you going back home to be with her?"

If only... "We'll see. If not right away, then soon. I hate the separation."

"Speaking of separation, you never told us where you've been the last couple of days."

"If I told you the full story, you'd think it was fiction."

He laughed. "Seriously, though, where did you go?"

"Cairo."

"Egypt?"

"Is there another?"

He shrugged. "Did you save the world?"

When I gave him the basics of how I took down Amadou and his coup attempt, he just stared at me and shook his head. "I overheard Karma saying you a Bond badass. Now I know why."

I chuckled so hard I almost spilled my glass of wine. Casper shot me a wink, then went to mingle with the others. I plucked a bottled water from the fridge and thought about the last words Charlie had said to me: *"There's someone else besides Amadou. Someone far more powerful. Far more devious. And I can't die without telling you that I know..."*

But Charlie did die before he could tell me. Leaving me with lingering questions that ate at my peace of mind.

"Two more missions," I muttered to myself before chugging the water. It was possible Simon would blackmail me beyond the two missions. Even if Simon kept the pact at four total missions, would they allow me to just walk away? Would they surgically remove the implant in my arm? It was hard to imagine.

And too overwhelming to think about.

One day at a time, Jack. Eye on the ball.

It was time for me to go.

After an abbreviated goodbye—Casper joked that I was a nomad—I walked out the door and peered into a deep sky filled with stars sparkling like diamonds. I reflected. So many harrowing moments. I took in a full breath, allowing the crisp air to clear my mind of the perils that had engulfed so many people. I thought about what dangers the future might hold, but also what would get me through them.

Two more missions until I was reunited with the one life that mattered most: my daughter, Maddie.

Two more missions, but I also knew I'd have to uncover the truth about Simon. Once I did, I would have no second thoughts in doing whatever it took to end the imminent threat they posed.

Goonies never say die.

61

Karma

The party ended, lights came on, and everyone worked together to clean up. Everyone except Jack.

"I can tell Jack is a vagabond at heart," Miss Patty said to Bailey, who was helping her at the sink.

"Mm-hm. He's got something on this mind."

"What do you think it is?"

"Something that requires the utmost focus," Bailey said. "And he won't stop until it's done."

"That sounds like our Jack," Miss Patty said, then turned her attention to picking up the dirty dishes and glasses from around the room.

Karma had overheard the conversation and smiled at the older woman. "You're such a good person, Miss Patty." Her phone buzzed, and she wiped her hands on a towel, then slid the phone out of her back pocket. "I'll just take it outside," she said and stepped out into the darkness.

After a brief introduction and one question, she offered her opinion while staring at a star-filled sky. "I've never seen anyone respond like he did to so much intense pressure, sir. And I heard he did even more in Cairo. I think he might be our guy." She paused to listen, her eyes falling to the old cobblestones beneath her feet. "I see. We'll wait, then. And hope that he's successful. If not…well, God help us all."

John W. Mefford Bibliography

The Jack Whitfield Thrillers
NEVER GO BACK (BOOK 1)
NEVER SAY DIE (BOOK 2)
NOW OR NEVER (BOOK 3)
NEVER AGAIN (BOOK 4)

The Alex Troutt Thrillers (Redemption Thriller Collection)
AT BAY (Book 1)
AT LARGE (Book 2)
AT ONCE (Book 3)
AT DAWN (Book 4)
AT DUSK (Book 5)
AT LAST (Book 6)
AT STAKE (Book 7)
AT ANY COST (Book 8)
BACK AT YOU (Book 9)
AT EVERY TURN (Book 10)
AT DEATH'S DOOR (Book 11)
AT FULL TILT (Book 12)

The Ivy Nash Thrillers (Redemption Thriller Collection)
IN DEFIANCE (Book 1)
IN PURSUIT (Book 2)
IN DOUBT (Book 3)
BREAK IN (Book 4)
IN CONTROL (Book 5)
IN THE END (Book 6)

The Ozzie Novak Thrillers (Redemption Thriller Collection)
ON EDGE (Book 1)
GAME ON (Book 2)
ON THE ROCKS (Book 3)
SHAME ON YOU (Book 4)
ON FIRE (Book 5)
ON THE RUN (Book 6)

The Ball & Chain Thrillers
MERCY (Book 1)
FEAR (Book 2)
BURY (Book 3)
LURE (Book 4)
PREY (Book 5)
VANISH (Book 6)
ESCAPE (Book 7)
TRAP (Book 8)

The Booker Thrillers
BOOKER – Streets of Mayhem (Book 1)
BOOKER – Tap That (Book 2)
BOOKER – Hate City (Book 3)
BOOKER – Blood Ring (Book 4)
BOOKER – No Más (Book 5)
BOOKER – Dead Heat (Book 6)

The Greed Thrillers
FATAL GREED (Book 1)
LETHAL GREED (Book 2)
WICKED GREED (Book 3)
GREED MANIFESTO (Book 4)

To stay updated on John's latest releases, visit:
JohnWMefford.com

Printed in Great Britain
by Amazon